More books in the Jack the Ripper Victims Series

Of Thimble and Threat
available in paperback, ebook, and audiobook

Say Anything but Your Prayer
available in paperback, ebook, and audiobook

A Brutal Chill in August
available in paperback, ebook, and audiobook

Apologies to the Cat's Meat Man
available in paperback, ebook, and audiobook

The Double Event
(comprised of the two novels *Of Thimble and Threat* and *Say Anything but Your Prayer*)
available in ebook, and audiobook

Each novel in the series is a standalone story.

Praise for the Jack the Ripper Victims Series

"*Of Thimble and Threat* is a terrifically absorbing read. A mature novel and superbly researched. The image of silver in the blood was woven expertly and made the ending luminous and poignant."
—Simon Clark, author of *Vampyrrhic* and *Night of the Triffids*

"Clark proves himself to be the ultimate double-threat, his prose every bit as evocative and compelling as his art. Steeped in Victoriana *Say Anything but Your Prayers* is a worthy edition to Ripperology."
—Steven Savile, author of *Silver* and *London Macabre*

"*A Brutal Chill in August*, one of a series wherein Alan M. Clark masterfully recreates the sorry lives of the Ripper's victims, is awash in atmospheric detail of those dark days in 19th century London. Exhaustively researched, Clark brings to life the plight of London's poor, and the extremes to which they must go in order to merely survive... or succumb as victims to disease, abuse, alcoholism, or worse. A great read."
—Elizabeth Engstrom, author of *Lizzie Borden* and *York's Moon*

"In *Apologies to the Cat's Meat Man*, Clark's skill shows through in terms of bringing the era and setting and characters to vivid life. Not a feel-good read, not a fun read, but another powerful one, and a stirring memorial for a woman who was more than a mark on a killer's scoresheet."
—Christine Morgan, author of *White Death* and *The Raven's Table*

Alan M. Clark has given us a great gift with his Jack the Ripper Victims series. I no longer care who the murderer was, for I know who his victims were. Exhaustively researched and true to period, Clark artfully relates their stories with clarity and compassion. *The Prostitute's Price* is the crown jewel of the quintet.
—Stephen T. Vessels, Thriller Award nominated author of *The Mountain and the Vortex* and *The Door of Tireless Pursuit*.

"I regard the five books that make up this series as unarguably one of the high points in Ripper fiction over the past 130 years."
—*Ripperologist* magazine

The Prostitute's Price

a novel by Alan M. Clark

IFD Publishing

P.O. Box 40776, Eugene, Oregon 97404 U.S.A.
www.ifdpublishing.com

The Prostitute's Price

This is a work of fiction. Although the novel is inspired by real historical events and actual human lives, the characters have been created for the sake of this story and are either products of the author's imagination or are used fictitiously. Any resemblance to actual events or locales or persons, living or dead, is entirely coincidental.

ISBN: 978-0-9996656-1-9
Printed in the United States of America

Thanks to Elizabeth Engstrom, Matt Hayward, Melody Kees Clark, Jill Bauman, Lisa Snellings, Mark Roland, Eric Witchey, Ross Lockhart, Michael Drewek, Cynthia Drewek, Cameron Pierce, Kirsten Alene Pierce, David Conover, Michele Green, Michael Green, Mad Wilson, Amanda Lloyd, John McNichols, Stephen T. Vessels, and, most of all, my collaborator on the *13 Miller's Court* project, John Linwood Grant, who graciously allowed me to write about his character, Mr. Edwin Dry, the Deptford Assassin.

To understand more fully events hidden from the POV character, Mary Jane Kelly, in this story, please read the companion novel, *The Assassin's Coin*, by John Linwood Grant, also available from IFD Publishing.

Author's Note
To Hell with Jack the Ripper

This novel, and the Jack the Ripper Victims Series of which it is a part, are not meant to satisfy curiosity about the identity of Jack the Ripper. Instead, they exist to take readers back in time to experience the circumstances in which those he preyed upon lived and suffered his crimes in Victorian London.

Many of the place names in the novel—Stepney, Spitalfields, Shadwell, Whitechapel, Southwark, Clerkenwell, Deptford, Poplar, Shoreditch, Limehouse, Chelsea Embankment, Knightsbridge—are in the greater London area. Some are the names of districts or parishes or what were towns in their own right until they were swallowed up over time by the expansion of the city of London. They are all within ten miles of one another, most of them within easy walking distance.

Having written novels about the first four victims, I found myself shying away from writing this one about the last victim, Mary Jane Kelly. With time, I realized that the crime scene photographs had discouraged me.

At least two exist, one that is perhaps the primary, taking in the whole scene, the other a closeup. Much of the "trash" in the photos exists because the images now available are from photographic products that have deteriorated with age. Those materials would be going on 130 years old. The pictures have what looks like dust and scratches or perhaps water damage that led to mold, mildew, fungus. Whatever the cause, the deterioration has a very dirty look, making what is a disgusting scene, usually seen in a brown sepia-tone, look even worse. Taken in London's East End in 1888, the images seem to speak accurately of what was a very filthy part of the world in the late Victorian period, indeed a place and time with some of the most impoverished people the world has known. Yet when the photos were first created, they probably had much less trash in them, and would have provided a clearer view of the victim.

The mutilation of the corpse in the photo is so extreme that it somehow wounds my sense of human worth and dignity. The outrage of the wasted humanity is bad enough, but seeing those pitiful remains on a bed in a small, squalid single-room dwelling, I also suffer an odd claustrophobia, a sense of being trapped in that tight space at 13 Miller's Court in Spitalfields, where true horror took place. With the dreadful feeling I get from the images, I didn't want to begin the work on the novel about Mary Jane Kelly.

I considered showing the pictures here, but decided that those who haven't seen them are better off. Unfortunately, these words may pique the curiosity of some who will look for the images.

Despite my revulsion, I have completed the series with this novel, and in a manner that took my distress over the crime scene photographs into consideration.

"For all the murder victims forgotten in the excitement over the assholes who kill." That is my dedication for *A Brutal Chill in August*, the novel in the series about the life of Mary Ann "Polly" Nichols, the first victim of Jack the Ripper.

We know much more about the women he killed than we do about him.

Likely, the women did not know the murderer.

As most do, I employ male pronouns when talking about the Ripper merely because of the name Jack, though we don't know for certain the killer's gender.

I have stuck to what history tells us about the women he killed as much as seems reasonable, while also trying to tell good stories. The available records that provide their reactions to given situations are limited, so we do not know what they said or felt in many cases. In broad periods of their lives we have mere outlines of their activities at best. Writing character-driven, dramatic representations of their lives, I have invented dialogue and emotional motivations for the characters that fit with their time and circumstances.

Survival within the environment of Victorian England took a heavy toll on the lives of the women the Ripper targeted. The first four, middle-aged and struggling to survive on their own, had taken to the streets to earn as prostitutes. They were worn down and weakened by the time they met their killer. The fifth and final, Mary

Jane Kelly, was a young prostitute, possibly twenty-five years old.

What we know about those he murdered tells us something about Jack the Ripper and offers a glimpse of the world in which he and they lived. In most ways, he would have been as vulnerable as his victims in a dangerous, often merciless world. Just like them, he was probably aware of the need to maintain appearances and to achieve the highest social position possible in order to ensure survival in a swiftly changing environment. I presume he knew that eventually disease and death would claim him without ceremony and that he would die alone like everyone else. If he considered these things after what he'd done and what he'd witnessed of death, perhaps he experienced a pitiable fear something like what his victims knew.

Most of us spend much of life feeling confidently alive, solid and incorruptible, not thinking about our demise, our eventual loss of facility and faculty, our loss of awareness and sense of identity and finally the decay of our flesh. Those of us who have not seen war, violent crime, or deadly disaster turn to face our demise slowly over many years as it dawns on us frightfully that we are like all those who have gone before us, that we all suffer and die. To see someone face that fear precipitously, the process demonstrated within moments, to be the playwright and director of that drama—that is what the Ripper experienced.

Considering the crime scene photos that show the severe mutilation of the Ripper's last victim, I have to wonder if the murderer could identify with the women he killed and feel their suffering. Having revealed to himself by his own cruel acts the heights of fear and pain, and the terrifying frailty and ephemeral nature of flesh and awareness, was his dread of a particularly intense nature?

If his freedom or his life were never taken from him in answer to his crimes, did he at least suffer revelations of his own mortality?

I would like to think that he did.

—Alan M. Clark
Eugene, Oregon
February, 2018

WEST HAMPSTEAD

↑ MUSWELL HILL   ↑ HORNSEY

ISLINGTON

CLERKENWELL
SMITHFIELD
HOLBORN

BLACKFRIARS

KNIGHTSBRIDGE

WESTMINSTER

·VAUXHALL

CHELSEA EMBANKMENT

LONDON AND

↑
-N-

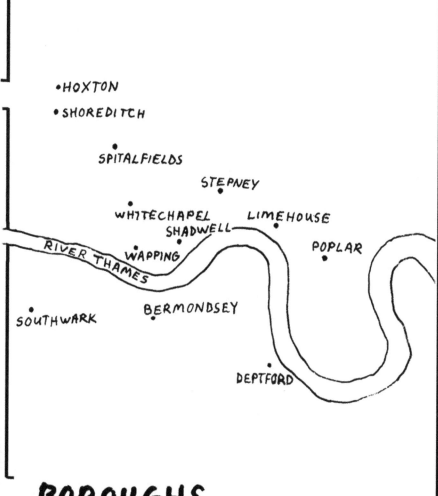

HOXTON
SHOREDITCH
SPITALFIELDS
STEPNEY
WHITECHAPEL   LIMEHOUSE
SHADWELL
RIVER THAMES   WAPPING   POPLAR
BERMONDSEY
SOUTHWARK
DEPTFORD

BOROUGHS

CATFORD

The Prostitute's Price

a novel by Alan M. Clark

Publishing

Eugene, Oregon

PRELUDE

Mary Jane Kelly, I am.

I am not the woman that died at 13 Miller's Court.

And I will speak ill of the dead.

The haybag what died there were as wretched and filthy as the crib itself.

A bit of jam, she'd been a toffer in a fine West End gay house. Were so mouthy, the Abbess of her house turned her out in the street. Fell to common tail, she did. Would bed any cove with enough chink. A blower, chaunting to the bleeders, she hurt a lot of women just trying to get on. Her street cokum would have her put down on a friend, or sell her own.

'Tis anger what brings out the street cant. I am capable of better.

Difficult as it is, I must become calm enough to consider carefully.

I argue with myself. Because I did indeed find the end of my life there in that squalid room, I have confused myself with that horrid buor. I've hated and even loved her. Yet, for all that makes us alike, I refuse to accept that we are one and the same. Hers is not a life what should make one proud.

Does that mean I am not proud of who I became when I were among the living? Perhaps. The haze that surrounds my thinking on the matter obscures the truth.

A desire for independence and adventure were my undoing.

In life, I knew both opulence and squalor.

Should the religions of the East be right, and I live again in some uncertain future time, give me a life of hardship and hatred or one of comfort and love, but not both. The knowing between the two is where true cruelty lies.

CHAPTER ONE

Stepney District, London's East End, September, 1886

In the drizzling early afternoon rain, Mary Jane left Thomas Morganstone's apartments in Harford Street intending to make the rounds of several pubs until she found a client. As she turned west into Bale Street amidst several others using the footway, a hand came out of nowhere, grabbed her left arm and twisted it. Mary Jane cried out, and went to her knees on the damp flagstones, trying to relieve the painful pressure.

"Let me go!" she cried.

Those walking nearby stopped and faced her; startled, fearful, some appearing ready to take action against possible threat.

She turned enough to see out of the corner of her eye the stocky man who had seized her.

A constable?

No, not a blue bottle, nor even a police detective, not in such fine clothing: a worsted blue suit and a black felt bowler.

"Help me," she said to those watching.

"This is a matter of crimes committed," the man said loudly.

In his fine clothes, he had the authority. Many of the pedestrians were already moving on, the increasing rain driving them away. Two men remained. They looked Mary Jane up and down. Her clothing and hair distinguished her as a ladybird. They seemed to decide she wasn't worth the trouble and went on their way as well.

"They have no care for a harlot," her assailant said. "They know *you* are truly the danger."

She recognized his voice, got a better look at him, and saw his ginger hair and whiskers. He was probably the same man she'd seen on the street months earlier, questioning a friend of hers named Bell. Mary Jane had been hidden from his view at the time, and had seen only his back. He'd asked about Andriette's whereabouts. Her friend didn't know Mary Jane had once gone by that name. When Bell offered nothing useful, he'd struck her to the ground and kicked her viciously.

"Get up," he told Mary Jane, pulling her up by the wrist with his left hand.

If indeed he was the same man, she'd heard his name. Just prior to his attack on Bell, Mrs. Buki, the proprietress of the Laughing Magpie, had warned Mary Jane that a red-haired gentleman had come to the brothel looking for her.

"The look of him told me he meant you harm," Mrs. Buki said. "I told him I had nothing for him without knowing his name. 'Stuart Brevard,' he told me. In return, I gave him a lie."

With the warning, Mary Jane had left her employment at the Laughing Magpie. She'd worked briefly at another brothel, Gander's Bush, before going to live with Thomas Morganstone. She'd been avoiding ginger-haired men since.

Most likely Stuart Brevard was related to the man, Harris Brevard, a client who had attacked Mary Jane in Paris. Defending herself against the attack, she had accidentally maimed Harris. She'd then robbed him of a valuable emerald and platinum necklace and escaped. No doubt, those were the offenses her assailant referred to. He, Stuart Brevard she presumed, wanted her to pay for the crimes.

He reached with his right hand to take her elbow.

She quickly moved toward his left shoulder, pivoting her wrist to parallel his. His rain-slicked grip loosened, and she nearly got away.

With his other hand, he grabbed her by the hair, just as his brother had done in his attack. He got behind her. His left hand let go of her wrist, moved out of sight for a moment. When it returned, she saw that it held a knife. He moved the blade up to the base of her ribcage, and pushed her toward the brick face of the nearest building, where the eave of the structure two stories above provided some protection from what had become a heavy downpour.

"I should gut you here and now," he said, "leave you swimming in your own blood."

"I would not do that, sir," she said. What arguments did she have? "Y-your fine suit."

17

He laughed with obvious delight.

Mary Jane sucked in her gut, swallowed hard, and held her breath. She would close her eyes so she didn't see what happened, but what little hope to get away she still possessed kept her from doing that.

"These people know you for what you are. They won't help. I can kill you and walk away."

"I passed a constable at the crossing." She tried to point westward.

He made a quick slice with the knife, cutting the underside of her left arm through the fabric of her chemise. So sharp was the blade, she didn't feel it until she lowered the arm and blood dripped from her elbow. Mary Jane stood trembling within his embrace, helpless.

He became still, and sighed softly. She'd heard that tone before from cruel clients—he savored her fear!

No professional bludger, this one. Too much emotion. A sudden move while he remained quiet might win her release, perhaps an elbow to his thick gut. Yet, if such a move didn't work, she'd be hastening her death.

"Oh, what I've been through trying to help my brother. Hopeless! Then the long search for you."

Harris's brother!

"You will die here today." Mr. Brevard said.

Mary Jane saw a woman, somewhat older, taller, dark-haired, approaching swiftly along the footway while adjusting her hands around the neck of a heavy laundry sack.

"No one will stop me," he whispered in Mary Jane's ear, clearly relishing his power over her.

As the woman moved, she lifted and swung the sack around. The burden lifted in an arc over her head.

Seeing what was coming, Mary Jane raised a leg and brought the heel of her boot down on the man's right foot. Her strike and the impact of the laundry sack occurred simultaneously. Mr. Brevard, a large man, bounced off Mary Jane, shoving her toward the brick wall.

He let go of her. She gasped for breath and tried to regain her balance.

"Run," came the woman's voice.

Leaning away from the man, glancing back, Mary Jane saw him teetering. Several leaves of paper spilled from his coat pocket in a spray upon the footway. He fell backwards onto his arse while reaching for her unsuccessfully.

She saw the woman lift her skirts and run away, having abandoned the laundry sack. The glimpse Mary Jane had of the woman's face stuck in her mind's eye, and she didn't know why. Her features seemed familiar.

Printed on the leaves of the paper on the footway, Mary Jane saw a sketch of a woman that looked much like herself, with the name, "Andriette," underneath. She grabbed one and stuffed it into her bodice.

Mr. Brevard tried to rise as Mary Jane leaned into a mad dash away from him. Her skirts tacked to lift seductively in front to show a bit of ankle when she walked, she ran easily without gathering her hems.

She looked back again, saw Mr. Brevard rise and take a few stumbling steps on his injured foot. With his pained expression, she knew she'd get away. The look in his eyes told her he would keep his word to gut her if he caught up with her again.

Mary Jane wanted to thank the brave woman who struck the man, but she'd gone in the opposite direction.

CHAPTER TWO

In August, 1885, a year before Stuart Brevard's attack in Bale Street, Mary Jane had found work at the Phoenix gay house.

The four-story stone building of the elegant brothel had a kitchen with dining tables, indoor plumbing with porcelain baths, basins, and flush toilets, a common room, several plush parlors, and twenty beautiful bedrooms. She was given one of the bedrooms with a feather mattress on a fine wooden frame, an eight foot tall armoire, a vanity and chest of drawers, the furniture all a matching walnut, finished with French polish.

On her first day there, a house seamstress named Bridgid took her to a room filled with fine clothing, said, "Please choose what you'd like to wear."

The woman made alterations to the pieces Mary Jane chose so they fit properly, and placed them in the armoire in her room.

Mrs. Elouise Arseneau, the elderly proprietress of the gay house, encouraged Mary Jane to set the limitations of what she would endure with clients. Mrs. Arseneau wrote down her subordinate's preferences in a book on a desk in her office.

"Those I send you shall engage only in the practices you allow," she said, gesturing toward the book. "Should a customer overstep his bounds, you shall give him warning that you'll call the house warders. Should he persist, cry out for help immediately."

Mary Jane got a sense that the proprietress valued her safety and service.

"May we call you Andriette?" Mrs. Arseneau asked.

"Yes," Mary Jane said. That became her name in all business with the gay house.

Her duties began with meeting clients in the parlors. Unlike her previous experience in Cardiff, price wasn't discussed. Within a month, she was attending gentlemen as a companion at events outside the gay house.

She learned that the self-made man, whose wealth brought him into demand socially, could take a prostitute who had sufficient ability with etiquette and language into certain social situations. Mary Jane had gained her position at the gay house by demonstrating her knowledge of social graces and the Queen's English in her interview with Mrs. Arseneau.

Some among the aristocracy held events to draw the well-to-do, self-made men into their circles. Among the peerage, many had too much debt, and had sold off so much of their holdings that little but their titles remained. They needed investment to rebuild the strength of their family lines. Those willing to compromise the standards of their kind in order to meet new, rich blood, looked for spouses with fortunes among the wealthy families of the self-made at home and abroad. Others had schemes to win money off the unsuspecting self-made men by drawing them into rigged gambling, or, through connections in the courts, manipulations of the legal system.

Of course, no one mistook Mary Jane for one with wealth. She had little more than the fine clothes on loan from the Phoenix gay house and the education she'd received when a child. Still, Mary Jane did get looks from titled toffs. She did not look or act out of place at the social events.

Was she happy? That would have been difficult for her to answer. She had certainly become impressed with herself and how far she had risen from humble beginnings. Mary Jane had a fascination for her new world and an eager willingness to be a part of the life around her.

Some of the peerage, once introduced to those of a lower station gained a fascination for what they called "slumming." She tried to steer clear of them, as they were known to turn cruel if they thought one didn't show the proper respect. That happened most unexpectedly at times to some of the women she knew.

The self-made man could also be cruel. Something in his outlook seemed to make his anger more predictable and manageable, though. He often had a sense that his money and influence should buy him whatever he wanted. Yet, whilst his wealth and power had been gained through his efforts, the circumstances of his birth did not suggest to him that he was a superior being. A spate of cruelty might easily be quieted with a few well-placed compliments to his character, appearance, or manner. As Mary Jane found out, that didn't always work, and sometimes the tactic made things worse.

Within a few months of joining the women at the Phoenix gay house, she made a trip to Paris with a gentleman. Mary Jane had met Harris Brevard, a bridge builder, on several occasions. She'd seen him eyeing her with obvious fascination from a distance, but each time, thankfully, she had been engaged with another gentleman. Round, thick-skinned, pink and balding, he had a porcine look, even in the best clothing. One of the self-made toffs, he carried a look of defiant pride, as if that helped prove his worth.

Through the gay house, he hired Mary Jane to go to Paris with him for two weeks in December of 1885. He had a large, two room apartment, a parlor and bedroom, on the fourth floor of Le Muerice in Rue de Rivoli, in the heart of the French capital. The fourth floor balcony, which ran the length of the building, gave a perfect view of the beautiful Tuileries Garden just across the lane. Though winter time, and most of the trees had lost their leaves, Mary Jane wanted to explore.

Gardens didn't interest Harris Brevard.

The first day, they shopped in delightful boutiques, where he bought her several small pieces of fine jewelry and a fur muff.

On a visit to the Musée du Louvre, Mary Jane discovered to her astonishment that each painting was as much a portal onto the soul of the artist as it was a window to a view.

"Too much yellow," Mr. Brevard said of the many worlds of vision they inspected that day. Upon leaving the museum, he said, "Shameful that they don't repair the damaged ones. There are painters who could touch up all those cracks." He stuffed his ugly head back into his silk top hat, and they strolled along the Seine while he tried to look important.

In bed, Harris Brevard was unremarkable. Mary Jane must have unwittingly revealed her lack of interest the first night because he looked at her sternly after his release. "You *must* do better," he said, pulling his stiff sinew from her notch with a sudden, angry jerk that left the sheath inside.

"Yes, Mr. Brevard," she said. "I beg your pardon. I don't wish to disappoint. I mean to do my best."

His features softened somewhat. "You are desirable in most every way. The look on your face needs work."

Less yellow? she wondered. *Fewer cracks?*

"Yes, sir," Mary Jane said.

He rolled over and slept.

At just ten o'clock in the evening, she couldn't sleep, spent a restless couple of hours listening to him snore and wishing she were not in his bed.

The next day, he presented Mary Jane with a beautiful rosewood box. "The emerald and platinum beauty you'll find inside is yours if you can earn it," he said.

Within, she discovered a gorgeous necklace of cut green jewels set in large white metal beads. She knew the sparkling delight with the glowing gems had to be worth hundreds of pounds.

Mary Jane's astonishment must have shown. He smiled, even as he took the box away from her.

"I did not tell you because I hadn't yet decided that you would be the one. I still have not decided, but thought you might need an incentive to earn what I have to offer."

She had the irrational fear that he was about to propose marriage. "What do you mean, pray tell?"

"This is the beginning of what will be for me a months-long tour of the continent. Although I have seen much here in my work, I have been too busy to see the sights of Europe before now. Should you improve the look you give me in bed, you may accompany me on the tour, attend to my needs, and, when all is done, you may have that necklace in addition to what I shall pay your house."

"Oh, sir," Mary Jane said, "that is generous. Yes, I most gratefully hope to earn your favor."

He seemed pleased with himself.

She was excited to have the opportunity to earn the treasure.

Her expression that afternoon in bed must have been persuasive.

He displayed a better mood.

That evening, they saw a show at the Folies Bergère; beautiful women in scant, colorful costumes performing gymnastics and dance. Bawdy at times, the tunes playful, yet grand, the graceful, supple bodies moving in time with the music took Mary Jane's breath away, while Mr. Brevard, seeing so much female flesh, sat with a boyish leer on his face.

The magical establishment itself, a fancy beyond anything she'd imagined, filled her senses until wonderment overflowed. The bright colors, the chandelier lighting, the variety of fascinating people, their elaborate dress and wild costumes, the rich food and drink—all had become a waking dream. The sounds of voices and music drew Mary Jane's attention in many directions. Turning this way and that, not wanting to miss anything, she grew dizzy.

With that, the experience began to sour. Expressions on the faces of those around her, especially the painted ones of the women, became pinched with a savage hunger of some sort. The odors of the place turned Mary Jane's stomach. The loud noises coming from the orchestra and audience confused and unsettled her. She fell ill, and knew she must find a privy quickly.

Mr. Brevard did not slow her as she excused herself. Mary Jane moved through the tables, fearing she might let go the contents of her stomach there in the hall, perhaps soiling some poor patron enjoying the show.

She did not speak the language, and was in too much of a hurry to ask where to go. Mary Jane stumbled out of the entrance of the establishment and vomited there in the street. Embarrassed, she glanced around. Thankfully none of the people coming in or going out took much notice of her.

Then a hand under Mary Jane's shoulder lifted her gently.

"Poor girl," said an English voice. "Let me help you."

Mary Jane thought the woman looked to be close to her age, possibly a bit older. She had a fair, pretty face with too much rouge, lip color, and eye shading. Her dress was that of a Parisian whore. "Miss Blanche Sayers," she said. "Did you come from inside?"

"Yes," Mary Jane said, "and I must return. A gentleman…"

"No need to explain. I see that you know life. The Demimondes are not to your liking, I take it."

She meant the hedonistic gathering in the cabaret, a word used to describe it. At the time, Mary Jane didn't know what she meant.

"Let's get you something for your stomach," Blanche said.

She helped Mary Jane, led her inside the cabaret to a marble-topped bar. "Warm rum and ginger," Blanche said.

The woman in lace and black velvet behind the bar seemed to understand her. While she moved about among the many bright bottles, preparing the drink, Mary Jane tried to locate Mr. Brevard. He sat where she'd left him, still watching the show. He glanced around a couple of times, presumably to find her, a look of irritation on his face.

Mary Jane turned back to her companion. She watched Blanche pour a few drops of amber liquid into a steaming cup that the barkeep must have placed on the polished surface. "Your drink," the woman said, lifting the cup and handing it to Mary Jane.

"How much shall I pay?" she asked.

"I've paid," Blanche said. "I put laudanum in your drink, a tincture of opium. With that, all this shall be much more fun." She waved her arms to include the entire cabaret.

Mary Jane knew of laudanum, but had never tried the drug. She also knew that some destroyed their lives with too much opium, yet she didn't worry that might happen to her.

"Perhaps I'll see you after the performance?" Blanche asked.

"Possibly," Mary Jane said, though she had no intention of seeking her company. "Thank you."

She took the cup with her back to the table where Mr. Brevard sat.

"You went for a drink alone?" he asked with a scowl.

"No," Mary Jane said. "I became ill. A woman helped me, gave me this to settle my stomach."

He gave her a look of disgust—may have thought she drank medicine—and turned his attention back to the women on stage.

Mary Jane sipped the drink until she'd emptied the cup. Strong flavors. Blanche was right, the laudanum made the rest of the evening much more tolerable. In truth, Mary Jane enjoyed too much the feeling the narcotic gave her.

Again that evening, when they had returned to his apartment at Le Muerice, she must have had an acceptable expression in bed.

And, again, after he turned over and went to sleep, she could not find slumber.

Thinking of the garden across the lane, Mary Jane decided upon an adventure. She rose, dressed in warm clothing, and quietly slipped out the door of the apartment.

By the dim gaslight, she explored Tuileries Garden. Alone in the night, there in that strange city, Mary Jane should have been afraid, but she wasn't. That may have been because of the laudanum. She had the impression no one saw her. That was to her liking.

She lifted the hem of her skirts and slipped from shadow to shadow in the chill air. The black limbs of the trees, with twigs like withered fingers, reached for the crescent of the moon. The stars, mere smudges high overhead, winked lazily to let her know they would keep her secret.

Looking up at them, Mary Jane tripped over something, and her knees struck the ground. She kept herself from falling all the way. The turf, dead that time of year, had blackened her stockings. Somehow, the stains seemed a badge of honor for her tidy adventure.

Mary Jane slipped back into Mr. Brevard's apartment, quietly undressed, hid her soiled stockings, and returned to bed without him noticing.

The afternoon of the next day they joined giblets again. Harris Brevard was crushing her. The fire on the hearth had been set too large, and the room had become sweltering hot. His sweat ran freely. As he pumped in and out, he gasped, groaned, and sprayed a bit of spittle. She pretended to find her pleasure with him, until he accidentally blew a clot from his nose into her face. She tried to relax, but all that was piggish and disgusting about him—perhaps all that Mary Jane had found loathsome in the men she'd serviced over the years—came back to haunt her in that moment. She panicked, and struggled under him in spite of herself.

He must have seen the soil from his nose on her face because he had a brief look of embarrassment.

Then he pulled away, jerked the sheath off his truncheon, and got up. "You've spoiled my coming bliss!" he said, his anger probably put on, not quite felt entirely.

"Me?" She regretted the one word question immediately because of the accusation it implied.

"You dare to blame me?" His embarrassment, possibly an unendurable blow to his pride, had quickly turned to rage. His eyes, menacing red-rimmed orbs, bore down on Mary Jane. "You disgusting whore!"

"No, o-of course you're n-not at fault," she said, stumbling on her words. "I-I should have aired out the room. 'Tis too hot. A fine gentleman such as yourself ought to be better served. I apologize."

"You patronizing pinchcock," he shouted. "Don't pretend to have respect for me. The look in your eyes tells me I'm not what you want. All I've wanted is a good show for my money. But I see that if I'm to have my pleasure, I must take it."

He struck Mary Jane in the gut. She rolled with the pain and tumbled off the bed. Trying to get away, she crawled toward the French doors that let out onto the balcony. He followed, struck her in the arse and back. She collapsed upon the floor, curled up to protect her middle. Mary Jane's head jerked back with a terrible ache in her neck as he grabbed her hair and yanked her toward the bed. Pinning her left arm up behind her back and holding the limb there painfully, he steered her onto the edge of the mattress. With his right hand, he savagely tore at Mary Jane's lower cheeks to open her. Wearing no sheath, he rammed his root deep inside. She feared he'd break her with the painful pounding her arse took. Mary Jane wailed and cried out until he shoved her arm up harder, the pain silencing her.

She would not, *could* not think. Trapped in a merciless agony, the need to get away from him could only eat at her. While she tried not to reason, unwanted memories came forth. She was back in her room in Cardiff, where a man had beaten her insensible and raped her. Should she survive Brevard's attack, another year of illness and convalescence might lie ahead. No, she would not think of that. All

27

she could do was to endure.

Brevard had wanted to be cruel all along. He would have got to the brutality somehow eventually, no matter how Mary Jane acted. She knew those things later as she recalled him spitting in her hair, digging his nails into her back and neck, gasping out guttural, half-formed curses.

Eventually, he stiffened. His flying, slapping flesh ceased to pound against her. He cried out in his release.

His grip on her arm weakened in that moment, and she twisted around hard to her left toward him. He seemed surprised to be looking her in the eye. He still quaked in the flood of bliss, and had little control of himself. Mary Jane got away, and hurried through the bedroom door into the parlor.

He got his feet under him quickly enough, and followed. She turned as she moved, saw that he was almost upon her again, saw the hatred in his eyes and his meaty hands clawing for her. Mary Jane swung wildly to fend him off, and her right hand struck him in the throat.

A long moment passed while he stumbled forward. She moved out of his path. His eyes grew large in his red face. He clutched at his neck, turned toward her with a frightful look of anger turning to fear. Wheezing with a pleading, childlike face, he flailed. Mary Jane dodged out of his way again and returned to the bedroom, shutting the door between them and holding it. He pushed from the other side. The latch tongue clicked into the frame, and the pressure let up. A pounding on the wood commenced, became weaker until it ceased.

Mary Jane dressed quickly, gathered her things into her travel bag. Taking the necklace from the rosewood box, she added that to her bag. She pushed to open the door, hoping he had fallen insensible. His right shoulder kept it from opening. He lay unmoving on the floor, his wheezing a thin reed of sound. Pushing with all she had, she created a gap large enough to pass through with the bag.

She left the door to the apartment open. Walking swiftly, but as casually as possible, her heart pounding, limbs shaking, fearing that he'd somehow catch her again, she fled the hotel.

Mary Jane had some money and the small jewelry Mr. Brevard had bought for her on their first day in Paris. She hid the necklace inside the stuffing of the fur muff he'd given her. Over the ensuing days, she used all her money and the small jewelry securing passage to the coast, bribing a sheep smuggler to return her to England, and making her way back to London. She arrived at the Phoenix gay house two days before Christmas, believing she had some time before word of what happened in Paris got back to Mrs. Arseneau. Once that happened, Mary Jane knew she'd no longer be welcome in the establishment.

She hid the muff with necklace still inside atop the eight foot tall armoire in her room, a dusty spot clearly too high for the charwoman to bother cleaning. The decorative parapet around the top of the piece of furniture totally hid her prize from sight. Mary Jane began to pack her things, leaving room in her travel bag to add the muff and necklace. She would add those just before she left.

Word of what happened to Harris Brevard arrived faster than she expected, two days after Christmas. Mrs. Arseneau came to her room with two of her punishers, big fellows with hard faces. Standing by in case they were needed, the men looked uncomfortable in their fine clothes. They didn't choose to look at Mary Jane.

"We cannot be seen to help you in any way," Mrs. Arseneau said, a stern look in her hooded blue eyes. The old, white-haired French woman stood stiffly and somewhat unsteadily in her finery. "If you leave now, we will tell the police nothing, should they come for you."

Mary Jane thought of the muff atop the armoire. "May I have a moment alone to gather my things? I have not finished packing."

"No," Mrs. Arseneau said.

The two men turned toward Mary Jane, their sharp eyes a clear warning.

"All of the gifts you've received are forfeit as recompense for the damage we've sustained by your actions," the proprietress said. "I see you've packed clothing. I assume you have your push."

Mary Jane had little money after fleeing Paris. Still, she nodded.

"I shan't go through your bag," Mrs. Arseneau said, "but you must leave now with what you've already packed."

Mary Jane had a sudden desire to strike the old woman, to tear her beautiful pink silk, to undo the white, matching curls of hair arranged so perfectly on her wrinkled brow. What might have been follow-me-lads in Mrs. Arseneau's day, were just jug loops now. As stylish as the woman was, why did she wear her hair in such an ugly, old-fashion manner?

Mary Jane held in her rage, knowing that to show the anger would do no good. Nothing more could she do at that time to retrieve the muff and necklace.

She allowed the two men to escort her to the door of the establishment.

CHAPTER THREE

Mary Jane ran from the site of Stuart Brevard's attack for at least a quarter of a mile. She took a northeastward direction through Stepney, across the Regents Canal at Bridge Street, to become lost in the neighborhoods of the Holy Trinity Liberty. Finally, Mary Jane slowed to a walk. Still trembling in fear, she continued to look back frequently, making certain the man hadn't caught up with her. Larger and no doubt faster than Mary Jane, he could be anywhere among the many using the footways and streets. Hidden behind the reflections on the glass of a carriage window, he might watch her that very moment. She could only hope that her heel had damaged his foot enough to slow him.

She took the bottle of laudanum from the pocket under her top skirt, pulled the small cork, and took several tiny sips of the bitter amber liquid. Though some time would pass before she felt the effects of the tincture, she became calmer even as she put the drug away.

Mary Jane continued through Holy Trinity at a slower pace, northward at one crossing, eastward at the next, wanting even more distance from the site of the attack, while confusing her trail. She did her best to tidy her disheveled hair as she walked, and used a handkerchief moistened with saliva to clean the blood from her arm.

Putting the handkerchief away in her bodice, she discovered the leaf of paper, now wrinkled, with the sketch of the woman printed on it. The name beneath the image, Andriette, had been Mary Jane's name while at the Phoenix gay house. She decided the woman depicted looked more like Gabriella Gorse, a beautiful flaxen haired prostitute she knew. Like Mary Jane, Gabriella had once worked in a fine gay house in the West End. With her angry mouth, she had burned all her bridges and now worked the streets. Mary Jane didn't trust her.

The attack having come so close to Thomas Morganstone's

apartments, she assumed Stuart Brevard had somehow tracked her there. Relentless, the man would keep coming for her until he succeeded in making her pay for what she'd done to Harris.

In Mile End Road, Mary Jane began to feel less unease and turned around, trying to think of where she might go. She couldn't return to Thomas Morganstone's apartments or Mrs. Buki's Laughing Magpie because Stuart Brevard had tracked her to both. After leaving employment at the Laughing Magpie, Mary Jane had gone to live at Gander's Bush, a brothel belonging to Mrs. Buki's sister, Mrs. Carthy. Despite the amount of time Mary Jane had spent in recent months away at Thomas Morganstone's apartments, she remained on good terms with Mrs. Carthy and could return to her brothel anytime, but her run-down house was a place of last resort.

Joseph Fleming's beaming face appeared ahead on the footway bobbing up and down as he walked. The two walking in front of him moved off to the left, and she saw his full form, dressed for labor. He was a handsome fellow, despite his slightly bowed legs.

Clearly he'd seen her.

Mary Jane looked about for an excuse for her appearance, saw the low limbs of trees along the verge, and came up with a lie.

Joseph Fleming, a criminal of all work and associate of Thomas Morganstone's, also worked as a plasterer. She'd made love to Joseph several times while staying at Thomas's apartments. Fleming had always been good to her and anything but demanding. Despite knowing her profession, he had shown a romantic interest in her and had recently asked her to come live with him at his room in Globe Road. He'd made it clear that if she did, he wouldn't expect her to cease her soliciting activities. That had surprised her.

Mary Jane had no interest in romance. She did want possible protection from the likes of Stuart Brevard, and a place to stay since she resisted going back to Gander's Bush.

"Mary Jane." Joseph said. Moving closer, he gained a look of concern. "Did you meet with harm somehow? There's blood on your arm, and your beautiful hair…"

"Yes," she said, "Clumsy, I were, allowed a low-lying limb of one of these trees to snag me as I walked past." She gestured toward the verge.

"Well, I'm glad it wasn't worse."

"I ought not to have given you my true name." she said with a playful, chiding tone.

"Oh… yes," he said, looking chastened, "Pardon me, Ginger."

"I forgive you," she said with a chuckle. "If your offer still stands, I would be delighted to come share your room."

His smile, like that of a little boy, knew no bounds. He laughed and caught her up in his arms.

Though Mary Jane giggled for him, she hoped she'd not just made a terrible mistake. Something about the man was too appealing. To her vexation, she'd found herself thinking about him when he wasn't around.

"I'm on my way to a job site," he said with a slight frown. "My lodgings are at 200 Globe Road, number 2. 'Tis at the crossing with Green Street. I can give you my key. I'll need to return shortly after seven o'clock this evening. I'll get you your own key as soon as I can."

Mary Jane didn't relish the idea of being alone with her fears in Fleming's room at such an hour, waiting to let him in.

"No," she said after consideration, "I have a place I can stay for the night. Shall I find you tomorrow, then?"

"Yes." He bent forward and gave her a delightful kiss.

Mary Jane didn't want to enjoy it as much as she did.

He walked away, glancing back with a smile.

She would go to Gander's Bush, after all. At least then she'd have a crib to satisfy a client if she found one.

Walking southwest along Mile End Road, Mary Jane seriously considered for the first time removing from London to make a start elsewhere in a place of safety, somewhere Stuart Brevard wouldn't easily find her.

Perhaps she would do well in America. Wherever she went, she'd need funds to make that fresh start.

The stolen necklace was worth two hundred pounds, if not more. Unfortunately, she could not get it from atop the armoire in her old room at the Phoenix without alerting those who would want to claim it. Still, if she could get the necklace, sell it to a fence, and combine the funds with what she had saved, about twenty-five pounds, then she'd have what she needed. Mary Jane had never had dealings with a fence, but thought that she'd gain at least half of the worth of the necklace. One hundred and twenty-five pounds would be enough for her to feel comfortable making the move. Of course she might go with less, since soliciting would always see her through, yet she would miss much about London, and the funds would be a small compensation.

When a child, I had no need of money to go on an adventure.

With fear still dogging her, she willingly retreated into pleasant recollection.

Always the same, Mary Jane's earliest memories came to her from a time in Ireland. There, she found Mum's beautiful green eyes and musical voice, Papa's stern gaze and hard mouth, her sister's petulance, and her five older brothers, each one a different mystery.

She also found rain so gentle it didn't fall, just hung in the air beneath woolen-gray skies. The complaints of long gone sheep and crows came to her magically out of morning mists that hugged the ground. She smelled the thick brown odor—like dirt burning—of peat smoke rising from chimneys. The vapor of Papa's breath on cold evenings, carrying the sweet-rotten aroma of whiskey, lingered there still.

Of Mary Jane's own concerns of the time, only the green stains on the knees of all her white stockings came to her. They were badges of honor, from slipping in the dew and falling in the weeds. Mum wasn't pleased, but the patches of color reminded Mary Jane of escapes from family, and her tidy adventures in the fields around their lodgings.

A small girl with few worries, Mary Jane had been happy and fearless.

"Do you know what danger is, girl?" Papa asked. Tall and thin, with straight, sandy hair and a pocked face, Papa could have been a frightening scarecrow.

Mary Jane's brother, Johnto, had captured her on that day and carried her home. He stood holding her head so she faced Papa and couldn't turn away.

She didn't understand Papa's question then. At the time, the word, *danger,* seemed a curious one. Beyond the stern look he gave her, Mum, behind him, smiled. For all Mary Jane knew, danger was the spanking she got, and still it was worth the pain to go missing.

No further recollections remained of Ireland. A gray body of water passed beneath her, separating Mary Jane from the land of her birth, and life had begun anew in Wales.

Though, we start as such foolish and vulnerable creatures, so often that is our time of greatest happiness.

A child may not need to earn, but I most certainly do. I must work to gain what I'll need in case I fail to recover the necklace.

Mary Jane turned south into Burdett Road, paused to use the urinal near the cabmen's shelter, and considered hiring the Hansom cab that stood at the kerb. To ride would be faster, more pleasant, and safer than walking the nearly two miles to Gander's Bush in Breezer's Hill.

No, her fear had diminished. She felt confident that she'd lost Stuart Brevard for the nonce, and she had to save her funds.

Having turned southwest into Bridge Street to cross back over the Regents Canal, Mary Jane saw the woman who had helped her earlier, walking along the other side of the road with what looked like the same sack of laundry she'd wielded as a weapon. Something about her large eyes and full mouth were hauntingly familiar.

Recklessly, Mary Jane hurried into the road, almost falling beneath the wheel of a fast-moving growler. She dodged by the vehicle and got to the other side of the road in time to catch the woman.

"All my thanks to you!" she said, somewhat breathless from her dash across.

Startled, the woman dropped her sack and stopped, her hands out to the sides, as if reaching for balance. "Oh...my," she said, "you're..."

"I'm Ginger," Mary Jane said. "You saved me from that bludger in Bale Street."

The woman appeared to be forty-something years old. Her dark hair had grayed at the temples. She stood a good six inches taller than Mary Jane.

"Miss Jennifer Weatherhead," she said a bit reluctantly, her beautiful gray-green eyes looking Mary Jane up and down.

A good thing she didn't take the time to look me over before deciding to help! She recognized in Jennifer the discomfort people often displayed when confronted with a fallen woman. Mary Jane didn't hold it against her.

Then it occurred to her why the woman seemed familiar—she looked much like Mum!

Mother had died a couple of weeks before Mary Jane's eighth birthday, less than two years after the family arrived in Wales and settled in Carmarthenshire. Recollections of Mum had always been precious. Her happy expressions, her laughter, and her warm and graceful bearing still lived in her grown daughter's memory.

Mary Jane beamed at the woman, and that seemed to make Jennifer *more* uncomfortable.

"I did what decency demanded," she said. "I'm glad to have helped." She bent to pick up the sack of laundry.

"Is that the same sack?"

"Yes," Jennifer said. "I went back for it. Had to wrestle it away from a woman who tried to claim the clothing. It holds my evening's work...." She paused uncomfortably. "...Mending for Bryte's Laundry." Again she paused, looking at the pavement. "Now, I must be on my way. I'm expected at home."

"Again, I am most grateful. You are truly brave to have helped. Good day."

"Good day to you."

Mary Jane watched her go. Looking at the woman brought her delight, as if she were seeing her mother alive again. She had a desire to follow, but didn't want to frighten Jennifer any more than she had already.

Instead, still thinking of Mum, she continued southwest toward Gander's Bush.

CHAPTER FOUR

In 1869, when the family arrived in Wales and settled in Carmarthen, Mum would have been about the same age as Jennifer Weatherhead. That year, Mary Jane became six years old.

Papa took a gaffer position at the Morganstone Ironworks.

The Kelly family—father, mother, and seven children—lived in a two-room, company-built brick cottage on the River Towy, alongside five other identical homes. The children had the back room. Their beds shared the chamber with six chairs and a table large enough for the family to all sup together. When that happened, three stood. Mary Jane and her older sister, Ruth, slept together in one bed, their brothers, Johnto, Jack, Dylan, Kevin, and Iason, wedged together like oiled herring in a tin, slept in another. Their parents had the front room, which also served as kitchen.

They had come from much humbler single room-lodgings in Limerick, Ireland. In the new house, Mary Jane felt smaller.

Papa warned of the River Towy, fifty yards down the hill behind the house. "Don't go within ten feet of the water. At least one child each year drowns in that river. Hasn't claimed the year's victim yet. Don't tempt it."

Alive with light and movement, with strange smells, swelling with the rains or running low in dryer weather to expose hidden treasures, the River Towy was home for all manner of fish and birds. The Kelly children had not known so much life before, and they all wanted to play in the water.

Papa away at work one day, Mum told them, "Want the adventure all the more, you will, to have it denied. Even if he does not know this, I do."

She helped her children find shallows where they could wade in the water safely.

They all kept the secret from Papa, a strict and demanding man.

Mary Jane's brothers found work so they might add to the household income. Johnto, Jack, and Kevin went to work at the ironworks with Papa. Dylan and Iason worked in woolen mills. Ruth and Mary Jane considered themselves lucky since they stayed home to help Mum with the housekeeping. She taught her girls to read and write, something denied her sons because they spent so little time at home.

Mary Jane enjoyed a good life in Wales for almost two years, until a day shortly before her eighth birthday, in the spring of 1871.

In the breezy afternoon of that day, she and Mum worked together hanging laundry out to dry. Ruth was spending the day with her beau. The clothesline, strung from posts, was protected from the strongest winds in a flat spot halfway down the slope behind the house. The fat clouds above started low and built high and fluffy into the bright blue sky. Good daydreaming clouds. A beautiful day in a lovely life.

"And what will you be wanting for your birthday," Mum asked.

Just as Mary Jane decided upon her wish, a frivolous desire for a yellow bonnet she'd seen in a shop window, the wind shifted and came down the hill. A damp bed linen lost its pins, billowed out in the stiff breeze and seemed to swallow Mum. She cried out, fell, and rolled downhill. The linen cloth twisted around her, pinning her arms to her sides. Running after, Mary Jane could not catch up until they reached the upper edge of the steep river bank. She leapt, gripped an edge of the linen. Though addled from a hard fall, she'd caught the cloth in her hand.

She knew some small relief, then saw the fright in Mum's eyes as she rolled out of the sheet, clawing for the verge. She caught the linen in one hand, and the cloth slipped from Mary Jane's grasp.

Hope turned to horror. Mum and the linen flew over the embankment. Falling several feet into the river, she went under, again, wrapped in the cloth.

Neither of them could swim. Too afraid, Mary Jane did not jump in to help Mum.

She struggled to the surface, but the current carried her downstream.

In a panic, Mary Jane followed along the bank, trying to find a way to help, looking for a way down and a shallow where her mother might come out. Mum rose to the surface several times, gasping for air, weaker each time. Mary Jane could not keep up. Her mother disappeared around a bend. Fallen brush and a thicket of small trees stopped Mary Jane. She turned back for help.

No one answered her frantic knocks upon the neighboring cottage doors. Those who lived in the homes, men, women, and children, were all away trying to earn a crust. Mary Jane saw no life on the river that day, no fish, no birds, just the cruel water and lifeless rocks. The wind had blown the daydreams out of the fat clouds in the cold blue sky. She returned to the fallen brush and tangled thicket, pushed through, and searched farther downriver to no avail. Passing through the thick wooded patch had not been as difficult as she'd imagined. With that realization, the child knew the depths of shame and regret for the first time, a pain greater than any she'd known before.

Johnto discovered where exhaustion had left Mary Jane, in a patch of violets growing beside the water. A few weeks earlier, she and Mum had picnicked there because they loved the violets.

Johnto carried Mary Jane home.

She wept for weeks, it seemed, hid herself away whenever she could.

Then came the blame from Papa. He didn't say how he felt, but she saw the anger, the accusation in his eyes.

Mary Jane had an accusation of her own.

Mum died because I didn't try hard enough. If only I'd pushed through the thicket instead of turning back for help.

Johnto moved into the front room with Papa. Ruth left home, married a cooper named Evans in Swansea. Mary Jane slept alone.

Life took a dark turn, and she thought her days would never truly recover their light.

On occasion, she went back to the flowering patch where she and Mum had picnicked. Mary Jane picked violets, and threw them into the water for her mother.

Papa sent Mary Jane to work for Mrs. Margaret Morganstone in 1872. Her husband, Douglas P. Morganstone, the owner of the ironworks where Papa worked, had gone missing in 1870 when the passenger steamship, The City of Boston, "disappeared" somewhere in the Atlantic between Halifax, Nova Scotia and Liverpool. Mrs. Morganstone had managed her husband's enterprises since.

She had asked those in trusted positions at the ironworks if any had a child about her daughter's age, ten years, willing to work as a live-in housemaid.

Papa offered Mary Jane, a girl of nine years at the time. The day he told her of her fate, she heard him saying "good riddance" though he did not indeed say those words. Of course, he would collect her wages for the family and Mary Jane would receive none that she might spend as she chose.

Even with a dread of displeasing her future mistress and the cruelty that might follow, she felt glad to leave home and go to live at Bryn Haearn, the Morganstone home. Not that Papa harmed her. Well…, one willow switch whipping that stung awfully for a lie she told. But worse, Mary Jane suffered his cold silence, the disapproving looks, his never once wanting the best for her. Even if Mrs. Morganstone whipped or starved her, that would be better.

A conversation Mary Jane overheard between Papa and Johnto sometime after Mr. Morganstone went missing gave her some hope that she'd be treated fairly in her future position. Home from the day's labor, they sat together sharing a pail of bitter Papa had brought home. Ignored, Mary Jane kneaded dough for dinner biscuits on the counter beside the pump.

"I thought to myself," Papa said, "a woman, a fine mess she'll make of the ironworks. Yet, she's done well."

"I much prefer the Missus," Johnto said shaking his head. "A hard man, Mr. Morganstone."

Papa nodded. "Rode me like a bit of blood." He shook his head slowly, staring perhaps into recollection. "I won't miss him."

"The men are much happier under Mrs. Morganstone."

"Yes, production is up. From Mr. Collins I hear she'll share some of the wealth with us this year." Papa paused to look Johnto in the eye. "You didn't hear that from me."

Bryn Haearn, a great two-story granite house of many rooms built on a hill, had projecting gables and a high, steep roof containing several dormer windows. The interior held ornate woodwork, decorative plaster relief, and leadlight windows, each a different design with stained glass at the top in blues and greens.

On Mary Jane's first day at Bryn Haearn, she had expected the housekeeper to greet her. Instead, she found herself with Mrs. Morganstone. Standing before the finely-dressed lady of the house in the marble vestibule of her beautiful home, Mary Jane suffered embarrassment for her worn clothes. Her heart in her throat, ringing her sweaty hands behind her back, she couldn't think how to act.

"Please call me Peggy," Mrs. Morganstone said.

"I couldn't do that, Madam."

"Yes, but you may."

The girl didn't know what to make of the woman.

"You may call me Mary Jane, should you choose to, Madam," she said sheepishly.

"Thank you. I'd be delighted to do that."

Though short and small, Mrs. Morganstone had a confidence about her. Her brown eyes had a youthful warmth. A single dimple appeared in her left cheek with her lopsided, slightly mischievous smile. She kept her nearly black hair with tidy pins. Among her sensibly drab clothing, one small brightly colored piece always stood out, perhaps peacock-blue cuffs, a new-leaf-green collar, or the edge of a red handkerchief poking out of a breast pocket. That day, she wore a purple enamel brooch of columbine blossoms.

She showed Mary Jane to her chamber, a cozy room in the below-ground area. The room had a chest of drawers, a coal grate, a small bed that looked soft and warm, and a window high in the wall that looked up toward a flower garden. A coral-colored rose in bloom stood outside the window in what she'd later learn was a walled garden behind the house.

"The water closet down the hall you'll share with the other servants."

An indoor toilet that Mary Jane would be permitted to use? She could not believe her good fortune.

The woman seemed an angel for a moment. Then, having heard adults in her life speak of their misgivings toward the well-to-do, and remembering Mrs. Morganstone's crooked smile, a deep suspicion of her set in, and Mary Jane wondered what sort of mischief she were up to. Had the woman made her out to be a fool somehow?

Trying to discern the truth, Mary Jane looked Mrs. Morganstone in the eyes.

The woman allowed the child's piercing gaze, smiled easily, comfortably. No mischief did Mary Jane see.

She set aside her misgivings, at least for the moment, and followed Mrs. Morganstone back to the ground floor and her daughter's chamber.

"Elen," she said. "We have a new housemaid, Miss Kelly."

"Mary Jane, please," Mary Jane said, and winced at her boldness.

She saw in one corner of the room a girl about her age, sitting at a small desk. She had an impression that the girl had been reading before she looked up. Elen had long brown hair and dark eyes, like her mother.

"So pleased to meet you," she said in a proud, crisp voice.

She didn't get up, which Mary Jane thought strange until she rolled out from behind the desk in a wheeled contraption.

Later, she would learn that Elen's legs never grew properly, yet a happy child she seemed. She had seating with large wheels in front and small ones in back. Below the seat, a foldout footrest rode high to support her little feet. The large wheels had pushrims so she could propel herself about.

"Will you play with me?" she asked. "I have lots of toys."

Mary Jane's eyes took in the rest of the room, the small bed in one corner, in the other a trunk and a set of shelves loaded with toys; dolls, stuffed animals, and miniatures, including a chandler's shop and a fine home.

Her eyes must have grown large, and she imagined her mouth dropped open. Mrs. Morganstone's dimple appeared with her broad smile. Elen giggled.

"Do you like my doll house?" she asked. "The wee housekeeper and the tiny valet are in love."

Mary Jane found herself frowning at the thought.

"What's the matter?" Elen asked.

"Domestics most often have to leave service to marry," Mary Jane said carefully, thinking she might regret the words. "How shall they earn?"

"Oh, I shan't worry," Elen said, "the master and lady of the house are not entirely stuffy. They approve. They shall permit the servants to stay on and live in the guest house."

Mary Jane looked for a smaller house, and didn't see one.

"The guest house is in the trunk," Mrs. Morganstone said. Her voice dropped to a whisper. "She pretends they have not built the dwelling yet."

"It is a surprise," Elen said, shushing her mother with a forefinger across her lips, "a nuptial gift. Now, be quiet, lest they hear."

Since Mary Jane could tell that Mrs. Morganstone was willing to play along, she made a show of vigorously nodding her support for Elen's admonishment. "You don't want to spoil it," she told Mrs. Morganstone.

Elen beamed at Mary Jane.

"Of course, you're right," Mrs. Morganstone said, smiling.

Then and there, Mary Jane knew she liked Elen.

Her mother seemed pleased that the two girls got along.

Back in the area, Mrs. Morganstone took Mary Jane to the housekeeper's office, and introduced her to Miss Mateland, a gray-haired woman with a pointy nose and something of a dewlap beneath her weak chin. Though all business in her black and white uniform, she had warmth in her tone when she spoke. Mary Jane was given two sets of a black and gray uniform. Miss Mateland explained the household rules and housemaid's duties, then gave Mary Jane a leaf of paper with all that she'd explained written down in a manner easy to read and understand.

Mrs. Morganstone stood by, listening.

All was much as Mary Jane had expected except for a curious two hour period after luncheon each day. For that time, the instructions read, "Help Elen with anything she desires."

"Get settled in today, and be ready to start tomorrow," Miss Mateland said.

"Yes, Miss," Mary Jane said.

The housekeeper left her office to attend to other duties.

"If you'd like," Mrs. Morganstone said, as they took the stairs back to ground level, "go play with Elen. Ask her to show you her collection of stereograms. My favorites are the ones of American Indians. Such interesting faces."

Mary Jane stood staring at her, not understanding. "Won't Miss Mateland become upset with me?"

"We have a special understanding."

"But the help doesn't play with members of the family they serve," Mary Jane said, feeling awkward to be telling Mrs. Morganstone her business.

"Do you like Elen?" she asked.

"Oh, yes," Mary Jane said.

Mrs. Morganstone grinned. "I'll tell you a secret if you won't tell Elen."

Mary Jane's vague suspicions about the woman returned.

"My beautiful daughter doesn't leave the house because she doesn't like feeling different from other children. She says they look at her funny. I have had companions brought to the house for her, ones that have a crippled family member and are accustomed to the limitations. Elen complains that I hire them to be her friends, and she shies away from them, embarrassed. We had a young scullery maid, Bethany, who became Elen's best friend. With the kitchen staff, I worked out adjustments to the schedule to allow Bethany time to play with Elen. My daughter was broken-hearted when the poor girl died of grippe nearly a year ago. Elen retreated from life afterward and lost interest in her lessons, especially those concerning social graces. 'I shall never need to know how to be with people,' she said. Nearly broke my heart."

"You brought me here to be her friend?" Mary Jane asked.

"Only if you want to be. I leave the decision up to you. You'll work so she doesn't believe I pay you to be a companion. Should you choose to take the time in the afternoon to play, please promise not to tell her."

Although unsure of the arrangement and still concerned that such a thing would draw the ire of the housekeeper, Mary Jane nodded her head. "Yes, I promise."

You mustn't let Papa find out, she thought, uncertain why that seemed good advice. Intuition told her that he wouldn't want her to have fun while toiling for the family.

She played with Elen that afternoon. Mrs. Morganstone invited Mary Jane to attend the lessons she gave her daughter in the early evening before dinner. The lessons had three parts—reading and writing, maths, and one concerning speech and social graces: elocution and etiquette.

During that first lesson at Bryn Haearn, Elen drew the new housemaid into the work at hand. They both read, competed to solve their maths, and practiced pronunciations with tongue twisters that made them laugh.

Their favorite was by an American woman named Carolyn Wells.

> Betty Botta bought some butter;
> "But," she said, "this butter's bitter!
> If I put it in my batter
> It will make my batter bitter.
> But a bit o' better butter
> Will but make my batter better."

"You'll be fine ladies yet," Mrs. Morganstone told the girls.

"Yes, we nearly have all the ingredients," Elen said, giggling. "We need but a—"

They laughed themselves to tears.

Elen insisted that Mary Jane attend all her lessons. Allowances were made in the work schedule to permit her even more time in the afternoons with Elen. As housemaid, Mary Jane did little work. While she feared the resentment of the other help, most of the domestic servants were so pleased to see Elen come out of her shell, they readily accepted Mary Jane's absence from duty.

Thus began the second happy period of Mary Jane's life. Four carefree years passed by too quickly.

When Mary Jane was twelve years old, Elen's cousin, Thomas Morganstone came to live at Bryn Haearn. His parents had perished when their home in Pembroke caught fire and burned to the ground. Thomas had jumped from a window to escape the fire, had spent months in hospital, and had come to Bryn Haearn with his limb healed.

Mary Jane found him handsome, his smile spellbinding. He had light brown, curly hair, gray eyes framed with dark lashes, and lively eyebrows. Though a sixteen-year-old boy, he became a companion for the girls. He loved making things. With tools he'd brought with him, he made a stable for Elen's miniature horses from the wood of crates discovered in one of the outbuildings.

"Would you make a gazebo for the lovers?" Elen asked.

"Yes, I'd be happy to do so," he said, bowing low as if he were not her equal.

Mrs. Morganstone bought better wood for him to use, hand tools, and a miniature lathe and saw, powered with a treadle.

When done building the gazebo, he said, "Let's make a whole village."

Elen and Mary Jane heartily agreed to help. Thomas did most of the work. The many buildings he made matched the scale of her doll house, guest house, and chandler's shop.

Mrs. Morganstone bought new pieces for their effort, furniture for the homes and businesses, small wagons, carriages, animals for the streets, and tiny people. Elen and Mary Jane sewed curtains for the windows, and clothes for the figures that populated the village. Mary Jane learned to paint, and created portraits, landscapes, and still lifes to hang on the interior walls of the houses and some of the establishments. One of the largest rooms at Bryn Haearn—what had been Douglas P. Morganstone's study—became home to their project. Most of the furniture was removed from the chamber to make room on the floor for the miniature village. The streets of the tiny town wide enough, Elen wheeled through them in her seating, careful not to upset the inhabitants.

Mrs. Morganstone brought in tutors for Thomas, and allowed him to go to worksites in Carmarthen to watch construction and learn from what he saw. He would tell the girls about what he learned and show them how he used the knowledge in constructing the miniature village.

Mary Jane fell in love with Thomas. Though he treated her sweetly, he never seemed to look upon her in the manner she did him. Still, she knew happiness just being in his company.

Papa never knew how her circumstances had improved until one day after her thirteenth birthday when he arrived at Bryn Haearn to collect her wages and discovered her playing badminton in the front yard with Thomas Morganstone while Elen cheered them on. Mary Jane knew he came once a month to collect her wages, but he had not asked to see her. She had not seen him in several years, except for brief moments each Christmas.

By the look in his eyes as he watched her playing, she knew she was in for trouble.

Papa took Mary Jane from Bryn Haearn. Having no choice in the matter, she lost all semblance of dignity. She fought, wept, and cursed him as she was taken away. Ashamed that the Morganstones witnessed her wild tantrum, she became quiet on the way to her family's home, the company cottage on the River Towy. Once there, she withdrew further into herself, while anger and sadness in equal measure roiled within.

At first, Mary Jane had hoped to return to the Morganstones. She fancied they might come quickly, perhaps in the night, and take her away with them. Somehow, she knew that could not happen, and that she'd have to wait out Papa's anger.

Still a girl full of fancy, her most troubling concern was that Thomas might go on with his life without her, and she'd miss her chance to one day become his.

Papa found work for Mary Jane at the woolen mill where Iason had a position. Sister and brother walked the mile and a half to the mill together each morning at five o'clock along a deeply rutted dirt lane with a few stands of sturdy ash and oak trees here and there along its length. Until her feet became used to such a long walk, Iason let her ride him piggyback some of the way. She found a bond with him that she didn't have with her other siblings.

He had advanced over time to a comfortable position at the mill. A doubler, he operated a machine that made two-ply yarn. Mary Jane became a bowlminder, and cleaned raw wool, a malodorous and filthy job. She was miserable, having little strength for such labor.

After years of many comforts with the Morganstones, to coarse living she had returned. Mary Jane's oldest brothers had left home, Johnto for the army, and Jack for Australia. With Ruth married and gone to Swansea, Papa gave Mary Jane the task of cooking and cleaning for the family. The cottage had become a filthy hole, the privy a reeking horror. Iason saw her unhappiness and helped with the work when Papa couldn't see. She prepared plain food, made cruder still by her inexperience. To fend off complaints from the family, and in defense of her own palate, she learned to do better.

Mary Jane continued her education by reading anything she could get her hands on. Those who could read at her place of employment shared their books and periodicals with her. When done reading copies of Charles Dickens's periodical, *All the Year Round*, a woman at the mill, Mared Jones, loaned them to Mary Jane. In their pages she read short fiction stories, and some longer, serialized fiction. She also read articles involving international affairs and cultures, and social criticism.

Whenever Papa found her reading material, he disposed of it.

"Women with idle hands need books," he said. "I mean to see that you have too much to do."

Mary Jane hated her father.

Mrs. Morganstone visited the Kelly home on three occasions after Mary Jane left Bryn Heaern, each time asking Papa to allow her to return. Mary Jane didn't hear their conversations. Iason told her something of what had been said during the woman's last visit.

"She offered to raise your wages and his," he said. "Surprised, I were, by what he turned down, as if he hadn't heard her. He were polite enough to keep his position at the ironworks, but later he grumbled about the insult of her visit. I cannot say I understand."

Then Thomas Morganstone came to the cottage. He arrived in the coarse clothes he wore to visit worksites.

"Please sir," he said, "at least permit your daughter to visit us."

Papa blocked the door so Mary Jane couldn't go out to greet him. "My daughter, she is," he said. "and I have decided that life with her family is best for her. One of us, she must endure what we do. Otherwise, my sons will not see the need for fairness."

Mary Jane could tell he didn't believe his own words. Obviously, he blamed Mary Jane for the loss of his wife and wanted her to suffer.

As Thomas went away, she cried.

Mary Jane missed her mother more than ever.

CHAPTER FIVE

Following the dreadful incident involving Harris Brevard in Paris, and her fall from her prized perch at the Phoenix gay house in December of 1885, Mary Jane had found a position at the Laughing Magpie, a brothel run by Mrs. Sarah Buki.

Standing two stories tall in St. George Street in the East End, the establishment had rooms for ten women, a kitchen, one parlor, and outdoor privies. Mrs. Buki hired two women to do the charring, and the place remained fairly clean, though much of the furnishings had fallen into disrepair.

Mary Jane settled in to seeing clients there in early January of 1886. Her second floor room felt drafty and cold. The once extravagant flocked red wallpaper had faded and peeled from the walls in places. The ceiling, which leaked when rain came, had a large brown bruise growing in its plaster. After the Phoenix, everything at the Laughing Magpie seemed difficult, especially waiting her turn for hot water.

In early February, 1886, Mary Jane made an attempt to get the necklace, going to the Phoenix gay house with the pretense of wanting a visit with a friend there, a prostitute named Dorothy Wostmann.

"Dorothy isn't here," Mrs. Arseneau said. "You may not come back here, Mary Jane. They say Mr. Brevard suffered too little air for so long that he's now an idiot. I suspect he deserved what he got, but I cannot help you. I'll tell Dorothy you asked after her, and you may leave your address with me."

Mary Jane had no concern for the man's condition, and turned away before her anger got the better of her.

A gloom settled into her outlook, one she could not shake as she went about the business of the Laughing Magpie; satisfying a much coarser clientele than what she had known at the Phoenix. The hardship and a sense of failure wore painfully on her spirit.

Following that first taste in Paris, Mary Jane gained a laudanum habit that helped her endure the hardship. She needed the drug to help her feel better or to at least feel less. Food held little interest for her, and she began to lose weight. Mrs. Buki treated Mary Jane with kid gloves, brought her extravagant meals, sat with her, and encouraged her to eat, "just a bit more."

In early March of 1886, Mary Jane had a chance meeting in Cable Street that brought about welcome changes. She was on her way to one of the pubs she frequented in Shadwell to find clients, dressed the part she intended to play. Her green bodice had panels of scarlet satin that matched the flounces of her green top skirt. She wore a shortened petticoat. As she did with all her ladybird skirts, Mary Jane had gathered and tacked the fabric in such a way that the garment swayed seductively when she walked and lifted in the front to show her slim ankles. The skirt lifted further still when she sat and crossed her legs. She wore no hat and allowed a few follow-me-lads to dangle from her coiffure.

"Mary Jane Kelly!" she heard a voice cry.

She looked toward the owner of the voice amidst the foot traffic. Seeing a grinning face stopped her in her tracks. Emotion caught in Mary Jane's throat, a sense that something good and hopeful, long since lost, had been found. She couldn't put a finger on the memories at first. Mary Jane stared at the figure in the fine double-breasted frock coat and curled-brim bowler. While his jaw appeared squarer, forehead higher, and brow heavier, she saw a young man from a past life, one with curly-hair and beautiful, pale eyes.

Sudden recognition forced his name to her lips. "Thom——," she began, and tears sprang from her eyes. Mary Jane stepped back, not understanding her response. He couldn't be real. That life had been dead and gone for a long time. Reborn, she'd been given the life of a whore.

"Pardon me," he said hurrying to her. "I didn't mean to frighten you."

Mary Jane took another step back, though she wanted to wrap her arms around him and never let him go.

He became still, with his palms out to his sides, his face open, concerned.

In recent years, she had rarely let herself dwell for long on her time at Bryn Haearn and her feelings for the Morganstone family, but not a day had gone by since she was taken from them that Mary Jane did not lament the loss of what she considered her second family.

"Thomas," she said, her weeping loud and open, "I have missed you *so!*" She folded up and collapsed on the footway.

Thomas lifted Mary Jane, held and supported her. She got an impression that Mrs. Morganstone and Elen also held her.

As people strode past on the streets, some turned to watch. And with the stares, the realization that Thomas must see her for what she was dawned on Mary Jane.

Again, she shrank away from him. He let her go. Under her own power, she got to the face of a building, and leaned against the brick.

Approaching cautiously, he asked "Are you ill?"

Mary Jane considered several lies, not liking any of them. He deserved better.

In the years she'd spent with him at Bryn Haearn, he'd never treated her with anything but respect, though she'd held a much lower station. As a child, four years his junior, she'd quickly realized that her crush on him would go unrequited. He and Elen had been Mary Jane's world, though, her family for a precious and magical time in her youth.

She realized that her feelings for him had not changed. Mary Jane still loved Thomas. Considering the many men she'd known since she'd last seen him, the fact that such sentiments endured took on the proportions of a miracle.

"No, not ill," Mary Jane said, "...*ashamed.*"

He looked at her with his mouth agape, clearly dumbfounded.

"You must see how I'm dressed," she said, her gaze cast toward the pavement. "Surely you recognize..."

His silence finally drew Mary Jane's eyes toward his. He had a troubled expression. "Yes, but you don't know what I am because I hide the truth so well," he said. "I am no better, and perhaps much worse." He shook his head, looked away.

Mary Jane didn't know what to make of his words. The world held people of all sort, so many of them worse than a prostitute. Not Thomas, though. Surely—

"Come with me," he said, taking her by the hand. "We'll take a meal together. You haven't known Thomas Morganstone for many years. I'll introduce you to him. There's nothing *much* to fear."

His smile, spellbinding still, encouraged Mary Jane. They walked to Shadwell Station, where Thomas hired a hansom to drive them to the Cock's Comb tavern in Whitechapel Road. Inside the establishment, he asked for a drinking box, paid the fee for the more private seating, and they were escorted to the booth for their meal. Thomas ordered from the barmaid a plate of cold meats, bread, and two glasses of bitter.

Over their meal, Mary Jane asked, "How are your Aunt Peggy, and Elen?"

"Elen is well. I think she's as happy as she can be. You know her, a little soldier, always clear-eyed and looking for the best. Still quite an imagination."

Mary Jane smiled, her heart swelling with a desire to see her one-time friend.

Impossible. I could not let her know me now.

"My aunt's business manager invested heavily in a company that developed new mining equipment. When that company collapsed in scandal, she lost a fortune. She sold Bryn Haearn and several other holdings."

"I'm saddened to hear that," Mary Jane said, finding the words hollow.

"They are quite happy in a smaller home. Some money remained from my parent's estate, more than enough to send me to school. Then I had an apprenticeship here in London with a wonderful master in the building trade, a man named Treecle. He died suddenly and I was on my own, my term with my master incomplete. Though he had spoken to some of my abilities in glowing terms, I had no letters of reference from him. No one wanted to hire me. I took what jobs I found, all the while losing funds I could not replace quickly enough. Should things have got much worse, I knew I'd have to leave the city."

Mary Jane understood the feeling of failure in the midst of a bustling city full of money, food, and other comforts; the frustrating sense that all one needed for a good life lay so close at hand, if only the treasure could be taken.

"I had made the acquaintance of a man in the Metropolitan Board of Works," Thomas said. "I went to him, asking if he could help. He did find me work, but it was secretive stuff, repairing a small bridge. The job went on forever, used inferior materials, and far more workers than necessary. When I discovered that I'd helped him commit fraud, I threatened to expose him. 'This is how the business of building is done in London,' he said. 'You can take my bribe and stay silent, or become known for your betrayal, in which case you will find no further work in the city.' He told the truth. I learned that even Mr. Treecle helped professional criminals to commit such crimes in order to have work. Since then, I have done no end of things for which I'd feel shame should my aunt or Elen find out."

Thomas took a drink of his bitter, set the glass down and looked Mary Jane in the eyes. "Now that you know something of me, please tell me something about you."

Mary Jane began a disjointed explanation of what had led her to soliciting, her words quickly turning to sobs. She looked down, and hid her face in her hands.

Thomas lifted her chin, and looked her in the eye. "Please tell me what happened after your father took you from us."

Mary Jane composed herself, took several deep drafts of her bitter. "Papa blamed me for my mother's death and life with him were unendurable."

"Your father is a beastly fellow, if you'll forgive my saying so."

Mary Jane laughed. "Thank you for saying that. Never has anyone described him so tidy. I've rarely allowed myself to judge him harshly because I suffered the same terrible loss—my mother— that took the hope and kindness from his heart, and turned him against me."

"Her death didn't turn you into a beast."

"Yes, well, I didn't have anyone to blame."

Mary Jane took more of her bitter.

"I married at sixteen to get away from Papa. My husband, Evan Berwyn Davies was a lushington, always drunk when home. A collier in Penygraig working the Pandy Coal Pit, he died in '81 in a mine explosion."

Mary Jane struggled to rein in the familiar pang of loss. The strong sentiment that came with thoughts of Berwyn had always confounded her. Either he represented a longed-for time of lost innocence or she'd loved him more than she was willing to admit to herself. She said no more about him to Thomas.

"My bitterness toward Papa stood in the way of clear thinking. I would have been better off if I had returned home. Instead I went to live with my cousin Carryl Hughes in Cardiff."

⚮

A pittance Mary Jane received from the fund that she and Berwyn had paid into for protection against mine accidents. She could not remain in Penygraig alone. Nor did she want to stay there with the memories.

She wrote to her cousin, Carryl Hughes, who lived in Cardiff, asking if she might come and lodge with her for a time. Mary Jane had met her cousin twice before when much younger and with Mum still among the living. With Carryl's pretty dark hair and eyes, and her clever way with words, Mary Jane had always thought well of her.

She received the answer she hoped for. In 1881, at eighteen years of age, less than two months after poor Berwyn's death, she removed to Cardiff.

With Carryl four years her senior and living on her own, Mary Jane thought she'd learn something from her about how to get on in life. Her cousin had better togs than what Mary Jane had become accustomed to since leaving the Morganstones. Carryl's home, two rooms in a three-story wooden building near the Cardiff Docks, with upholstered furniture, papered walls, and a metal bed, was grander than Mary Jane had expected. The building housed a number of unmarried or widowed women, all rather neighborly, given to standing on the landings and talking. The doors to lodgings, including Carryl's, often stayed opened, perhaps to encourage the chumminess. Mary Jane worried about thieves taking advantage, but realized that never did a time come that someone wasn't about. As they might have done with any newcomer, Carryl's neighbors became quieter when Mary Jane drew near. She had confidence that, with time, they'd warm to her.

Carryl took Mary Jane to eat a fine fish dinner at a tavern her first night in the city. Several times during the meal, men and women approached their table to make small talk with Carryl. One gentleman, rather fashionably dressed, left her his calling card. Her popularity dazzled Mary Jane, and that encouraged her feeling that her cousin would indeed make a good guide to her new life.

Until Mary Jane arrived in London much later, she would not see so many kinds of people. Those living and working together around the Cardiff docks were of all sorts. New faces appeared often, as seaman came and went, some from far-flung parts of the world, of different colors and creeds. Along with the dockworkers and merchants, most of those in the city labored in positions that in some way aided the shipping of coal and iron. From its posh homes to its beggarly hovels, Cardiff remained a stew of activity. Mary Jane found the city exciting, yet unsettling too, a dirty and at times dangerous place.

Sitting at dinner in the noisy tavern, she made a confession to Carryl. "With the loss of Mum, the cruelty of my father, and the mine explosion taking Berwyn, I have become fearful of life itself."

"There *is* much to fear in life," Carryl said, "but taking control of your own fate will help you bear up. What happened to your mum, your poor husband's death—those were accidents. Your father chose to handle you roughly. That is the sort of cruelty one finds in most employment."

"I'll find it again, then, should I find work," Mary Jane said, shaking her head.

"No woman should be a slave to man," Carryl said, "as long as man's desire for union with womankind is so strong. You are gifted with a clever head and a beautiful form. Your father is perhaps the only man immune to your charms. All others you might twist round your little finger. Use your wiles and your bosom to better your lot in life." She gave Mary Jane a piercing look. "Use them to get your way."

She welcomed the idea that she possessed gifts that could win her the better things in life. Carryl had said the words with such confidence that, although Mary Jane didn't understand fully what her cousin meant, her fears were calmed in that moment. She felt grateful to Carryl for that. Mary Jane had a sense of power over her future, something she needed so desperately that she became willing to overlook what rigors might stand in her way.

A mystery, Carryl slept through most of the following day. Mary Jane was not in a position to question her cousin, but wondered if she did that often, and if so, what that meant about how she earned her living. Possibly Carryl worked a nightshift somewhere.

That evening, they made their way through a light rain to her lodgings after eating a meal at a pub. A voice beckoned to Carryl from a carriage waiting at the kerb.

"A moment," Carryl said, and went to speak with one Mary Jane presumed to be an acquaintance inside the carriage. With the increasing rain, the driver on the exposed seat of the vehicle bundled into his blanket and pulled his hat on tighter.

The one inside the carriage, a man, leaned on the door sash, his head, shoulder, and arm emerging into the light. His clothing told Mary Jane that he had wealth. The brim of his fine woolen hat had been pulled down low over his face, possibly to keep the rain off. Carryl spoke briefly to him before returning to Mary Jane. The man called to his driver and the carriage moved off.

"Would you be a darling and bide on the street for an hour to allow me to satisfy a client?" Carryl asked.

No explanation did she have ready, and no shame appeared on her face. Clear as day was her meaning, though. If Mary Jane had not been so naive and guileless, she might have seen the truth before that. She must have stood with her mouth agape too long because Carryl asked, "Would you do that for me? 'Tis how I earn my keep."

"Yes," Mary Jane said simply, her voice unsteady. Her cousin left her standing in the increasing downpour. Others on the street moved around her. She watched Carryl go until she'd slipped from sight.

Confused and feeling oddly wounded, Mary Jane sat in a coffee shop and sipped a cup for well over an hour, thinking about her situation. Had she taken up with a fallen woman? Would she have to return to Papa? Could she quickly find another situation in Cardiff so she wouldn't have to?

No good answers came for the questions.

Then Mary Jane began thinking about what she'd just learned of Carryl in light of what she'd said the night before: "No woman should be a slave to man, as long as man's desire for union with womankind remains so strong." She'd made a business of satisfying that desire. Mary Jane didn't know why she'd never truly thought of prostitution in such simple terms until then.

Carryl had said that Mary Jane was clever and beautiful, and that she might use those qualities to gain what she wanted from men. Her cousin spoke from experience, because Carryl had made a life for herself by those selfsame means.

Pondering these things, Mary Jane's view of the world changed. Some might have thought Carryl a fool, who would end her days in misery for going against the common notions of goodness. Mary Jane began to see her cousin as one with enough brains to see past the prosaic day-to-day concerns and stifling morals of most folks.

With the protection of a sheath, what was sex but a bit of lather, one that when done well felt very good indeed? And to get paid for it too—what was to dislike?

The management of the coffee shop asked Mary Jane to have another cup or leave.

The rain had stopped and she thought she might walk for a while with her thoughts.

She discovered Carryl outside, casually leaning against the worn gray stones of the establishment's exterior.

"You found me," Mary Jane said, not certain what else to say in that moment.

Her cousin nodded.

"Why didn't you come in?"

"I saw you lost in your own thoughts" Carryl said, "and knew you would find your own way out with time."

Mary Jane was past judging her. Still, she didn't know how to look at her cousin, and kept her eyes downcast.

"His name is Martin Bowers," Carryl said. "He give me this." She lifted her right hand to show that she wore a beautiful silver ring with a bright ruby. "Supplies iron mongers, he does, and he's getting richer by the day." She laughed. "Says but for my coarse mouth, I'd be on his arm once his wife has gone."

Mary Jane frowned, not understanding.

"Consumption," Carryl said. "He says her suffering is almost at an end."

Although what Mary Jane had learned that night troubled her, she did want the best for her cousin, especially as Carryl seemed to have Mary Jane's best interests at heart. "I can teach you how to speak the Queen's English," she said, making a clear change in her voice.

"Where did you learn?"

"I became a companion for a young lady in Carmarthen, and shared her lessons."

"Yes, that would be a fine thing!" Carryl took Mary Jane in her arms and hugged her like a sister.

Even then, she could not seem to look at her cousin.

"What troubles you, my dear?" Carryl asked.

Mary Jane's thoughts ran too fast to answer at first. Finally, she had what she wanted to say, and the words surprised her. "Can you teach me how to do it safely?" she asked, hoping she would not have to explain herself.

Again, Carryl nodded. "First lesson," she said. "Never go by your true name. How do you like the name Ginger?"

"I *do* like it."

"Well, then, Ginger, come with me." Carryl took Mary Jane's arm and led her home.

She remembered her father asking when she was a small child, "Do you know what danger is, girl?"

Still, Mary Jane had no answer.

She paused to give the impression she'd finished her tale. Her shame had returned, and she wasn't certain she wanted to tell Thomas more.

He gave her an expectant, warm look, placed a hand atop one of hers affectionately. "There's more because you are now here."

"Yes," Mary Jane said. She took more of her bitter. "Would you excuse me?"

"Of course."

Mary Jane got up and went to find a privy. The tavern had stalls indoors. She slipped into one, relieved herself, then took several sips from her bottle of laudanum.

Exiting the privy, she considered fleeing the tavern, though she knew she could not do that to Thomas. Instead she returned to their drinking box. A fresh glass of bitter stood at her place. She sat, took a couple of deep drafts from it, and continued her tale.

"What little innocence remained to me, I quickly lost..."

Carryl made certain Mary Jane had safe and pleasurable experiences at first, the men she serviced handsome and kind. That changed with time as her cousin foresaw a certain toughening of Mary Jane's spirit. Rarely did she enjoy the sex. Much of the time she found it merely disgusting. Many of the men, if not openly cruel, had a cold disregard for her. Every now and then, she'd have a man who played some sort of role for himself, one that had little to do with her, and she had the frightening feeling she was just another object in the room for him.

Carryl had many ways of managing the dangers of the business, her weave of friends and business associates a great help. She and Mary Jane paid protection to the Beloved Ratters, a gang like the High Rips of Liverpool that preyed upon prostitutes. The payment was demanded under threat of violence. Most not soliciting on the streets didn't know that the gang would do little to protect prostitutes. Mary Jane did as Carryl suggested, and mentioned the Beloved Ratter's when talking with new clients to put a fear into them so they'd behave.

Mary Jane felt safe enough.

The earnings did not amount to much, since the competition on the streets of Cardiff set a going rate. That unspoken starting point dragged down the price for even the best of ladybirds.

Mary Jane often stopped on the landing outside Carryl's rooms to talk with Daphne Michaels, who lodged across the hall. "My sister what lives in a London gay house earns at least two shillings a customer," she said one day. "That's after the cut as goes to the house where she gets free room and board."

Perhaps overhearing the conversation, Carryl came from her room. "That's quite a tale, Daphne," she said, rolling her eyes.

Indignant, Daphne said, "'Tis God's honest truth,"

"Spoken by a pious member of the Church." Carryl made a mocking face for Mary Jane to see, one hidden from Daphne, and returned to her room.

"I don't doubt you," Mary Jane said.

"She's afraid I'll put grand ideas in your head and you'll leave her. Her business was never so good 'til you come."

Mary Jane couldn't complain. What she earned was better than Berwyn's wages had been and might have been as good as Papa's. That thought made her feel good.

Of course, she did dream of earning more, and tucked away the idea of one day going to London to seek her fortune in a gay house.

To all appearances a generous heart, Carryl shared her room and her clientele with Mary Jane, all but Martin Bowers.

"He asks about you," her cousin said in passing one day. "'Who's the flaxen-haired beauty I've seen with you?' Mr. Bowers asks. 'My uneducated cousin, Ginger, from Carmarthen,' I says. 'She's my personal maid,' I tell him, 'still a virgin, worse mouth than my own.'"

They laughed together at that. Mary Jane had no desire to compete for his attentions.

The cousins looked out for one another and had good feelings between them for at least two years.

Hard feelings began to come between them when they entertained clients together and a time came for a man to choose which one of them to bed. Carryl had been comfortable enough the first few times a man chose Mary Jane. As the choice came more often, something in her cousin's gaze turned dark.

In a foul mood after waking late one afternoon, Carryl said, "Time you took a room of your own."

Mary Jane felt stung, though she did look forward to having more room. She removed to one recently vacated in the building on the same second floor landing. Still, the cousins came and went from both lodgings often enough that the doors remained open much of the time.

One night, the evening's clients had gone away satisfied. Carryl and Mary Jane were straightening the rooms before bed. They'd finished with Mary Jane's single room, and had started on her cousin's bedroom. Carryl had begun to undress for bed when she looked up with that dark gaze.

"'Tis you wearing my best silk and velvet bodice what gives you the advantage," she said. "Ginger ain't nothing without my borrowed flash."

Mary Jane had fewer fine clothes. Carryl's much grander dunnage fit them both, and she'd been generous with lending. Indeed, Mary Jane had done most of her borrowing at her cousin's suggestion. She thought Carryl's words a jest of sorts, a way of admitting her pettiness and getting it off her chest at the same time. Mary Jane simply smiled.

"Think it's a delight, do you?" Carryl asked. She spit on the floor, bent to loosen the laces of her boots. "Well, you stay away from my armoire from now on. Spend some of the money I've taught you how to earn."

Recognizing true anger, Mary Jane felt embarrassed and upset. "Yes, I will," she said. "I didn't mean to trespass."

"Mr. Bowers saw you again when he came for me at the Sea Anchor," Carryl said. "Should you know he's about, keep out of sight."

Mary Jane had tried to show her sorrow, and her cousin had come back with more anger. Now, she was angry too. But for her efforts, Carryl might not have had him at all.

"Too bad I can't take away that tidy language you wear like an ill-fitting gown," Mary Jane said, a bite in her tone.

"Oh, the cat's out of the bag, is it?" Carryl said. "The reduced cat, I see, mere pussy. Little Ginger shows her claws. Isn't that cute?"

Her words did their job—Mary Jane felt small.

She'd done her best in giving her cousin lessons in elocution, yet hadn't managed to break Carryl's worst habits of speech. And, like Mary Jane, in moments of high emotion, the slang spilled forth. She had learned at a younger age, and could control herself with a minimum of concentration. However nicely Carryl dressed and held herself with good posture, at the first distraction, she'd lose her way. Mary Jane might have felt the same trying to gild a wooden spoon.

"If you'd done a better job teaching, the gents wouldn't think I were putting on airs."

Carryl spoiled for a fight, so Mary Jane tried to put some of her anger away.

"Hasn't the better language helped with Martin Bowers?"

"He knows me for what I am," Carryl said bitterly. "There's no fooling him."

"You might have known that."

She glared at Mary Jane. "I have little time left before he takes a new wife."

"Mrs. Bowers has passed away?"

"Last month. Took her long enough." Carryl threw her right boot at the wall, cracking the plaster. "You stay out of sight when he's about. If by chance you speak with him, Ginger ought to sound like a laborer."

She threw her left boot at Mary Jane.

She dodged in time.

"Get out!" Carryl cried.

Mary Jane left her cousin with her bad mood and went to bed.

Hoping Carryl's feelings would mend, Mary Jane wore only her own clothes and kept her distance for a time.

⚓

Carryl interrupted Mary Jane in the midst of seeing a client. The door to her room had been open and they'd not got to business yet. They sat together, talking, enjoying glasses of wine.

"He wants you now!" Carryl shouted. "You've been seeing him behind my back."

Her angry words drove the client away. No great loss, Mary Jane thought, as he slipped through the door. He'd been a rough one.

"Who?" she asked, though she knew the answer.

"Bowers, of course."

"He found me in the Sea Anchor, a chance meeting. Bought me a drink, he did, and I spoke to him briefly. I made certain to sound like a muck boot. Gulped down my gatter, then made my excuses quick as I could. "

"Weren't no chance meeting—he's been looking for you."

"Why didn't you tell me so I could avoid him better?"

Carryl had no answer for that. She bared her teeth. "He were my chance to get out of this life," she shouted.

"I thought you liked the business."

"Nobody likes soliciting for long."

"Yet you brought me into it."

"You had nothing else, you ungrateful wretch!"

"Ungrateful? I've had only the best intentions toward you. I've offered nothing but kind words."

"Oh, that's the way, use the jemmy mouth. Makes you out to be my better, doesn't it?"

"Better than your bloody bone box, what can't help you land a floundering fish."

Carryl struck out with a metal-toed boot, kicking Mary Jane in the shin.

Though she thought she deserved the blow for her cruel tongue, the pain enraged her. She lifted an empty wine bottle from the floor and threw the thing. It hit Carryl on the forehead, glanced off and broke against the open door beside her. A shower of green glass shards fell in her hair and on her shoulders. Her eyes went wide, and she stumbled back against the wall, pieces of glass falling from her hair into her clothing and on her face. She moaned and clutched at the collar of her bodice.

Mary Jane saw blood at her cousin's neck. "Don't move," she said, horrified at what she'd done.

"You wicked child!" Carryl said, her tone vicious. The pain must have been more powerful than her anger. She became still.

Without a word, Mary Jane shut the door, and helped her cousin out of her clothing. Carryl didn't speak, merely stood, red-faced, staring into the distance. Mary Jane carefully picked the bits of glass off the bare skin of her cousin's face, neck, and right shoulder and gave her a dressing gown.

Carryl gathered up her clothes, and paused at the door before leaving the room. "I'm done with you," she said. "Don't come in my room again. Don't try to talk to me. Stay away from Mr. Bowers."

With that, she left, and Mary Jane never spoke to her cousin again. She was glad for that. Still she wept for the loss.

～❖～

Less than a month later, a new client turned on her. She'd picked up a pillow, buried her head in it, and hung on for dear life through the horrible dewskitch. He struck her in the head so many times, and so hard, she later had no clear memory of what happened.

Mary Jane seemed to recall her cousin coming into the room afterward and standing over her with a gloating look. Mary Jane couldn't be certain of that, though.

The man would have had a written reference. She took no clients without one. Again, uncertain as to the truth, she seemed to recall it was from Carryl. He must have taken the reference away with him because later she couldn't find the piece of paper to confirm that.

He'd used a sheep's gut sheath, something Mary Jane didn't accept because they'd seen a bad batch come through town. They leaked, and the ladybirds had taken to calling them broxy sheaths. Word was that even when whole, the ones made of sheep's gut weren't reliable at keeping disease away.

Daphne Michaels told her about the sheath. She had found Mary Jane and helped her get to the infirmary. Daphne said she discovered the thing lying on the floor beside Mary Jane's bed. Since her falling out with Carryl, most of the Cardiff ladybirds had turned against Mary Jane due to her cousin's lying gossip. Daphne had stayed friendly, though, and was trusted in return.

Since Mary Jane did not accept the sheep's gut with clients and had plenty of the rubber ones, her assailant must have forced himself on her before the beating, or he'd done so afterward.

Mary Jane remained in the Cowbridge Road Workhouse infirmary for nearly a year, from March, 1883 to November of the same year. One infection followed another. She lost the ability to bear children. Once they'd had enough of her at the infirmary, she found herself destitute and still not fit.

As a fallen woman, she was sent to the Monmouthshire House of Mercy to be reformed. Mary Jane heard from other inmates there that if she'd been much older, they would have considered her too hardened to save, and would not have taken her. For all the hard work they gave her, though, she knew they merely wanted strong, young backs.

They spoon fed Mary Jane religion with every meal, something her parents had thankfully neglected. In the house where she spent her days as a lavender, Matron Moss told her, "Doing laundry without pay is one of the best forms of contrition. Endless scrubbing to remove stains reminds us of the hard work needed to remove the taint of sin from our souls."

"Her prater mouth made me feel a right mark, it did," Mary Jane said. "I played the role of the penitent until I could lie no longer. Once I felt fit enough, in March of 1884, I left the House of Mercy and spent a month working my way to London."

Thomas released a shuttering sob, struggled to hold himself together. He took her in an embrace. "Oh, Mary Jane, how after all that is your warm heart still whole?"

His response set her off. She bent into his shoulder, biting down on her lower lip to push the pain and shame away. Her eyes dampened his jacket.

Finally, having composed herself, she sat up. "It got better," she said, and laughed through her tears. "Perhaps my memories of life at Bryn Heaern helped. I dreamed often of returning to my second family there."

Thomas seemed lost in memory for a moment. Then, for all the sadness expressed, he let out an odd, short laugh.

Throughout the telling, Mary Jane had looked to him each time she'd revealed what she considered a lapse in her character. His steady and caring gaze had assured her each time that he didn't judge.

Another laugh, and his handsome lips bent almost to a smirk.

"What do you find humorous?" Mary Jane asked.

"We were *indeed* your family," he said, "and you never truly left us. Even after your father took you away, I saw you in the corner of my eye from time to time flitting among the rooms of Bryn Haearn. On my last visit, I caught a glimpse of you in the great mirror in the main hall."

"Such fancy," she said.

Did he miss me that much? The thought gave Mary Jane a thrill. She wondered if he'd like to take up with her, though she considered such fancies on her part unwise.

"Seems you've shown great resourcefulness in the face of adversity," he said at last.

Mary Jane scoffed, said, "I'm considered a fallen woman."

"Yes, but I frequently work for criminals who do much worse." He paused and sighed. "Misery loves company. Criminals need coconspirators, and they'll get them by hook or by crook. Once you've worked for them, they'll hold it over you or find some other way to make you do it again. I grew more willing with time. Having gained a tidy reputation among thieves, I am kept busy and live quite well now."

Mary Jane nodded her head. "Just so, I've discovered that to get on in life, I must break the rules of polite society. I have nothing else. Of course, my crime involves sex, a thing hidden away as beneath human dignity, even when the engagement is innocently used to get children."

Unexpectedly, Thomas laughed. His laughter persisted, and, again, Mary Jane thought he must be laughing at her.

He saw her confusion, and calmed himself. He clasped her hands between his own, leaned in, and gave her a warm smile. "You ought walk in my shoes for a time," he whispered. "Should the wrong person find out that I'm a homosexual, I could go to prison. That's if I'm truly unlucky. As it is, I often find I have a fight on my hands."

Startled to silence, Mary Jane stared at him. Then, remembering her adolescent daydreams of a tumble in bed with Thomas, she laughed.

"Do you mock *me*?" he asked, grimacing slightly. "I don't admit that to *just* anyone."

"Not in the least," Mary Jane said. "Surprised, is all. I...well, ... when we were young, I had *such* a crush on you."

"I knew that, and love you still for your affectionate smiles."

She felt herself blushing.

He rolled his eyes and his smile grew larger, showing a gap in the lower left jaw. Perhaps he'd lost the tooth in a fight.

"Do you get in a lot of fights?"

"Sure, but I'm good with a bunch of fives." He made a comically fierce face and showed a fist. "I'm a bully trap."

They laughed, and held each other, rocking together in the drinking box.

The spell of shame broken, Mary Jane told about her employment at the Phoenix gay house, losing the position, and her situation at the Laughing Magpie, leaving out the most unseemly details. Surely his imagination filled in the rest. She did not tell him anything about what had happened in Paris with Harris Brevard.

"I have apartments near the Stepney Gas works," he said. "You have a standing invitation to escape the Laughing Magpie and stay with me whenever you want."

Mary Jane's crush on him had not gone away. She understood that her amorous sentiments would remain unrequited. The knowledge stung a bit. With all that, she felt glad to have him back in her life.

Following that chance meeting, the beginning of spring brought warming weather, and Mary Jane's heart became much lighter, her mood lifted.

During one of her stays at Thomas's apartments in Stepney, she had met Joseph Fleming. The fellow began to flirt with her the moment they met. Although she usually found that sort of thing irritating, something about the way he went about it made for a fun game. He came to the Laughing Magpie a couple of times to take Mary Jane out to a music hall performance. On the occasions she stayed at Morganstone's apartments and Fleming was present,

Thomas encouraged him to stay over. She got the impression that the two had been lovers at one time, but Fleming always spent the night with her. She said nothing of her suspicions. Thomas didn't seem the least unhappy that Joseph bedded Mary Jane.

Since she spent much of her time in Stepney, Mary Jane located cribs that let by the hour, where she could satisfy clients. She made an effort to get to know the local Ladybirds, and found a coffee shop that made for a convenient place to organize them. "A weave of friends," Carryl had called her own similar efforts to organize the prostitutes of Cardiff. The idea was that, with a meeting place and a willingness to communicate their experiences, ladybirds might work more safely.

CHAPTER SIX
Wapping, September 1886

Stuart Brevard's attack having come mere hours earlier, Mary Jane continued to look back in worry that he would find her even as she arrived at Gander's Bush and Mrs. Carthy welcomed her at the front door of the brothel. Mary Jane took one more glance back before entering.

A woman in her late thirties, Mrs. Carthy had prematurely gray hair, almost white, framing a sweet face. In silhouette, her figure cut a pear shape: small bust, thin arms and shoulders, large backside. Over her rather plain, white calico chemise and gray top skirt, she wore a kitchen apron.

"My sister has finally done as you suggested," the proprietress said, walking into her kitchen, "and gone to the Phoenix after your things."

Excited by the news, Mary Jane followed, almost stepping on the small woman. "Did Mrs. Buki come away with anything?" she asked. Although so hopeful she could hardly contain herself, Mary Jane shut her mouth before saying more. She had confided in Mrs. Buki about the necklace, but not Mrs. Carthy.

"I don't know. I'll send my boy around to ask her here to tell us. I'm sure she'll come—I have a new recipe for plum duff to try out on her."

Both proprietresses had a love of puddings and enjoyed sharing recipes.

"You can use Bell's room," Mrs. Carthy said. "She's finally gone to the infirmary, poor girl."

The young woman had suffered stomach pains for the four months since Stuart Brevard kicked her. Ashamed that she hadn't gone to the young woman's aid at the time of the attack, Mary Jane made a promise to herself to go to the Whitechapel Union Infirmary to visit her friend.

"You're third in line for bath water if you want it," Mrs. Carthy said, bustling about her kitchen, beginning preparations for the pudding. "You're welcome to look for something in the wardrobe."

"Thank you, Ma'am," Mary Jane said. "I'll look for clothing, but I shan't be wanting the water."

She went to a room off the entrance hall, one that housed a large wardrobe, picked out clothes that would fit her, and took them upstairs to Bell's room.

Mary Jane currently knew with a certainty that the fault lay with her for Bell's injury at the hands of Stuart Brevard.

Returning to the Laughing Magpie following a stay at Morganstone's in early May, she had heard from Mrs. Buki about Stuart Brevard coming to the brothel to ask about her. Not long after that, hidden from the man in shadows, Mary Jane saw him injure Bell. When the violence began, another man nearby came to Bell's aid, while Mary Jane remained hidden. Even though the Good Samaritan had stepped in to help, the poor girl had been severely harmed. Mary Jane had retreated before she was seen. She felt cowardly doing so. Returning to the Laughing Magpie, she told the proprietress about what happened.

"You shall both go stay with my sister, Elsa Carthy, at Gander's Bush," Mrs. Buki said, "Just until this bludger has given up on you. You'll be safe there. She is married to John McCarthy, a landlord of some reputation."

Mary Jane remembered being unable to look Bell in the eye on the day they both removed to Mrs. Carthy's rotting two-story wooden house in Breezer's Hill off the Ratcliffe Highway. After settling Bell into a wretched little bedroom upstairs, the proprietress took Mary Jane to a similar room down the hall.

A cell for labor, she thought, looking at the tiny, ill-furnished chamber. Yellow and gray with stains, the exposed ticking of the sagging straw mattress on the small rope bed disgusted her. Roughly folded, frayed bedclothes lay upon the foot of the bed. A battered washstand with ewer and basin sat against the rear wall, a small mirror above. Mary Jane believed she could smell the odors of the men and women who had struggled for release together in the room over the years, their sweat, their now rancid sexual fluids absorbed into the wood, the cloth, the plaster. The atmosphere gave a dizzying emptiness to the pit of her stomach.

To fall even farther from the heights of the Phoenix gay house brought back the melancholy that had lifted after she found Thomas. The room would do as a crib for satisfying clients, but she would spend as much time as she could at Thomas's apartments.

"I understand you were at the Phoenix for a time," Mrs. Carthy said.

Mary Jane swallowed hard before answering. "Yes, for a short time."

"My sister has always been a good friend to the abbess there."

"Mrs. Arseneau?"

"Yes. Mrs. Buki knows everyone in the business in London. Mrs. Arseneau has depended on her several times for information and introductions."

Now that was good news.

Shortly thereafter, Mary Jane had a talk with Mrs. Buki about the hidden necklace.

"We could share the earnings from a sale of the jewelry, should you succeed in retrieving it," Mary Jane told her.

At the time, Mrs. Buki had seemed doubtful about the idea.

Four months after making that offer, Mary Jane saw recovery of the valuable item as necessary for her escape from harm. She vividly recalled the violence of Stuart Brevard's attack on her earlier that day, his apparent glee at having her under his control. Relocating to some place where Mr. Brevard would not find her had to be her ultimate goal.

Since Mary Jane had been staying so often at Thomas Morganstone's apartments, her room at Gander's Bush had been given to another ladybird, and her possessions put in storage in the cellar. In Bell's room, she undressed and cast aside the damp clothing she'd worn on the walk from Stepney, then dressed in a Prussian-blue linen skirt and bodice she'd taken from the house wardrobe with Mrs. Carthy's permission.

Waiting for Mrs. Buki to come to Gander's Bush for plum duff and conversation, Mary Jane began to worry that the woman's cut of the necklace might reduce the possible earnings too much.

Too late to change the bargain now.

She took out her bottle of laudanum and took a sip.

"Mrs. Buki has arrived," Mrs. Carthy called up the stairs.

Mary Jane joined the two sisters in the kitchen.

At forty-five years of age, Mrs. Buki still had the figure of a young woman, and might have easily been mistaken for one if not for her heavily lined face. She looked good dressed as a ladybird, and with her dark hair done up with pins. As far as Mary Jane knew, she did not seek clients of her own.

While Mrs. Carthy was gone from the room, fetching cream from the cellar, Mrs. Buki spoke. "I recovered some dunnage and paste jewelry that Mrs. Arseneau said belonged to you. They are bundled in a blanket in the entrance hall. I was not able to secretly get to the top of the armoire."

Mary Jane did not like the news.

Mrs. Carthy returned and served the pudding.

Downcast and thoughtful, Mary Jane took little notice of eating the fruity delight.

Of course, London is a great, frightening labyrinth, filled with many people and goings-on. Stuart Brevard shall not find me as easily a second time. I have survived the violence of men before. Should I be careful, I'll avoid him. His red hair stands out like a sore thumb. Moving south of the river might be all that's needed.

Again, she remembered how she'd felt, the urgency of her earlier fear.

No, across the river is not enough. Those thoughts come from my desire to stay in London! I just need the chink to make a fresh start elsewhere.

"That was truly delicious, Elsa," Mrs. Buki said when finished with her plum duff.

"Thank you, sister." Mrs. Carthy said.

"Yes, quite tasty," Mary Jane decided, tasting its remnants on her tongue as if for the first time.

"Excuse me for a moment," Mrs. Carthy said, and she stepped out to take the cream back to the cellar.

Once she'd gone, her sister placed a warm hand on one of Mary Jane's. "Of course, I said nothing of the muff and necklace to Mrs. Arseneau, so that you might still have the opportunity to get them one day." She paused for a moment as if considering something. "That man what came to call on you at my house, the bow-legged one with the spattered togs—he a plasterer?"

"Fleming?" Mary Jane asked. "Yes, he is."

"The Phoenix has shoddy plaster, needs work, possibly near the ceiling beside the armoire in your old room there."

"Thank you," Mary Jane said, clasping and squeezing the woman's hands.

"Look at your face!" Mrs. Buki said, "your shining eyes!"

Mary Jane's mood had improved.

When Mrs. Carthy returned, Mary Jane said, "I'll just get my things from the cabinet in the cellar and be off. Thank you for the delicious pudding."

"You're welcome, dear." Mrs. Carthy said. "You know you are always welcome here."

Mary Jane retrieved her belongings from the cellar storage cabinet, picked up the bundle Mrs. Buki had placed in the entrance hall, and left Gander's Bush, headed for the crossing of Globe Road and Green Street. With so much to carry, she decided to pay for a cab to take her there. She would arrive well before Joseph Fleming did—he'd said after seven o'clock in the evening—but the idea Mrs. Buki had given her awakened new hope in Mary Jane, and she was too excited about the possibilities presented to wait.

Mary Jane waited at the Green Man pub across the street from Fleming's room for two and a half hours before he arrived home after his day of labor.

He proudly showed her his crib. The new brick tenement at 200 Globe Road had water closets on each landing. His room, a large one in the corner of the first floor, had a bay window, built-in shelves, and counters.

"The flue draws properly," Fleming said, "In colder weather, the room holds its warmth well."

Although Mary Jane knew better than to present her pressing need right away, she could not wait to speak of it. She told him about the necklace and the difficulty in retrieving it from the Phoenix gay house. His brow rose at the name of the fine brothel, and she got the impression he knew the place.

"The necklace were a gift from a client when I worked at the gay house. The proprietress holds that I owe her, and would claim the jewelry if she knew it were there."

Thankfully, he did not pry into why her circumstances had been reduced to the likes of the Laughing Magpie and Gander's Bush, and what had led to her leaving the necklace at the Phoenix.

"Surely your treasure will be found in short order, if only by the charwoman."

"The decorative parapet around the top of the armoire hides it," Mary Jane said. "Even should one stand on a chair, the place cannot be seen, and is difficult to reach. I had to toss the necklace and muff there. The spot is so high and dusty, I don't believe anyone has ever cleaned it. We would split the proceeds of the sale of the necklace, should you succeed in retrieving it." She described a plan she'd developed on her ride to Globe Road, one based on Mrs. Buki's suggestion involving his services as plasterer.

"Is that why you accepted my offer to come stay?" Fleming asked with a look of worry.

"No, certainly not," she said persuasively, since that had indeed not been her initial reason.

He seemed to accept her answer as truth.

"I see your cokum," he said. "The lurk will have to be considered carefully. It shall be more difficult than you suggest."

"But you'll think about how the job might be done, won't you?" Mary Jane said, leaning in to give him a deep kiss.

He responded with enthusiasm. Then, in the midst of the kiss, he seemed distracted. When he pulled away, she worried that he was not sufficiently charmed.

"If Mrs. Arseneau owns the building," he said, "I'll have to come up with a fakement to account for offering a bid low enough she cannot refuse."

Indeed, I do have his interest.

"Should she have a landlord... well, that is a matter Mr. Morganstone might best handle, should you be willing to cut him in."

"Yes, I would do that."

He shook his head. "No, no, my dear, I cannot work on that yet. We'll sort out your necklace later. I do one piece of *what-if* at a time. You're right to think the dust says no one cares about the top of that armoire."

But not well enough.

When he said, "what if," he meant a criminal scheme. She knew little about his work, only what he and Thomas spoke about openly.

"I thought you two worked a job bona fide."

"Oh, no, we're working again for family people. Nothing dangerous, mind you, and it shall pay well enough."

Mary Jane knew he meant professional criminals, a family of such.

At least he'd thought about her proposal. He saw no urgency in the matter because he didn't know about Stuart Brevard.

She didn't want to say anything about Brevard for fear that Fleming might break with her to avoid exposure to danger.

"You can see clients here if you wish," Joseph said, "as long as I'm not here. I'll be sure to let you know my schedule."

He continued to surprise her with his tolerance of her profession.

With time, I will persuade him to retrieve the necklace.

In the meantime, the Globe Road address was far enough removed from Thomas Morganstone's apartments for her to feel that Stuart Brevard would not find her easily. She also appreciated that Fleming's room was close to her haunts in Stepney; she could continue to earn soliciting, while remaining within the area where she had organized a protective weave of ladybird friends.

Mary Jane grew so busy over the following month that she never took the time to go see Bell in the Whitechapel Union infirmary. Shame welled up in her every time she thought about that.

CHAPTER SEVEN
Stepney, Monday October 1, 1886

Mary Jane nodded her head periodically to give the sailor the impression that she listened to what he had to say. One of three men vying for her attention in the Angel and Trumpet pub in Stepney High Street, he sat across the sticky table from her.

The dose of laudanum she'd had before entering allowed her to sit at ease in the pub. Prostitution among the coarse and unwashed became more bearable with a dose of the drug.

Soon, I'll be free, she told herself. *Once Joseph retrieves the necklace, I'll be done with the East End entirely.* She'd been telling herself that for a month, ever since taking up with Joseph Fleming.

"What shall I call you?" the sailor asked.

The other two at the table, the laborer sitting to her left, and the older fellow, perhaps a tradesman of some sort, on her right, both leaned in to hear her answer over the surrounding noise.

"Ginger," she said. As far as Mary Jane knew, Stuart Brevard didn't know her by that name, so she felt safe using the moniker.

"Pretty," the sailor said with a grin. "I like a little ginger."

She produced a demure smile and took a dainty sip of her bitter.

For a Thursday afternoon, the Angel and Trumpet had drawn a rather full house, with raucous groups at several tables. The haze of tobacco smoke helped obscure the many distracting glances and occasional stares aimed at Mary Jane from persons, mostly men, at other tables, and aided her pretense that she could see no further than ten feet. The tactic had always promoted the idea that her glances alone had value. If a man wanted to catch her eye, he'd have to approach.

The dark oak furnishings of the Angel and Trumpet, the local events ephemera decorating its walls, and the limited selection of victuals available were no more remarkable than the clients she found there. Mary Jane liked the taste of their bitter, though, and she wasn't well-known to the establishment since she'd spent most of her time in the area down the street at the Crown and Dolphin or at Dresser's Coffee Shop. That gave her what she knew to be a false sense of security. The pub stood within a quarter of a mile of Thomas Morganstone's apartments, as did Dresser's. Yet she had persuaded herself that with so many people and so much activity in the neighborhood, Stuart Brevard would not locate her easily, even if he still searched the area.

Mary Jane had grown so weary of being hunted—the continuing sense of unease, and frequent realization that, at any moment, she might need to run from the man—she'd looked for ways to dampen her worries. Assuming Mr. Brevard would turn violent again if he caught her, or at the very least take her to the police and make her answer for her crimes against his brother, she'd got a knife that fit in her boot and asked Fleming to teach her how to use it. In her mind's eye, she'd practiced what to do in a possible future attack. She imagined that since she hadn't come up with a knife the last time, and he plainly wasn't a professional bludger, he'd be so surprised to see her blade that she'd somehow gain the advantage. Her fear of the man had faded some with time.

Two fellows approached and stood behind the three men already seated at her table, as if queuing up for their chance at her. Possessed of uncommon beauty, Mary Jane never had difficulty attracting men to her table at a pub. She would consider which of the current batch of three would be the best prospect, or dismiss them and consider the other two. If she dismissed them as well, there would always be more.

Seeing the woman who had rescued her from Stuart Brevard's attack in Bale Street, Mary Jane became distracted from the business at hand.

Jennifer. Yes, that was her name, Miss Jennifer Weatherhead.

She sat alone, four tables away. Dressed nicely in a plum-colored skirt and a dark brown bodice, she clearly had done herself up to meet someone. She'd removed her hat and shawl so that the gloss of her dark hair and the slim shape of her shoulders could be seen. Her glances about suggested that she searched for a prospect of some kind. Even so, she obviously didn't want to talk to anyone.

A moment passed before Mary Jane realized that Jennifer Weatherhead was soliciting. New to the game, though, she wasn't winning, and had her tail down.

Because Jennifer looked like Mary Jane's mother, seeing her felt good, as if Mum indeed sat there in the Angel and Trumpet. That coupled with the way Jennifer had defended her, Mary Jane felt a great warmth toward her. Finding herself thinking of Miss Weatherhead *as* her mother, Mary Jane wanted to dissuade the woman from taking up prostitution.

She wanted to get up and go to Jennifer, but stopped herself.

I would only be frustrating her efforts, and at her age, she is surely frustrated enough as it is.

The tradesman at the table pushed toward Mary Jane. She drew away from his breath, a strong odor of gin and rotting teeth. Earlier, he had introduced himself as simply Franklin. "Give us a kiss," he said, "and I'll have the barmaid bring you another glass of bitter."

All three of the men were the worse for drink. Franklin, forty or fifty years old, had a shiny round face with a spiderweb of tiny blood vessels across his cheeks and nose.

A rusty guts lushington.

She'd decided he was a tradesman because he had no callouses on his hands and his clothing carried the confused smells of a chandler's shop of household goods. He wore a gray wool jacket and trousers, the cuffs and hems worn. The watch chain that dipped into the pocket of his faded black linen waistcoat flashed a dull brass color. By the quality and condition of his clothing, Mary Jane judged that Franklin had met with small success in life or significant debt.

"No, thank you," she said.

Trying to avoid the tradesman's foul breath entirely, she found herself looking at the laborer to her left, a burly blonde fellow somewhat blackened with a residue of coal. With the darkness rubbed into the creases of his face and hands and his clothes made a colorless dark gray from the dusting, he reminded her painfully of her deceased husband, Berwyn. The laborer had been trying to catch her eye for some time, and she'd avoided talking to him. Possibly a coal backer, he would have few funds to spend on her.

Unbidden, she recalled a black smear of coal on her pale skin as she lay naked, holding her Berwyn. They had been married a month and she'd been so eager to make love to him on that day she hadn't let him wash after his hours of labor in the coal mine. He put up a fight when she tried to drag him to their bed. Finally, he'd relented and let her have her way.

What a mess that were to clean, but the prigging were worth the trouble.

The memory, bitter-sweet, brought more pain than pleasure.

She turned away from the coal backer. Setting aside the pretense that she could see no further than ten feet, Mary Jane focused on the one she chose to think of as Mum.

Jennifer rubbed her face, perhaps to rearrange the features and give herself a new look, one that would belong in the pub. Still, her face displayed unease. She looked up at a gentleman passing by her table with his companions. Catching her eye, the fellow quickly turned away. Although attractive enough, Jennifer's appearance held an unavoidable dread of her very pursuit. Mary Jane had seen the look before, especially in young, green tail. She'd been that way herself, five years earlier.

Franklin gripped her under the arm, trying to lift her from her seat. "You have a crib nearby, somewhere we can go?"

Mary Jane became deadweight in her chair, looked toward the sailor.

"Here, now," the sailor said to the tradesman, "I had her talking. You wait your turn."

Franklin turned slowly toward him, said, "Look at your hooks, Jack Tar."

The sailor's hands were stained black with rope pitch. Mary Jane had known worse. He looked fit enough and had a moderately handsome, if weathered face.

"You think she wants those touching her?" Franklin asked.

She knew the angry words would end with fisticuffs. Men had fought over her since her days as a mere dollymop in Cardiff. To see one suffer for desiring her seemed to make men want her all the more. She'd played that to her advantage on occasion.

"My name is *Tedward*," the sailor said, his tone cold. "*Not* Jack Tar."

Mary Jane hoped he would win. He had spoken to her with some respect. Probably of able seaman grade, he no doubt earned less than the tradesman, yet was more promising. The Royal Navy withheld much of sailors' pay until they reached home port to prevent desertion. He still smelled of his ship, the tar on his hands, and the sea, so he had likely returned to London that day. If his voyage had been long, he might be in a mood to squander his funds.

"*Tedward?*" Franklin shouted. He bellowed his laughter.

Heads turned toward the sound. Jennifer Weatherhead's eyes, four tables away, grew large with a look of concern. She obviously wasn't accustomed to pubs and loud men.

Mary Jane hoped to catch her eye, and couldn't tell if she had.

"Who would *give* such a name?" The tradesman asked. "Mum couldn't decide between Edward and Theodore?"

The sailor rose swiftly and shoved the tradesman. Franklin clung to the back of Mary Jane's chair as he fell. The legs of the rickety seat gave way, dumping her in the sawdust on the floor. Tedward fell upon Franklin, pounding with black fists.

The coal backer fled.

Mary Jane crawled under the table.

From her new vantage, she saw the beautiful blonde prostitute, Gabriella Gorse, at the entrance to the pub. The woman had always been ill-mannered, if not insulting to Mary Jane. Because both had once been prostitutes of high standing, perhaps a competitiveness came between them. Folks called her Gabby because she chatted up all the fresh tail in the neighborhood. She seemed too helpful to the new girls; the daily crop of inexperienced pauper women of many ages that landed hard on the streets with but one commodity left to them.

Remembering that the woman in the printed sketch Stuart Brevard had dropped in Bale Street looked more like Gabby, Mary Jane had a notion that he might find and beat the churlish prostitute one day.

No, I shan't want cruel thoughts, just because I don't like her.

Gabby took half a step into the pub and stopped, holding the door open. The ugly, scarred face of Nick Shears came into view behind her, looking into the establishment over her shoulder. He'd become the most feared Demander of the Gully Bleeders. A gang like the Beloved Ratters of Cardiff and the High Rips of Liverpool, the Bleeders took protection money from prostitutes. Mary Jane had to pay what Nick Shears demanded. He carried sheep shears in his belt. Thinking about what he'd done with them to women, her hands moved involuntarily to cover her breasts.

Still in the doorway, Gabby nodded toward the table where Jennifer sat.

"No!" Mary Jane said aloud, the word drowned in the sounds of the struggle between Tedward and Franklin.

Nick also nodded, palmed something to Gabby, and they parted company without fully entering the Angel and Trumpet.

I have to warn Jennifer.

The fight between Franklin and Tedward moved in Mary Jane's direction. Out of the confusion of tumbling bodies emerged a clawing arm, probably trying to find something to grip as a weapon. The hand closed on Mary Jane's booted right ankle. Noting that the palm wasn't blackened with tar, she brought the heel of her other boot down on the hand's exposed digits, and it withdrew instantly.

Keeping her head down, she got up, and moved toward Jennifer's table. When she got there, she discovered an empty chair. Looking toward the front of the pub, Mary Jane saw the woman's plum-colored skirt. Jennifer passed through the door to exit the Angel and Trumpet.

Mary Jane had to catch up with her.

Out in Stepney High Street, Jennifer could be seen fairly running from the pub, despite a limp. Mary Jane hurried forward to catch up. They slipped quickly between the many people using the brick footway. Drawing closer, Mary Jane reached to touch her shoulder. Not wanting to startle, she hesitated, pulled back, and said a bit too loudly, "Excuse me, Mum."

Jennifer looked back at her without breaking stride, then faced forward again as she continued. The limp became more pronounced, but whatever the injury, it didn't seem to slow her much. She had not been limping on the day she came to the rescue with her laundry sack.

Mary Jane realized she must look a mess, with saw dust from the floor of the pub caught in her hair and clothing. Still, she sped up and placed her left hand on Jennifer's right shoulder. The woman stopped and turned. Her six inch advantage in height added to the illusion that she was Mary Jane's mother.

"*Yes?*" Jennifer said, her eyes narrowed, brow furrowed. She didn't seem to recognize Mary Jane. "I saw you in the pub. Those men fighting…"

"Yes, at my table," Mary Jane said. She forced a chuckle. "Tedward and Franklin. I had to get away from them."

Mum raised her brow with a disapproving look. "*And…?*"

"I am the woman you helped in Bale Street about a month ago. You struck a man with a sack of laundry. He were molesting me, and that allowed me to get away. I saw you again later that day on the street and introduced myself."

"Yes, I remember you." Jennifer looked around distractedly, then fixed her eyes on her feet.

For what had been a brave, helpful woman, she seemed timid and uncaring at present.

Mary Jane struggled to find a way to talk to her. "You were… *ill at ease* in the pub," she began.

"I'm glad I could help. Now, I must—"

Mary Jane pressed on. "Y-you wanted—"

"I wanted *out*, just as soon as they—" Rather than finish, the woman shook her head, pulled her checked woolen shawl tighter. She adjusted her felt hat, and began to edge away.

"No, not *then*," Mary Jane said, shaking her head, "*before* the trouble started, you…" Again, she didn't know what to say.

Jennifer looked nonplussed and impatient.

"Pardon me, I've forgotten my manners. I remember your name, Jennifer. You may not remember mine. Miss Mary Jane Kelly, I am."

She immediately regretted giving her true name.

"I am Miss Weatherhead." Jennifer turned her face away from a biting wind.

Because Mary Jane had seen the woman as much like her mother, until that moment she had not thought of her as a spinster. *How painful it must be for her to learn soliciting. No wonder she is so irritable and guarded.*

I should try to persuade her to give up the trade, yet her choices are truly none of my business, and she must have her reasons.

"Did you have a purpose in stopping me?"

Mary Jane wanted to warn her about Nick Shears straight off, but didn't want to frighten her away. Instead, she said, "Street cokum, you need."

"Say what you mean," Jennifer said with a frown.

"I can help you learn—"

"Learn what?" The frown deepened.

How shall I allow for her dignity whilst...? Arguing with herself, Mary Jane didn't answer quickly enough.

"How to find *clients*?" Jennifer offered.

Her expression had turned to a defiant challenge, a common response, Mary Jane knew, for one keeping shame at bay.

"Well...yes." she said, not knowing what else to say. *And something of the dangers of the street,* she thought, *like Nick Shears and the Gully Bleeders.*

She'd stood up to Harris Brevard and a variety of blackguards over the years. Mary Jane had kept a cool enough head to manage all that, yet with the way Miss Weatherhead looked at her, she felt cowed.

Jennifer gestured back the way they'd come. "Clients—like the ones you found at the Angel and Trumpet?"

Mary Jane felt herself blushing. "I *do* take risks." To admit such things to her mother—or so it seemed! "Exciting, I find it..." She looked down, then she raised her head to look Jennifer in the eye, "I manage the risks *because* I have cokum. Advice, I can give you. I'd like to help."

"*You* have experience?" Jennifer said. "*You* are cunning? I should think you were but a girl a few short years ago."

"Twenty-three years old, I am. I've been a ladybird for five years, five *long* years. Solicited, I have, amongst both toffs in the West End and laborers in the East End. I know my business."

Jennifer turned away and began walking again. Competing with the woman's long, limping stride, Mary Jane struggled to keep up.

"I made mistakes you might avoid," she said, "spent nearly a year in an infirmary in Cardiff healing from what a client gave me."

Jennifer kept walking. Mary Jane fell behind.

Why should I bother? I have my own concerns.

Mary Jane watched the woman stumble and recover. Holding her head high, Miss Weatherhead marched onward.

Another small blow to her dignity. She wouldn't have it, but I pity her.

I must do something to help!

What advice could I give quickly that might have helped me?

"Don't use the sheep's gut," she called. "Use the rubber ones."

Jennifer stopped and turned suddenly, her eyes wide, lips pressed tightly together.

Mary Jane grimaced at what she took for anger.

The older woman lifted a hand to her face. Glancing around to see if any others walking on the footway nearby had taken notice of the conversation, she crossed her lips with an index finger.

Mary Jane knew she had spoken too loudly. Jennifer had no doubt become embarrassed.

She approached, said in a quiet, cracking voice, "I bought the sheep's gut." Her expression had broken open to reveal that of an innocent child, the flesh around her eyes straining, her mouth small and worried. "This is *hopeless. I* am hopeless. We shall all end up seeking relief in the workhouse, I'm sure of that now." She bent forward and shook her head. Tears rolled down her cheeks.

"Come with me, Mum," Mary Jane said. She placed a warm hand on the woman's back. "I know a coffee shop where to we can talk without any bother."

Jennifer hesitated, and Mary Jane thought she might turn and flee again. She waited patiently.

Finally, the woman stood straight and turned to look her in the eye. "I am Miss Jennifer Weatherhead," she said with a return of some of her earlier pluck. "I *do* need help."

When the woman took her arm and allowed herself to be led, a thrill ran through Mary Jane.

She remembered her cousin, Carryl Hughes, offering an arm in a similar circumstance, and the distant echo of her father's question that followed: "Do you know what danger is, girl?"

I hope I am not leading Jennifer into peril.

CHAPTER EIGHT

Mary Jane guided Jennifer across Stepney High Street and into Durham Row, a lane running along the northern edge of St. Dunstan's Church. Trees in the churchyard had taken on yellow fall color, the leaves beautiful beneath an unusually crisp and clear blue sky.

Entering the Ashfield Place footpath to head northward to the coffee shop, Mary Jane noted that Jennifer's limp had lessened.

"While soliciting, I use the name Ginger. If you would, please use my true name only when we're alone. You should find a name to use other than your own, one that feels comfortable."

"I'll think about what that might be," Jennifer said. "My friends call me Jennie."

Mary Jane considered the last statement an invitation.

She saw a man with red side whiskers and mustache moving toward them among the other pedestrians ahead. With the warm color of his whiskers and the hair that poked out from beneath his brown bowler, he stood out, even at a distance.

Brevard!

Her heart beat quickened, and a tingling at the back of her neck told her to hide. She didn't want to frighten Jennie.

"Look at this hat," Mary Jane said, taking Miss Weatherhead by the arm and tugging her into the recessed doorway of a Milliner's shop. "Now where is it?"

Though clearly surprised by the sudden deviation, Jennie seemed willing to concentrate on the hats displayed in the window. "Which one?" she asked. "They're all quite beautiful."

Mary Jane hadn't got a good look at the man, and she didn't think he'd seen her.

Jennie stands out too far! He might recognize her.

"Excuse me for a moment," Mary Jane said. "I have a rock in my

87

boot. Would you steady me?" She offered her left hand.

Jennie took it and turned toward her.

Good. Now she faced completely away from the approaching man and had her face down.

Mary Jane crouched and pretended to attend to her foot with her right hand beneath the cover of her skirts. Then she realized that if the man had noticed her, crouched down as she was might prove her undoing, since she would not be able to sprint away quickly. She gathered in her hand the hems of her skirts in case she did have to make a dash for it.

The fellow walked by, taking no notice of the women in the Milliner's shop doorway.

He was not Stuart Brevard, yet she had felt the return of the fear from a month earlier, and regretted taking a more casual view of the threat he posed.

Mary Jane realized she'd been holding her breath. With relief, she took a gulp of air.

Remaining in her crouch for a few moments to compose herself, she leaned out of the recess to watch the man walk toward the pretty trees of the churchyard and turn eastward into Durham Row.

"Did you remove the stone?" Jennie asked somewhat impatiently.

"Oh…yes," Mary Jane said, standing.

The two women continued up Ashfield Place.

Mary Jane dreaded a possible future in which Stuart Brevard tracked her to her new lodgings in Globe Road, an eventuality that seemed inevitable. She'd gone to live with Joseph Fleming initially to confuse her trail and gain some male protection. Persuading him to help her recover the necklace was taking more time than she'd anticipated. If Stuart Brevard found her in Globe Road before Fleming agreed to help, and she had to move again, she might lose her chance to get the necklace altogether.

"Here we are," she said, leading Jennie into Dresser's Coffee shop, an establishment run by a man named Sean Dresser. They served tolerably good, strong coffee, different types of tea, and a few simple comestibles. Perhaps a nod to the name of the place, many old, battered dressing screens stood between the numerous tables.

The patrons were allowed to move those about to create pockets of privacy.

Mary Jane regularly visited the coffee shop with potential clients, sometimes to sober them up, but more importantly she used the place as a neutral territory to get to know a man before committing to a transaction. She had organized numerous ladybirds of the area at the coffee shop, confederates of sorts. They all used the establishment for the same purpose, and shared their knowledge of the men they met in an effort to identify and, hopefully, avoid the dangerous ones.

Around the edge of a screen, Mary Jane saw May Wildash glance up at her from her seat at a table. The woman purposely caught her eye.

"Good afternoon, Ginger," May said. She adjusted the screen as if she wanted a better view of Mary Jane. The true purpose was to reveal the man with whom she sat, a tall fellow in a dark gray jacket. His thin face held heavy side whiskers and a curling mustache. They sat with cups of coffee and slices of bread. The gentleman busied himself brushing crumbs from the table, and then from his lap. He obviously didn't want the intrusion.

"Good afternoon to you, Kitty," Mary Jane said.

She had met the man before, knew that he had hired a mutual acquaintance, and that the transaction had gone off without incident. Pretending to adjust an errant lock of hair, she pulled on her right earlobe with her left hand.

"We'll have to find time to do a tightener, the three of us," Mary Jane said, "so I can properly introduce you to my new friend." She nodded toward her companion. Mary Jane didn't want to force a name on Miss Weatherhead, yet felt awkward not giving one.

Jennie, quick on the uptake, nodded and smiled. "Emma Lizabeth Smith," she said.

"Very good to meet you," May said. "Yes, I'd like that." She smiled, and turned back to her gentleman.

Mary Jane adjusted a green screen made of spilt cane or bamboo so that panels largely surrounded a table in the corner. She and Jennie took chairs at the table.

A young girl brought cups for the two, poured coffee into them, and left without a word.

"Emma Elizabeth Smith?" Mary Jane asked.

"No," Jennie said. "Emma Lizabeth, after a strict and proper school marm I had as a child in Yorkshire." She chuckled. "A small revenge for the many times she rapped my knuckles with her stick. And Smith because, well, the name is common."

Mary Jane smiled. "A good thing that you can jest. You'll need the humor. If I were to do you kindness, it would be to persuade you not to take up the life."

"My fears alone *are* a persuasion, but there's nothing for it. My family and I have lost nearly everything. I can but try."

Mary Jane saw in the woman a kind and generous gaze, now that Jennie's fear and shame had been put away. The lines around her mouth and pale eyes, deepened from worry, formed open, pleasant expressions that further reminded Mary Jane of Mum.

Obvious from Jennie's voice and manner, she had not been poor for most of her life, and had received a good education. Mary Jane longed for more stimulating conversations than she had with most of the women she currently knew, almost all of them East End prostitutes with little if any education. She got a sense that she might eventually have that with Jennie.

"Will you tell me something of your circumstances?" she asked.

"My brother, Lieutenant Charles Weatherhead, was the bread winner for our family. He died from eating bad victuals while serving aboard the HMS Penelope. Several others onboard the ship died from the poison food. His family—widow, Clarissa, and two children, Benjamin and Maisie, our mother, Levinia, and I—tried to hold a man named Caille accountable. With help from the families of the other victims, we paid a solicitor to bring the claim in civil court. The costs to trial took what little we had and we lost the case. The other families suffered the same loss. My family now survives on my brother's pension, cut in half for a surviving spouse, and what work Clarissa and I find. Levinia, my mum, has taken ill—grippe, I think—and cannot help. My cousin, Catherine Weatherhead, visits from Southwark on occasion. She earns as a widow's companion, and is able to provide a little assistance from time to time. She is so very lucky to have found a position, but then she is young—twenty-three years old, I believe—strong, and well-spoken."

"Little worse for a woman in the East End than to be left to earn for her entire family," Mary Jane said.

"I have Clarissa. I must say, though, she doesn't have the wind for some of the labor we take in." Jennie's face reflected the frustration in her tone.

"What sort of labor?"

"You saw me with it. I used it as a weapon." She smiled crookedly. "We take in work from Bryte's Laundry. Stain removal and renovation. Clarissa cannot scrub for long, so I do most of the stains. Childhood illness stole half her breath away and she doesn't have the wind to give to the effort. She does the mending instead. Well, we both do that. The children help some, when they're not in school."

"I knew there must be hardship for you to turn to…"

Jennie nodded her head rapidly with a grim smile. Mary Jane didn't finish.

She watched the older woman sip her coffee. *Yes*, she decided, *Jennie has it in her to keep herself safe while soliciting. She needs to follow a few simple rules. She will not want to discuss what's needed, though she knows she must.*

"Don't hurry," Mary Jane said, getting down to the business. "Get to know a man a bit with conversation first."

Jennie nodded, clearly listening intently and thinking about the words.

"Bring him here, if you can. Women I know what come here will take a look at him and give you a signal." She demonstrated with a slight tug on her right earlobe with her left hand. "*Right ear should the man be right and true, left ear if he's left you black and blue.* A simple shrug says you don't know. Introduce you, I will, to those willing to show you the ropes. Once you get to know the local clientele, you can help too. When you make the signal, always use the opposite hand so there's no confusing, and do so as easy as you can. Some men are so wary, they'll flee should they suspect a conspiracy, even if it's harmless to them."

91

Jennie took a deep breath, sat straighter, exhaled slowly.

"Always use a sheath, the rubber ones."

Although the words had been spoken so quietly that none but Jennie could hear them, she glanced about uneasily.

She could be a virgin, still. At the least, she has little experience.

"If a man can speak only of the act..." Mary Jane said.

Seeing the question in her companion's eyes, she paused, said, "Engagement."

Still, a lack of understanding.

"*Tupping*, then."

Finally, Jennie seemed to understand, nodding with fresh embarrassment.

"Should he want to talk about the particulars at length, that is his manner of having his way with you. Should you allow such a thing at no cost, unlikely he'll be to commit funds. That, or possibly he's dangerous."

Jennie's eyes became wide, and Mary Jane placed a warm hand atop one of hers.

Poor thing. Would that I might hold her hand when her first time comes. She would have laughed at the thought if the look in Jennie's eyes had held any real sense of hope.

"The going rate for a *casual* is four pence. They are unfortunates with little or no experience."

Jennie frowned, as if confused.

Mary Jane forced a tight smile. "The muck snipes you see wandering the streets."

She immediately regretted using the derogatory term, and knew she'd revealed her unavoidable resentment toward the innumerable amateur prostitutes, something of which she wasn't proud.

Jennie's expression changed, her eyes narrowing with suspicion.

"They are, I know, just trying to get on in a hard life," Mary Jane said quickly. "The casual, she is most often a poor woman who has lost her man."

Jennie's frown deepened. "Or her brother," she said with a look of challenge, "the family bread winner?"

"I should not have called them muck snipes," Mary Jane said, speaking more rapidly still. "I do not truly look upon them with scorn. The crude term I use so there's no mistaking. You are not like them, and we intend that like them you shan't become. The casuals drive down the prices for all of us. Attractive, you are, and your tidy clothing will do for now. We'll make improvements as we can. You should ask for six pence to start. A tanner is respectable."

"*We* intend?" Jennie said indignantly.

"I don't mean to speak for you," Mary Jane said, shaking her head.

A bitterness had entered the conversation. Appearing uncomfortable in her seat, Jennie looked away, placed her hands on the table, her mouth forming a tight line. "*We'll* make improvements?"

Mary Jane knew she'd upset the woman again. She couldn't think what to say to mitigate what appeared to be a return to mistrust. "I meant only to show my eagerness to help."

Jennie ran her right hand over the stained, pitted wood of the tabletop. With a look of hurt, she rose slowly from her seat, and looked down her nose at Mary Jane. "If you know so much, what are you doing *here*? You say you have experience with the well-to-do, yet no gentleman would have a woman on his arm who speaks as you do. By your manner of speech, I should think you grew up on the streets."

"I don the voice I need," Mary Jane said calmly. "Quite capable, I am, of the Queen's English."

Jennie frowned, and shook her head. "I might need help, but I shan't need a whore's minder, nor your pity." Her eyes flashed with accusation. "Who are *you* to decide what *I'm* worth?"

She turned to leave. Mary Jane grasped her left hand. "Please, I don't wish to gain anything from you, save, perhaps, friendship. There is more to tell to help keep you safe."

Jennie pulled her hand free, hesitated. Her expression suggested that she couldn't decide whether to stay or go, that a desire for help warred with a fear of being played.

Mary Jane realized she'd been presumptuous. She had indeed somehow got the feeling that Jennie was family. That had driven her words too much. Portraying herself to be a ladybird of a higher station had set a barrier between them. The older woman's pride might not permit her to share her problems so intimately with a woman half her age.

Her face, so much like Mum's, will haunt me if she walks away.

Telling how I came to be here might put her at ease. Then she might listen.

"My story, I'll tell, if you'll sit with me. It may well be instructive."

Moments passed as Jennie shifted restlessly from foot to foot. Finally, she sat with a look of resignation, her eyes downcast.

With a sense of relief, Mary Jane sat back, and tried to relax. Unaccustomed to explaining herself and unsettled by the conflict, she wished she had whiskey rather than coffee. Better still would be another dose of laudanum, but when others saw her take the drug, they often had questions she didn't want to answer. *Jennie already looks upon me doubtfully. No sense in making that worse.* She took a deep draught from her cup of coffee before beginning.

Mary Jane told of the loss of her mother and her father's anger. "With hard feeling toward Papa, I left my home in Carmarthen, Wales when sixteen years old and married the first man what'd have me, Berwyn Davies. He were a collier, a coal runner, killed in '81 in a mine explosion in Penygraig. I don't miss the drunkard much."

Jennie looked up at her, possibly to assess the feelings behind the words.

Mary Jane didn't mean to sound uncaring. "Difficult he made my desire to love him." The familiar sadness filled her heart. She gasped slightly and swallowed hard to keep the feelings down. Embarrassed to think that the emotion showed on her face, she gestured with her hands aimlessly.

A small flash of sympathy in Jennie's eyes said that the woman recognized the pain. She clearly knew much about loss. "Tell me," she said, a bit of demand in her tone.

Mary Jane didn't want to tell her, yet wanted to gain her trust. "A woman who worked by my side at a woolen mill in Cartmarthen, Mared Jones, introduced me to her brother, Evan Berwyn Davies. He had come from Penygraig for a visit. He worked the Pandy Coal Pit there. I saw my escape from Papa when Berwyn took a romantic interest in me. At such a young age and selfish, I thought little of the poor fellow's feelings. Because my father disliked me so and wanted to see me suffer, I knew he would accept my marriage to one of such a lowly station. Once Berwyn and I were wed, I removed to Penygraig, a village of dullards and drunkards. The color at sun's set was the best part of each day."

Dabbing it up with Berwyn had felt good while it lasted. At that age, she had not learned how to manage a man. His pearly shower came too quickly. Afterward he got a bad case of lobcock. She became pregnant once, but lost it.

"Berwyn looked at me at times with a certain light in his eyes, as if proud to have me. Turning his lamps on me like that, I felt worth something after the poor treatment of my father. Made my heart to skip a beat. I found Berwyn handsome, if a bit rough.

"He were a lushington. Weary once home from his labors at the mine, he drank too much and fell asleep early most evenings. I missed him, even when I had him home. I wanted to talk, go out for a drink, a meal; anything to break the monotony of my days.

"Bored in a way that told me I didn't truly love him, I grew upset with myself. I'd become spoiled, as Papa would have it. Though I do believe I had feeling for him, my interest had waned quickly. I tried to talk to Berwyn about my restlessness. He wouldn't talk about it. I fought a desire to sneak out alone to the bottom of Amos Hill and drink at the Steamer Seam pub.

"On one occasion that we drank together, I cursed him, turned petulant and contrary. 'You are as dull as the others in this dirty village,' I told him. 'Take care to keep me interested, or you'll find yourself alone again.' Those words I regretted most in my short marriage. They weren't all of my ugliness.

"As time passed, I made little effort to be fair with him. I took to teasing him for his rough language, his lack of maths, and inability to read. I looked for ways to bring into our conversations things I'd learned and read about that I knew he would not understand. Enjoyed his lack of understanding, I did, and a feeling that I were his better.

"The day I lost the battle with my desire to go to the bottom of

Amos Hill, Berwyn died in the mine while I drank at the Steamer Seam. The constabulary took me to see his lifeless body. The light had gone from his lamps."

Remembering the pain she'd experienced with Mum's death, Mary Jane had held in her grief, regret, and shame. Perhaps that was why the sentiments had to sneak out.

Jennie looked at her intently, squeezed her hands, but remained silent.

Mary Jane wiped the moisture from her eyes and nose with a handkerchief.

"My pride and anger toward my father wouldn't allow me to return home. I went to live with my cousin, Carryl Hughes, in Cardiff. A prostitute, she led me into that life. We had an affection for one another, with a sense that we'd taken charge of our own lives."

Mary Jane paused briefly, trying to untangle the love and the hatred she felt for her cousin before saying more about her. Her cousin's betrayals, large and small, loomed large in recollection. Impossible to sort her feelings quickly, she went on with her story instead.

Mary Jane described the attack in Cardiff and her many months recovering in the infirmary. She told of journeying to London and finding a position at the Phoenix gay house.

"Born of a low station, by twenty-two years of age, I were riding about London town in carriages with wealthy industrialists. On the arm of fine gentlemen, I've attended extravagant social gatherings where our kind is tolerated. I partook in the ways of the well-to-do; enjoyed fine food, fine lodgings, comforts of all sorts.

"But they wanted a lot in return, too much at times. Suffer abuse, I would not. I stood up for myself." Mary Jane recounted the incident with Harris Brevard in Paris. "That ginger-haired man, Stuart Brevard, what attacked me the day you helped, I believe he is the brother of Harris Brevard."

Out of shame and a desire to avoid frightening Jennie, Mary Jane offered little description of the severe violence suffered on both sides in the incident with Harris Brevard. She also held back much of the emotion associated with the memories, and didn't admit that she'd robbed him.

Held back or not, she did relive those feelings some. Following a long pause in which she struggled to compose herself, she realized that Jennie still waited for her to finish.

"The gentleman what I harmed in Paris were a client in good standing with my gay house in the West End," she said. "Because of what I done to him, they turned me out in the streets."

Jennie had covered her mouth with a hand. Mary Jane couldn't tell whether the gesture hid an expression of shock or disdain. *A good thing the full story I did not tell.* Whatever the case, she had begun the tale, and must find an appropriate end if she hoped to regain the woman's trust.

"In high society, I dare not show myself for fear of that brother. Destroyed what I had gained in life, I did, such as it was. I've returned to the dreadful work I began at age eighteen in Cardiff, yet my experience remains, and much the wiser for it I am."

Mary Jane paused for a moment, took another drink of her coffee. "I speak before thinking at times. Please forgive me, and allow me to help."

Jennie seemed to relax. When her hand moved away from her mouth, Mary Jane saw that her ire had melted away.

A wing of the bamboo screen opened outward to reveal Rachel Bowles and a handsome fellow in a pale grey suit.

"Good day, Ginger," Rachel said.

Jennie's eyes grew wide.

"Good day to you, Rachel." Mary Jane said brightly.

Jennie tugged on her left ear repeatedly, no subtlety to the effort.

"Has the earache returned, Emma?" Mary Jane said quickly. "Excuse us, Rachel, My friend hasn't been feeling well."

"Of course," Rachel said. She and the gentleman retreated and swung the wing of the screen back in place.

Placing a hand on Jennie's arm, Mary Jane raised an index finger to her smiling lips. After a moment, she said, "They're gone now, I think. You know the man?"

Jennie appeared embarrassed. "I know I did a poor job of the signal. I used the wrong hand! Please forgive me." She waved a hand before her face, as if brushing away her mistake. "He came for me in the Crown and Dolphin, just at the end of the street. He grabbed my…" Again, she looked embarrassed. "Well, I didn't expect his touch, and I complained loudly. He savagely stomped my foot."

"Ah, the limp." Mary Jane felt her smile grow as she thought of the older woman's frantic earlobe tugs.

"Yes."

Mary Jane chuckled.

Jennie gave her a cross look, seeming confused as well as indignant. "My misfortune amuses you?"

"No, just the face you made when you gave the signal." Mary Jane laughed. "You'll have to work on being nonchalant when you make it."

Jennie must have seen the humor. She smiled and burst out with her own chortling.

"But you did well to give it. Wrong hand or not, I'm certain she got the message." Mary Jane tried to quiet her amused response. "Pleased Rachel will be with you," she gasped, her laughter resuming.

"Yes, I shall practice it now." Jennie tugged both ears and screwed up her face in a foolish grin.

Mary Jane broke into uncontrolled guffaws.

Jennie covered her mouth to stifle her own growing laughter.

The good humor slowly died out, and the two women sat silently and comfortably for a time.

At length, Mary Jane said, "One more piece of advice have I for you today. If you heard nothing else I've said, should you think I am a fool or a danger, still, please, hear this well."

Jennie sat up, shaking her head. "I believe you, and am most grateful for your advice. What would you have me know?"

"The Gully Bleeders will come to you for protection money."

"Protection? Protection from whom?"

"'Tis a shakedown. You pay them to protect you. Should you fail to pay, a nobbling they give you."

"Nobbling?"

"A beating. You pay them for protection from their abuse. Nick Shears, a man with a scarred face, or one of his underlings will come for it. Don't be afraid, just pay the price. If you don't, they'll cut you badly, leaving permanent scars."

She saw Jennie's horror grow in her expression. Mary Jane had nothing for it—she had to finish the warning. "Should they decide to make an example of you, they will maim you. Find a way to pay you must. From a casual, they take a half-shilling per week. Should the Gully Bleeders see that you make more than a casual, they'll demand more."

The look of concern on Jennie's face said that she considered a tanner a dear price to pay. Carryl had paid Mary Jane's protection to the Beloved Ratters for a time. A tanner, just six pence was a small burden—she could pay that for Jennie for a few weeks. Jennie would be able to pay it herself with time.

"If you haven't the chink, find me and I'll pay for you."

"I could not let you—" Jennie began.

Mary Jane cut her off. "Yes, you can." She gave the woman her most grave and piercing gaze.

Then, something of the woman who had swung a laundry sack at Stuart Brevard emerged. "You stood up for *yourself...*" Jennie complained.

"Yes, and have someone after me for my trouble, yet he may never find me. He is an amateur. The Gully Bleeders are different. Eyes and ears, they have, everywhere in the East End. Promise me you will come to me if you cannot pay them."

With a fragile smile, Jennie nodded. "It isn't at all fair."

Mary Jane returned the smile with a grim one, chuckled dryly. "What's fair rarely visits the East End."

CHAPTER NINE

Mary Jane remained at Dresser's to finish her coffee following her new friend's departure. On her way out of the establishment, she saw a fellow named Mansfield—whom she knew to be dangerous—seated at a table. If he sat with a prostitute, Mary Jane wanted to give her a warning. She approached the screen that hid the other side of the table. Behind it sat beautiful Gabriella Gorse.

Although they didn't get along, Mary Jane thought she should warn the woman. She reached for her left ear with her right hand as Gabby glanced up.

The woman gave a scornful, lop-sided smile. "I have no need of your quaint intrigues," she said.

"You might have, without knowing," Mary Jane said, and nodded subtly toward the man.

He huffed, and glared at her.

"Be gone, Ginger," Gabby said.

Ungrateful termagant. "Suit yourself." She left Dressers to head back to the Angel and Trumpet.

The next day, while passing through Stepney Green, Mary Jane saw Gabby with a black eye.

Serves her right, Mary Jane thought, assuming that Mansfield had beaten the woman. *She's lucky she only copped a mouse.*

Gabby, seeing Mary Jane, approached. The closer Miss Gorse got, the more bruises could be seen on her face. She held out folded pieces of paper. "Is that you?" she asked.

Mary Jane took what looked like three sheets of half-foolscap, unfolded them, and saw the printed sketch of a woman with the name, "Andriette," beneath.

The pictures Stuart Brevard carried!

"No," she said, remaining calm while her brain raced.

He is still here, and could be anywhere. Has she led him to me? She wanted to look around, searching the area to see if she could spot him, and she wanted to question Miss Gorse, but decided that either effort would reveal her answer to be a lie.

If she believes that's a picture of me, did she tell him so?

She would probably not know that Mary Jane went by Andriette at the Phoenix gay house.

"The fellow what had those thought I was the woman in the picture," Gabby said, then pointed to her face. "He give me this before deciding maybe he'd made a mistake."

Mansfield hadn't given her the black eye, Stuart Brevard had.

Does she know she took a beating meant for me?

"You ought to take more care in the company you keep," Mary Jane said coldly. "Do you know his name?"

Gabby spit on the path at Mary Jane's feet, turned, and walked away.

If he is still here, at least he's confused about who he's after.

Mary Jane worried that Gabriella Gorse had detected her lie, and that she might find and tell Stuart Brevard that Andriette was now going by the name Ginger.

CHAPTER TEN

Mary Jane asked Joseph Fleming to fetch her possessions from Thomas Morganstone's apartments. He borrowed a friend's coster's barrow and hauled what were mostly clothes over to the room in Globe Road.

She continued to see as many clients as she could. Though Fleming had allowed she might see them at their lodgings while he was out, she made a deal with Rachel Bowles to share her crib in Eastfield Street, since the place was closer to Dresser's Coffee Shop. Mary Jane had satisfied an average of twenty clients a week in the almost two months since taking up with Fleming—although some were repeat customers—earning just over sixteen pounds. Of course, the money wasn't nearly what she'd earned working at the Phoenix gay house. Fleming didn't expect her to contribute to household expenses. She added seven pounds to her savings, bringing the funds she could depend on for relocating to a new city to thirty-three pounds.

Instead of seeing clients in the late afternoon of Tuesday, October 23, Mary Jane spent time with Jennie Weatherhead at Dresser's Coffee shop. They sat together in relative privacy behind a dressing screen while the older woman told about her first successful transaction with a client and what followed.

"The act was not as bad as anticipating it," she said, attempting a brave face. "Then the scarred man you told me about came to me outside the Crown and Dolphin…" Her words caught awkwardly in her throat. "…demanding I pay a half shilling per week to…" She shook with sobs, unable to finish.

"Nick Shears of the Gully Bleeders." Feeling that further words would be hollow, Mary Jane fell silent.

"Yes," Jennie said. "That's the one. He cut me under the chin with a small knife." Quaking in renewed fear, she tilted her head back to show a small, scabbed nick. "'That's my mark,' he said, 'just like my Christian name. You'll not be wanting more of those. Each one is bigger and they lead to my surname.' He showed me sheep shears, then took the tanner I had earned."

He likes to think he's clever. Mary Jane nodded to show she recognized the ritual marking.

Two days earlier, upon passing south through the East London Cemetery, she had seen Nick Shears, four of his bludgers, and Gabby Gorse among the grave markers. Out of curiosity, Mary Jane slowed to see what they were up to. She'd paid her protection money for the week, so she had nothing to fear if they saw her, yet didn't want them to think she intentionally spied. Fairly well hidden among uneven markers, she felt safe enough. Nick and his young men remained too quiet to be engaged in a shake down. Gabby spoke to Nick calmly. She counted out something on the fingers of her hand, said something, and Nick nodded. He gave her something, and she smiled. That was the second time Mary Jane had seen Nick Shears give Gabby something. The woman had to be working for the man in some capacity.

"If I were my young cousin, Catherine," Jennie said, "I would not be so afraid. She is a tall woman with and iron jaw. Not that I would wish my lot on her, but she would succeed on the street much better than I do. Would that I could be more like her."

Jenny covered her eyed with her hands. "Such self-pity! When I think of my mother, now on her deathbed in our miserable lodgings, I know I should feel fortunate that I have my health. She will not be with us much longer."

When Jennie's emotions had quieted, Mary Jane pressed a shilling into her friend's hand, and would not take the coin back despite protests.

Finally, the older woman accepted the gift with thanks.

They finished their coffee, and Mary Jane walked Jennie back to her lodgings, a room in an old, wooden tenement in Brantridge Street. They took a rather circuitous route to avoid going by Thomas Morganstone's apartments, just in case Stuart Brevard watched the neighborhood.

"Please allow me to introduce you to my sister-in-law, Clarissa, and her children," she said.

"Thank you, but no," Mary Jane said.

Jennie wanted her soliciting to remain a secret, had come up with a lie concerning a position as a housemaid, and seemed fairly confident that Clarrisa believed it.

"You've changed," Mary Jane said, referring to Jennie's clothing, "but I haven't. I don't want to give your family any suspicions."

The door of the tenement opened, and a tall, young woman with some family resemblance to Jennie emerged.

"Oh, Catherine, good to see you. I spoke of you earlier, and here you are."

The woman seemed surprised, as if her thoughts had been far away. "Cousin, yes. Good to see you, also."

"My friend, Ginger."

The young woman looked Mary Jane up and down, made the merest nod of acknowledgment, then turned back to Jennie. "I don't have time to visit at present. Perhaps soon." She strode away at a fast pace.

"Your cousin, Catherine Weatherhead?" Mary Jane asked.

"Yes." Jennie shrugged sadly. "She saw you. Hopefully nothing will come of it."

"She *was* making haste."

"I will see you at Dresser's, then."

"Yes, or at the Angel and Trumpet. There is still much more for you to learn."

Jennie nodded. "Thank you," she said, and entered the building.

Mary Jane headed north and west toward home as the sun set. The afternoon with the woman had been strangely more exhausting than seeing most clients.

She had become accustomed to walking in the night. Usually she did that with other women. Stepney had dangers aplenty any time of the day. In the benighted streets, illuminated unevenly as they were with gas lamps—which oddly deepened the areas of shadow—the activities of the pickpockets, both child and adult, the mug-hunters, and various other rampsmen became easier to conceal. Though the stone streets and footways were busy with traffic and pedestrians, and a feeling of being lost in the herd came easily enough, Mary Jane knew the predators were good at singling out those walking alone. She made frequent casual-seeming glances around and behind her as she made her way toward Globe Road.

Nearing her lodgings, Mary Jane had troublesome thoughts about her situation with Joseph Fleming that she had difficulty pinning down. While the room had been comfortable enough, and she remained at ease in his company, something about the arrangement didn't sit right with her.

He paid her nothing, and treated her like a lover. The lack of payment perhaps gave him an impression that she was indeed his. Mary Jane had not been honest with him about her reasons for taking up with him. She had not told him about her need to get away from Thomas Morganstone's apartments because of Stuart Brevard. And, of course, in part she remained with Fleming because she needed his help with the necklace. Her role as lover did not mean the same to both of them.

She'd done worse, so why was she so troubled?

Possibly, the answer lay in an earlier experience of the day.

Around noontime, as Mary Jane and Joseph had left their room and walked south on Globe Road amid the heavy foot traffic, she resumed her efforts to wheedle him into helping her with a plan for recovering the hidden jewelry.

She'd made the mistake of telling him she needed the funds from a sale of the necklace to make a fresh start out of London, a city for which he'd expressed much affection.

Briefly, he'd looked hurt. She should have expected he wouldn't like that. If she left, he'd be torn between losing her or his beloved London. He wouldn't want to leave the city. Thankfully, he had not asked her why she wanted to leave.

"We'll talk about that when I return from Deptford," he said.

Thomas Morganstone had taken a job at the Deptford Victualing Yard, just south along the River Thames. The work required Joseph's presence for a few days.

Entering Mile End Road where they would part company, he

leaned down and kissed her goodbye.

"I'll return late Friday night," he said.

Mary Jane saw a warmth in his expression that troubled her.

He'd been acting rather queer, and she feared that he'd fallen in love with her.

"Perhaps give poor Miss Laudanum a rest," he said. "You've been hitting her hard lately. Should she become fed up, she'll turn on you."

Mary Jane punched him lightly in the chest, gave him a stony look. Her habits were none of his business.

"And don't sell *all* your wares while I'm away," he said, grinning.

She had been neglecting him while she increased her efforts to earn from clients. They'd enjoyed sexual relations much more often when she stayed at Morganstone's apartments. Some sexual distance could make her more desirable. Too much and he might lose interest.

"Leave some for me to enjoy upon my return," he said. Laughing, he walked eastward.

Moving westward, Mary Jane felt herself smiling as she thought about his performance in bed; his graceful movements, his affectionate gaze, and the thrust of his proud instrument within her.

Then his laughter came again from a distance, his guffaws heard over the noise of a tram rolling by. She chuckled.

He would rendezvous with Thomas Morganstone in Deptford at the job site. She had headed for the Angel and Trumpet.

Blast Joseph, she had too much fun with him. From the moment they met, she'd liked the jocular fellow. He was handsome enough, attentive, kind to her, not particularly demanding. He had few nice clothes, a modest embarrassment for her when they were out together. Similar, yet strangely quite the opposite of her husband, Berwyn Davies, who had rarely been seen without a coating of black powder from the coal mines, Joseph, a plasterer, frequently had a dusting of the lime used to make plaster white. Somehow, the sprinkling looked good on him.

Mary Jane didn't want to fall for Joseph. Her mysterious feelings for poor Berwyn were quite enough unwanted sentiment. Her primary goal had to be to resettle somewhere away from London.

If he *had* fallen in love with her, she might use that to help get her way, though not quite knowing the depth of her own feelings for the man complicated the matter.

Yes, *that* was the problem, the source of the uneasy feeling about her situation with Joseph. Not understanding her feelings for the man left her troubled.

Of course, she could always leave him. She could go back to Gander's Bush if need be, yet the idea of returning to the run-down brothel held no attraction.

Mary Jane turned into Devonshire Street, and intentionally dropped some of her wariness. Why she liked doing that when close to home, she could not say. As if playing a game, she ceased to glance around and behind her, choosing instead to pretend blithe innocence to potential threat. A foolish habit, but somehow an exciting one, especially in the moments her lodgings came into view. She'd get the oddest feeling she could outrun any danger that might appear, imagining herself dashing inside her abode and slamming the door to shut out menace. Mary Jane hadn't actually run home since she was a child. The fancy, merely played out in her mind, gave her a pleasant surge of vigor. Along with the sense of danger and risk came memories of the knees of her childhood stockings stained green with adventure.

Of course, just because she did not turn her head to look for danger did not mean that she wasn't aware of what went on around her. The sound of rapid footsteps from behind startled Mary Jane. Turning, she saw shadows flitting across the dampened street, heard an odd chuckle that sounded like it might belong to Gabriella Gorse.

Is she following to find out where I live? To tell Stuart Brevard?

Mary Jane strained to make out the features of those behind her. The people she saw in the lane were mostly silhouettes in the spotty gas light and the misty drizzle of rain. None seemed suspicious of anything, yet Gabby would not necessarily raise anyone's suspicions either running or laughing, not in London.

Still, having the nagging feeling that someone stalked her, Mary Jane picked up her pace.

Turning into Globe Road, and approaching the railway viaduct, the feeling increased. She saw a dim form moving in her direction through the darkness beneath the arches toward the east. Lifting her skirts, she ran as the road passed beneath the viaduct. Seeing threatening shadows emerging from between the stone arches and the mission hall, she ran with all she had.

Those around her stared in wonder. Her skin felt tight. Her lungs burned from the exertion. Mary Jane gasped for air, and pounded on, past Portman Place and Digby Street. She knew someone was at her back, though she would not turn to look.

She saw the tenement on the left, and entered the road to cross to the west side through moving traffic. Mary Jane fouled her boots in the "mud," and came so close to a dray, its driver reined his team of horses to a halt to avoid her.

At the door to the building, she fumbled with her key, her heart pounding in her neck, vision disturbed with bright flashing stars. She got the door opened, glanced left before entering, saw a male figure hurrying toward her. Did he have red hair?

She dashed through the threshold and pushed it shut behind her.

The figure banged into the door. She saw his shadow through the small window at its top.

"Let me in," he called out more calmly than she would have expected. The voice did not sound like Stuart Brevard's. The fellow rattled the door in its frame, trying to get in.

Mary Jane rushed toward her room through the darkened hallway. The broken gas jet had not been fixed.

"Please, I lost my key," said the one outside the building's entrance.

She unlocked her door by touch alone.

Once inside, she moved to the bed and collapsed.

Her heart beat slowed, and her skin seemed to relax. The stars swam out of her vision. Had Gabriella Gorse followed Mary Jane home to find out where she lived? Had anyone at all chased her? Had there been genuine danger or had she merely played an exciting game? She had felt actual fear, yet the danger she'd sensed could have been pure fancy.

Mary Jane heard the door at the building entrance being rattled again, presumably by the man who said he'd lost his key.

Deciding she had indeed let fancy get the better of her, she felt foolish. Even so, she was not about to go find out if the fellow truly needed help.

Mary Jane missed Joseph Fleming already.

Eventually, she sat up and took a large dose of laudanum, at least twenty drops. Since the attack from Stuart Brevard, she'd increased her daily doses of the drug, often having the largest one at night to help her find sleep.

Though much of the evening remained, she needed rest. Mary Jane ate a light meal of bread and cheese, then lay down on the bed again.

CHAPTER ELEVEN

"…I have great affection for you, Mary Jane," Joseph said. "I do not like Miss Laudanum. Come, I've decided you *must* give her up."

Groggy from her narcotic nap, Mary Jane looked up at him somewhat confused. Moments passed before she knew she lay in her bed in their room in Globe Road. Little light came through the thinly-curtained bay window. The night had begun Friday, October 26, and Saturday might have arrived while she slept. Joseph sat on the edge of the bed, her empty bottle of laudanum in his hand. He must have just returned from the work in Deptford. She'd done little in his absence but see clients, and school Jennie Weatherhead in the ways of the ladybird.

Despite his words, his features did not suggest he made a demand. He set the bottle down.

"Before you left, you were on *her* side," Mary Jane said, "wanting me to not *hit* her too hard."

"I've tried to have good humor about your habit. The truth is, the time you spend with her is time away from me. I don't resent your clients half so much as I do her. They are not with you when I am. Laudanum is. In the grip of that stuff, you seem to have one foot in the grave. You're hardly here with the rest of us. I *miss* you."

"You were not here tonight," Mary Jane said flatly.

"I have returned, and I'd had some hope you'd be awake and in a mood for a bit of…." Joseph slipped his right hand into her chemise and cupped her right breast softly, lovingly. "Did you sell everything you had in stock while I was away?"

Though his touch felt good, he'd brought up the subject of her laudanum use again. "The hour is late." She pulled the watch from the pocket of his spattered waistcoat, held the timepiece in the moonlight coming through the bay window. "Past two o'clock in the morning."

He unfastened the chain with his left hand, took the watch from her, and set it on the bedstead. "The work is progressing, but now we have a short deadline. I'll be returning to Deptford in the coming days." He lightly pinched her right nipple, twisted the softness gently. "Seems we might need your help."

Mary Jane tried to ignore the pleasant sensation within her chemise. "In what way?"

"Morganstone took an innocent job at the Deptford Victualing Yard, the renovation of several buildings. That's where Royal Navy ships take on victuals. I'm part of his crew working the job. Then this ordinary-looking cove comes to speak with Morganstone. Oddly, I can't remember anything about the fellow. When they're done talking, we're suddenly up to a bit of *what if* that I don't understand completely. I'm certain Morganstone knows everything. He's keeping quiet about the full lurk. I *do* trust him."

Mary Jane nodded. "So you're not renovating anymore?" she asked, disappointed—he'd said that he wouldn't consider her plan to recover the necklace while he was already engaged in what he called "a bit of what if." With his near constant involvement in the shady side of Morganstone's work, she feared that Fleming might never find the opportunity to help her if she didn't keep bringing it up.

"Yes, we're still doing the renovation, and those who hired Morganstone to do the job know nothing about what the cove asked us to do. Along with the renovation, we're secretly creating a detailed map of the Deptford Victualing Yard, particularly certain parts of the buildings we're working on and the grounds around them."

Joseph slid his left hand beneath the bedclothes, caressed the soft, furred lips between her legs.

Without thinking, Mary Jane shifted her hips and legs to give his hand more room. "What's my part? What do I get paid?"

"Seems night rounders at the yard stand between our client, the ordinary looking cove, and what he's after." He paused, his face screwed up in a strain of concentration. "Curious that I cannot recall a thing about *that* man."

"And *my* part?" Mary Jane asked impatiently. If his caresses hadn't felt so good, she would have pushed his hands away.

"I don't know how it would work. You'd provide a distraction of some sort to draw the night rounders away. We'd make certain there would be no risk for you, and you'd earn a piece. I just don't know what that is yet."

As his fingers found their way into the cleft of her cunny and massaged lightly, she let out a soft moan, despite intending to show little interest.

"I'd do about anything for Thomas, I would," she said.

Again, an involuntary moan.

How did Joseph do that? What made his touch so delightful when it felt little different from that of many men to which she responded with indifference or even disgust? To her frustration, she realized she was intent on hiding her pleasure from Joseph, the one person who should know how she felt, quite the opposite of the pretense of enjoyment she practiced with clients.

"And for me?" He inserted a finger deep inside her. "Would you do just about anything for me?"

I am falling for him, and haven't wanted to admit that to myself.

Mary Jane pushed his left hand away, gave a warning look meant to remind him that he was still earning his privileges with her. "I haven't known you as long," she said. "I'm not certain our *dalliance* is worth the risk of being *lagged*."

He seemed to take the slight of being a mere dalliance in stride. "Ah...*prison*," Joseph said. "Well, it won't do to worry about that." He looked thoughtful for a moment. "But, should you help, I would feel better about our chances if you and Miss Laudanum had parted on good terms by then."

More harping!

She pushed his right hand away, tried the warning look again.

Joseph plucked at the bedclothes in a distracted, ill-tempered fashion.

Hopefully, he is weighing what he might risk to win my heart.

"I'm quite troubled that you care more for Thomas than you do for me, given..."

No, he wants to compete with the man! Why can't Joseph say what he means? Does he secretly scorn Thomas?

The tattered end of her dose of narcotic warned her against starting a fight. *A message from Miss Laudanum*, she decided.

Joseph would never understand the feelings she had for Thomas.

Despite knowing better than to quarrel, Mary Jane couldn't help herself. "Given that he's a *gal-boy*?" she asked sharply.

When she had learned the truth about Thomas, she'd experienced a strange relief, deciding that she could continue to love him without sex, and the large role it had in her life, coming between them.

"Well, yes," he said sheepishly. "Although I have nothing but respect for him, I know *he* could not please you like *I* do."

"Could he please *you* as well as *I* do?" she asked, showing more anger.

Joseph gave her an innocent look.

Time is your enemy, Miss Laudanum seemed to say. *You cannot risk the hard feelings, or worse, a falling out.*

Yes, showing more anger might hinder her efforts to persuade Joseph to help her. Once done with his latest business with Morganstone, he'd be on to the next job, like as not another bit of *what if,* unless she could shift his priorities ahead of time.

Mary Jane forced a smile, guided his right hand back into her chemise to her dairy. She caressed his arm, and his shoulder.

Joseph held the fingers of his left hand to his nose, took a deep breath, and smiled. Mary Jane's entire day was there for him to smell; her moments of discomfort and emotion with potential clients, with Jennie, plus the long walk home and her frightful flight at the end. He clearly liked what he found. Was it her quim that he liked, or would that of any woman do? She suspected he liked the odor because it belonged to her. The idea pleased Mary Jane.

"Did you sell all your wares," he asked, "or did you save something back for me?"

Like it or not, she must prevent him from believing he could have her easily. To hide the smile growing on her face, Mary Jane leaned away from Joseph toward a panel of the bay window at the head of the bed.

Where do these feelings for Joseph come from? Why can't I shut them out?

She pulled the curtain aside, looked up and out through the sooty pane, saw the moon riding the coal smoke haze in the sky above.

All the emotion hopelessly confused her efforts. His touch drew her to him, while he angered her, insulting their good friend. She had to give him hope and yet keep him at arm's length; persuade him that her love remained a possibility if he offered enough, without explaining exactly what she required—all in the midst of falling for him in a way she'd never experienced with a man before. How could she sort all that out to best advantage?

Would that I could ride above it all, Mary Jane thought, considering the bright moon high in the night, *so serene and unconcerned with what happens down here.*

"You do want me," Joseph said, "I can tell. I am possibly the best you've had, else you would not find so much satisfaction. I take you to the heights easily."

Yes, he was the best she'd had in her bed—something she ought not to admit. Still, what braggadocio!

"I am no bee, but a hornet when it comes to the sting of pleasure." He spoke with good humor. "I lay you low with the agony of bliss and bring the sweet, sweet death."

Mary Jane couldn't keep herself from chuckling. Wiping her smile away, she turned back to him, expecting to see the joke on his face. His gaze had turned serious. She gave him a sour, questioning look for his boldness. At the same time, she found herself oddly pleased with him.

"Well, of all the men you might have…" he said, "*have* had…"

Now he'd gone too far. With a look of hurt, Mary Jane gave him a punch to the chest.

Again Miss Laudanum counseled her, *You don't have time for a fight.*

Mary Jane knew she wanted a return to anger *because* he was right. Not only did he perform in bed the best of all the men she'd had, he'd also been the kindest to her.

Silence stood between them for a moment.

He slowly slipped his hand back into her chemise, caressed her breasts. "I'll make a bargain with you," Joseph said. "You give Miss Laudanum her freedom, and when the *what if* at the Deptford Victualing Yard is finished, I *will* find a way to get your necklace from the Phoenix gay house. Perhaps we can go away together, after all."

Mary Jane sat up so that her eyes were level with his. "Truly, you'll help me?"

"Yes. You mean more to me than you know."

Mary Jane giggled with delight. Somehow, she'd got her way in spite of herself.

"Will you agree to my terms?" he asked.

"Yes!" she said.

Mary Jane threw her arms around him, and dragged him down into the bed with her.

His deep kisses brought her fully awake at last. She cast off the slight discomfort that had come with the ebb of the narcotic tide and responded with eager passion.

Joseph shed his clothing, pulled the chemise off Mary Jane. She smiled to see that he'd already placed a rubber sheath on his standing root. He grinned, spread Mary Jane's soft, pale thighs, and quickly found his way inside her. As he had on other occasions, he inclined his body to keep from crushing the ripe fruit of her bosom, or possibly to see the pinkness more clearly. With the repeated warm, wet thrill of penetration, Mary Jane struggled to stay quiet. The thin walls of the building permitted sound to travel easily. She didn't want to disturb the neighbors so late at night.

His smell filled her nose, a strong odor of sweat, yet somehow fragrant and healthy, bringing with it something of his day of work, a sense of the flexing and relaxation of his muscles as he'd gone about his labors.

Her imagination revised what had led up to the moment. She imagined they stood in a shop she'd once seen being renovated in Cleveland Street, an empty, unfinished room with tall windows that allowed those outside to see in. Working naked, he'd filled a giant crack in the rear wall with her naked body, then spread warm plaster around the edges to seal her in place, all except between her open legs where a triangular gap in the lath would give him access to her cunny. Scrutinizing his work from a slight distance, the intensity of his gaze brought out the best planes of his handsome face, particularly his jade-green eyes. Her eyes fell to the taper of his slim hips, and his proud instrument. Over his shoulder, she saw passersby on the street outside pausing to look in.

Positioning himself in the gap, he thrust himself into her over and over, the sensation exquisite, the idea that they were seen by others adding to the sexual excitement.

Those watching from outside became more animated, gesturing, talking, laughing, their expressions jubilant, appreciative, envious, delighted.

Mary Jane struggled silently to touch Joseph's chest, arms, head, to draw him closer, but her hands remained trapped. His face was too far away to kiss. She had to break free and take control.

She quaked in time with his thrusts, heard the plaster crack, felt the pieces begin to give way. First, her head pushed forward, the plaster falling from her ruined coiffure. Their lips touched and stayed together, moving hungrily. Her tongue penetrated his mouth to taste him, to caress his tongue.

The loving sensation of his warmth penetrating her own moist heat at both ends gained power and presence within her. A shuddering pleasure, a release more intense than any she'd known before took her out of the wall entirely, out of the fantasy, and back into their bed. She turned away from Joseph for a moment to let go of a strangled cry.

He moved atop her more rapidly, thrusting more deeply within her, his sweet mouth on hers again, the soft hairs of his chest brushing across her nipples maddeningly. She strained to touch him more fully, to leave no gaps between them. Mary Jane raised her legs across his muscular back, pressed the heels of her feet into his flexing buttocks to pull his manhood in deeper still. Her sensation of release came repeatedly, the muscles of her cunny and back avenue contracting in pulses of ecstatic, wet acceptance around the gift of his warm, thrusting steed. She turned away again, used a handful of the bedclothes to help stifle her cries.

Finally Joseph shuddered and made several small cries of his own. He gripped her arms with clasping hands. All his muscles seemed to flex at once. Inside her, despite the sheath, Mary Jane felt a slight pulsing, like a tiny heartbeat, and suddenly the bedding between her legs grew much wetter.

Her intense sensations ebbed as he relaxed atop her. Their heavy breathing slowed together.

He turned to look at her, his cheeks pink, lips open in a satisfied smile, eyes mere inches away from hers. In them, she saw something she'd not seen since Berwyn died: a look that suggested she was loved. Joseph's guileless, open gaze told her that he took pride in her presence within his life, that he had an acceptance of who she was, and that he wanted to protect her and what they had together. She'd never found anything like that in the eyes of a client.

"I love you too," she said without thought, the words coming from her unbidden and catching somewhat in her throat.

His eyes widened, he sat up suddenly, and looked down at her, a confusion of emotion playing across his face.

Mary Jane felt foolish. He had not said as much. She'd presumed. She closed her eyes, grimacing in shame.

"I-I do not say it well," he said, "so I shan't. But it's true, and you are right to say it in that manner."

She opened her eyes and looked again. The qualities she'd seen remained in his eyes.

"We'll have to decide what to do about it," he said.

Relieved and happy with his response, Mary Jane took a deep breath.

I am loved! Such a simple thing. How has that eluded me until now?

She smiled and discovered some hope, imagining the bright days to come in which the two of them continued together. The vision brought a giddiness, an out-of-control feeling somewhat disturbing. She pushed the discomfort away.

Leaning in, he gave her a long and loving kiss.

Joseph sat up, pulled the sheath off, folded it, and placed the wilted thing on the bedstead. Mary Jane got up and washed at the basin with a moist flannel. He lay back down and closed his eyes.

She donned a robe, let herself out onto the landing, and went to use the water closet.

Upon returning, she found Joseph asleep.

She lay awake next to him. Thinking of the personal and social responsibilities involved with a feeling of love frightened her. She'd treated Berwyn so badly.

Mary Jane could not find sleep and her craving for laudanum returned. Once the idea of taking another dose of the narcotic occurred to her, she couldn't shake the thought. The desire became too intense to ignore. Finally she got up and located a bottle of the stuff she kept in a small box of her jewelry.

"One last dose," she whispered to the darkness in the room, "just to help me sleep. He'll never know."

CHAPTER TWELVE

On November 5, Mary Jane and Joseph sat together, having a meal at the Cock's Crow Tavern in Mile End Road.

"Our efforts will clear the way for a theft at the Deptford Victualing Yard," Joseph said, pushing his plate away and finishing off his glass of ale, "the ordinary-looking cove I told you about is the client. I don't have his name to give you. On the night of the theft, there will be two night rounders, Sims Overton and Roy Nagel, who stand in our client's way."

Mary Jane repeated their names to better fix them in her memory. She took another a bite of her rump steak pudding.

"Though they are Government employed," he said, "as are the stevedores, much like lumpers, they are organized at a local pub. Their master works out of the Evelyn Arms just across Grove Street from the entrance to the Deptford Victualing Yard. They are required to eat and drink at the pub before their shifts. Often they spend breaks there as well. Their shifts are twelve hours long, eight o'clock at night 'til eight o'clock in the morning. They take breaks around midnight, one at a time for fifteen minutes. On Saturday nights, during his midnight break at about a quarter to twelve, Overton goes to the Evelyn Arms, hires a Judy and takes her back to the south gatehouse. The small building is part of the gated entrance to the yard, and has a back door, so she can slip out should anyone come. The hire is prearranged, so you'll have to attract his attention in the week before, then be available that Saturday night, November 20. Overton and Nagel each take a turn with the woman, one having his way with her while the other stays outside to act as crow, ready to signal should someone approach the gatehouse."

"They're helping us without knowing," Mary Jane said with a smile. Though she had little enthusiasm for the job, she wanted Joseph to see her willingness. She had agreed to help because of the money offered, ten pounds, and because both Joseph and Thomas were important to her.

"Very nearly. You'll spend some time at the Evelyn Arms. Some sort of story for how you wound up there will be needed."

"I'll have to talk with Mrs. Buki," Mary Jane said. "She's acquainted with most of the ladybirds and their minders along the docks and can make what introductions I might need to smooth the way."

"You will hear distant alarms shortly after midnight. We'll be setting fire to a barge on the Surrey Canal that we will have wedged under the Blackhorse Bridge to the west. Also we'll set fire to a rail car on a siding in the Brighton & South Coast Railway depot just north of the victualing yard. That should draw the police of R Division away and give them something to do. You'll need to find a way to occupy both men for about ten minutes in one of the gatehouses. You ought to be out of the yard by half past twelve."

"Both men at the same time?" Mary Jane asked. "You said one watches as the other has his pleasure. They shan't both want to be in the gatehouse at the same time."

Joseph frowned, then smiled. "You are much more captivating than any of the other ladybirds in that neighborhood. I think you shall not have too much trouble."

Mary Jane did not have his confidence. He could be a leg when need be, good at pulling a ruse. With the right mark he had no difficulty swindling. Even though he had a good heart, he'd grown up hard on the streets of London—"a gormless shit of a guttersnipe," he'd said. He expected she'd been made of similar stuff perhaps, but all she could think of was how their plan could go awry if she didn't keep her two pigeons sufficiently entertained.

After so many years of solicitation, she had little trepidation about tupping strangers for money; yet doing so as part of a scheme designed by Joseph to satisfy the needs of a client of Thomas's was several steps removed from the sort of control she preferred to have over her work. Joseph had told Thomas that her part of the lurk would not have to include actual prigging.

"If we see success," she said. "it will be because of my willingness to dab it up with the night rounders, whether it comes to that or not. Will you promise not to tell Thomas if it *does* come to that?"

"Yes," Joseph said, "but you're a bricky girl. I have every confidence in your ability to play the crooked cross. Just look at the way you've got me under your thumb." With the smile that followed, he seemed to be saying that he knew she'd been playing him, and he remained happy to have her.

Were I that obvious with my wheedling before? Well, yes, she supposed she had been. That was part of the problem with love— she'd become comfortable enough with him to allow her facade to slip from time to time.

Somehow, they had both changed after she professed her feelings for him. He'd begun to say things to her that he might have held back before. Afraid of too much familiarity, she'd found herself wanting to manage his impressions of her even more than she had before. At present, she held back her lack of confidence concerning her part in the lurk, and the continuing discomfort she experienced in her withdrawal from laudanum.

In the week and a half since they'd made their deal, she'd kept her word to herself—the dose of laudanum she'd had that night after he'd gone to sleep had been her last. She meant to stay with the decision, even though doing so had been far more difficult than she could have imagined. She silently cursed Blanche Sayers, the prostitute in Paris who had provided the first taste of the drug.

Mary Jane's part in the deal with Joseph had been compromised two days earlier when he'd discovered the bottle of laudanum she kept with her jewelry. They'd had a row. She'd left the box open— almost, she thought, as if she'd wanted him to find the tincture.

"I'd forgot about that bottle," she'd protested.

He'd given her a look that said he didn't believe her. "Should you want my help recovering your necklace," he said, "you know you'll have to give it up."

That he'd dispensed with the charming phrasing that suggested laudanum was a woman told Mary Jane how serious he'd become.

"Would you dump what remains in the privy?" he asked.

She agreed to do that and went to the water closet on the landing.

Foolish that he didn't come with me to watch.

Standing alone beside the toilet, considering the laudanum, she decided she shouldn't waste what amounted to a couple of soothing doses. She'd paid for the drug, after all.

No, I must give it up for his help, and for my own well-being.

She had poured the tincture in the toilet and pulled the chain to wash the amber liquid away.

At present, sitting at dinner in the tavern with Joseph, she couldn't help wishing she hadn't done that. Fearing that she'd fail to keep the two night rounders entertained, an indispensable part of the scheme, left her feeling weak and cowardly. She wanted the escape from those feelings the drug could provide. The insidious craving had taken hold of her thoughts again.

Of course, she could always go to a chemist's and buy more.

No!

Mary Jane considered the remains of her meal. The bits of sodden pastry, the coagulated fat and gravy didn't look tasty now that the food and her gut had gone cold. She looked around the tavern at the other diners, most of them laborers eating inexpensive meals. She alone experienced severe unease, while those around her enjoyed their food and drink, talked, and laughed.

Earlier, when she'd expressed doubts about the scheme, Joseph's frown had told her he expected more than a smile to confirm her willingness to take part.

Mary Jane decided that if she wanted him to take a risk for her, to find a way to secretly recover the emerald necklace from the Phoenix gay house, then she should not question his plan further. She would find a way to do as he asked on November 20 at the victualing yard because that would go a long way toward restoring his trust and motivating him. The ten pounds offered would add considerably to her savings and bring her closer to making a fresh start out of London.

Being gone to Deptford for a week also had its advantages. Even though she believed the notion emerged from the realm of fancy, she couldn't help thinking that Gabriella Gorse had followed her home the night of October 23, and that the bitter prostitute might relay the location to Stuart Brevard. Mary Jane would feel better getting away from Globe Road for a while.

She gave Joseph another smile and nodded. "Yes, I can do that."

"Don't worry," he said, "we'll go over the lay again once you've been there and had a look around."

On Mary Jane's behalf, Mrs. Buki made an agreement with a whore's minder and magsman nicknamed Alister the Onion, a tall, rail-thin fellow with oiled brown hair and a waxed mustache. His clothing, though that of a swell, had been tailored for someone heavier and shorter. He sported a fine new brown bowler. The Onion operated most of the ladybirds of Deptford that frequented the Evelyn Arms. He had a reasonable disposition for a cash carrier, habitually ate raw onions, and took strange pride in his terrible breath.

When Mary Jane arrived in Deptford on Saturday, November 13 to meet with the man for the first time, she asked, "Aren't you troubled that the night rounders will want to do you harm after our work here is done?"

"No, love," Alister said. "They shan't want to own that the yard were robbed while they entertained tail in the gatehouse. Even if, I have a family behind me, and Overton and Nagel are jus' little men."

Deptford by day was a noisy place, with the incessant sounds of equipment, vehicles, and ships in motion, men moving about, talking and shouting to one another as they organized their labors, the sounds of hand tools in use, the whistles and the horns from the river and the rail yards. Although the industrial area remained a busy one at night, with fewer laborers working after hours, and most of the night shifts indoors at the slaughter houses, the saw mills, the warehouses, and the factories, a relative calm came to the community once the haze-swaddled sun had set.

The Evelyn Arms was small, with a simple rail before the taps, and about ten dilapidating tables. The drinks, both strong and mild, were watered down. The hardworking men who came to the establishment stank from the sweat of their labor, and the river rot along the docks. Most of the women who came in did so to earn from servicing the men. Like any other pub, the patrons talked, laughed, and argued. They played games, got into fights, or drank themselves into insensibility.

With Alister the Onion's help, Mary Jane's reception as Fair Rose at the Evelyn arms went uneventfully well, but for one prostitute, Sally Fourth, who eyed her with mistrust.

What a ridiculous name, Mary Jane thought. She had begrudging respect for the woman's ability to spot the suspicious.

Sally Fourth was not one of the Onion's Judies. The blonde, raw-boned, and bow-legged woman had a deeply pocked face that seemed like a piece of leather that had suffered in severe weather, then dried and set up, holding its distressed shape; in her case a permanent expression of scorn.

Like Sally Fourth, the Judies that frequented the Evelyn Arms were a slatternly lot. Most had a cordial manner once Mary Jane broke the ice asking them about themselves and showing interest in their answers.

"I'm from Cardiff," she told them. "Come to Deptford to attend my sick mum. She died, poor old soul. Now I must earn enough to return home."

Monday afternoon, Sally Fourth approached a table where Mary Jane sat with another prostitute, a heavy woman named Deborah LaFluer. "Too good for the likes of us, I see," Miss Fourth said to Mary Jane. "Haven't seen you try to earn a single farthing."

She didn't answer, assumed the woman suffered envy because nearly all the men at the pub stared at Mary Jane with a frequency difficult to ignore. She'd spent much of her time fending them off.

"I suppose that's a good thing," Miss Fourth said, "You ought to go back where you come from, and leave *our* men alone."

"Leave Fair Rose be," Deborah said. "Poor manners are like a contagion. You don't want me to come down with them, now, do you?"

Miss Fourth clearly saw the stout woman as a threat. She grumbled and wandered off.

Concerned that Miss Fourth's dislike might get out of hand, Mary Jane and Joseph Fleming decided to stage a meeting at the pub, one in which she'd seem to accept him as a client. While working at the Victualing Yard, he'd spent enough time in the pub to fit in. Since the previous Saturday, he'd been meeting her following her hours at the pub one road to the west, where Windmill Lane crossed Hanlon Street. Then they'd walk across the Surrey Canal on the Windmill Bridge to catch the Lower Road tram back to the inn in Plough Road where they had a room. Tuesday night, after they staged their meeting in the pub, they left from there together.

The Onion introduced Mary Jane to both Sims Overton and Roy Nagel when they came into the Evelyn Arms on Wednesday.

"Fair Rose is me cousin-what's-died's daughter, me second cousin," Alister explained to Overton the next day. "She's a toffer in Cardiff, but is far from home, fallen on hard times, and has no push. She must earn the price to get home, and will take one and a tanner for a storm of heaves." He winked at Overton. "Though it's more than you've paid in the past, she's well worth the chink."

Mary Jane smiled pleasantly and remained silent.

The man took on a thoughtful frown, perhaps unable to accept that a woman of Mary Jane's looks would come so cheaply. He might also have been bargaining with his own willingness to pay the price.

They had anticipated he might think she could earn her fare home more easily elsewhere.

"Fair Rose has a debt she must pay before she goes," Alister said.

Overton's eyes narrowed doubtfully.

"I am under obligation to the Onion," Mary Jane said. "He paid a debt I had in Cardiff to free me up to come help my mother, then he paid for my way here. I agreed to work for him for a week, to help him rebuild his reputation."

Overton gave a skeptical look.

"Remember Little White Bumps?" Alister asked.

Overton nodded. "Glad *I* never partook."

Mary Jane knew from talking to the Onion that Little White Bumps was a prostitute who had worked for him, one with what looked like raised white freckles on her face. The young girl had made several men deathly ill, or so the story went.

"Seems her bumps," the Onion said, "cute as they made her, were a pox, an *unknown* contagion. When she left Deptford, my reputation went with her."

Overton's jaw became set in a satisfied manner—he seemed to have been persuaded. "You'll come to me Saturday night, then, Fair Rose? You have but to knock on the south gatehouse."

Mary Jane nodded.

Waiting impatiently for Alister to make the suggestion they had worked out, she saw Sally Fourth enter the pub with a laborer. The two took seats at a table in the northeast corner of the room, the woman staring at Mary Jane with undisguised hatred.

During their planning session on Saturday, when she'd arrived in Deptford, she'd asked Alister to help her come up with a plan to occupy both night rounders simultaneously.

"I've been thinking about that since Mrs. Buki offered the job and described the lay," the Onion said. Then he chuckled unexpectedly. "As luck would have it, our marks have provided the solution. Overton asked me just last week to find a woman what'd take him and Nagel at the same time. Can you take both at once, Fair Rose?"

"Describe the inside of the Gatehouse," she said.

He did so.

"Yes," she'd said, "I can see a way." Mary Jane described it to the Onion.

"I like that. Would that I could watch."

Obviously, he'd assumed she'd be willing to prig the two night rounders, and had been surprised when Mary Jane asked him not to tell Joseph about it.

She'd experienced some relief with a plan in place, but at present feared Alister had forgot it.

Overton got to his feet.

"She'd take two men at once for two bob," the Onion said.

Overton's eyes grew large. He settled again in his chair, and glanced at Mary Jane. She gave him her tiniest, most charming crooked smile of confirmation.

Experiencing a small thrill of some sort, he quaked. But then he frowned. "Couldn't do that. There'd be no one to keep watch."

"I could loiter at the gate as your crow," the Onion offered, "knock on the gatehouse door should I see someone coming."

Overton's smile grew slowly, became large. He nodded toward the Onion. "I'll sing your praises, I will," he said with a laugh.

"Good man." Alister clapped him on the shoulder.

The two men rose together and left the pub.

Mary Jane found a seat at the table to her left, next to Edith Gilcrest, a friendly young woman close to her age. The spot also had the advantage of placing Mary Jane out of Miss Fourth's line of sight.

Friday night, when she met Joseph at the crossing of Hanlon and Windmill, she saw Sally Fourth watching from the recessed door of one of the terraced houses along the lane. Though Mary Jane tried not to worry about the ill will of the woman, the weather had turned cold, somehow raising a chill feeling that the mistrustful prostitute might be the undoing of their carefully laid plans. Needing to feel protected, Mary Jane clung to Joseph on the walk to the tram and the ride to their inn.

"I like your cuddling tonight," he said.

She didn't respond, deciding he *wouldn't* be pleased to hear the reason she stuck so close.

Saturday, Mary Jane watched to see if Sally Fourth communicated with Overton or Nagel. The men finding out that Mary Jane didn't seem to have any clients from the pub could compromise the plan. The men did not speak with Fourth. At the end of the day, as a light snow began to fall outside, she realized that her fear had been for nothing. The woman was just trying to protect her territory from an intruder. By one o'clock Sunday morning, Mary Jane would be out of her life.

Saturday, near midnight, Alister the Onion and Mary Jane stepped out of the Evelyn Arms pub together and walked across Grove Street to the south gatehouse at the entrance to the Deptford Victualing Yard. Little traffic moved along the lane at that hour.

Halfway across the road, they heard the door to the pub open again, and Sally Fourth's coarse voice cut through the cold air. "He's one of mine, Overton is."

Mary Jane and the Onion turned to face her.

The woman, drunk and stumbling, heedless of an oncoming van—the only vehicle moving within several hundred yards—stepped into the lane, forcing the driver to steer out of her way.

"Glocky buor," the driver cried angrily.

We don't have time for this, Mary Jane thought. She'd looked at the clock above the taps in the pub. They'd left the establishment with one minute to spare before midnight.

"He's never asked for you before," Alister said to Miss Fourth.

"Not so's you'd know he'd done," she said, her sloppy, scornful gaze fixed on Mary Jane. "I don't work for you, Onion Man."

"Best take a better tone with me, bunter," Alister said.

"We don't have time for her." Mary Jane edged away toward the south gatehouse.

"*She* don't work for you *either,*" Miss Fourth said. "She come here from somewhere else, taking away some of *my* chance to earn."

"I have to go," Mary Jane said.

"Off with you, then," the Onion said. "I'll deal with her."

"Don't go, coward," Miss Fourth said, "we's just getting started."

Mary Jane knocked on the gatehouse door.

"Keep your voice down, Sally," Alister said.

The door opened. Sims Overton poked his head out into the chill night. "What's all this? You want to wake the dead?"

"I'm here," Mary Jane said. "Let me in."

Hearing the sound of rapid footsteps, she turned to see Sally Fourth rushing toward her. Alister caught her in mid-stride and took her to the ground. The woman's head hit the cobblestones hard.

"We can't be knocking away in here with a disturbance outside the gate," Overton said.

"I'll take care of the problem," the Onion said, "and be your crow."

Mary Jane pushed her way into the gatehouse. Inside, the air felt nice and warm. She doffed her shawl, dropping it on a chair. Overton lingered by the door with a worried look, watching the two outside.

"Come," Mary Jane said, tugging gently on the man's coat sleeve.

"We have an agreement. Call Mr. Nagel."

Overton gave her a look of unease. "No, h-he'd better stay without to keep watch. The Onion won't be watching."

Before the gatehouse door shut, Mary Jane saw Alister carrying Miss Fourth away. She seemed to be insensible.

"He'll return quickly," Mary Jane said.

"Perhaps we'll do it another night," Overton said.

Mary Jane broke the buttons on her bodice and chemise opening them quickly. She laughed to pretend delight. Having dispensed with her corset for the evening in favor of ease of movement and speed in dressing, her creamy breasts were instantly exposed.

Overton's mouth dropped open. His eyes wide, he reached for her.

Mary Jane backed away, shaking her head slowly. "Call Mr. Nagel," she said.

He seemed to come out of a trance.

She teased with seductive poses.

Overton appeared to consider possibilities. Finally, he turned to the back door, the one that led out into the yard, opened it, and called quietly. Nagel appeared quickly, and entered.

Mary Jane doffed her top skirt and tossed it over a support beam that ran across the small room about eight feet off the floor. From a hidden pocket of her bodice, she took a small leather pouch containing coconut oil, and applied some as lubricant between her legs. She handed each of the men a rubber sheath, and they got down to business. Both ends of her skirt hung down from the beam, the hem on one side, the waistband on the other. Mary Jane clung to the ends for support as the men had their way. At the peak of their pleasure, both men had achieved penetration, and were working up a sweat. All three stood together, a beast with three backs; Mary Jane between, Overton in her cunny, Nagel in her back avenue.

The distant sound of a fire alarm came from outside, probably to the west. That would be the burning barge on the Surrey Canal.

The men paused for a moment, seemed to decide simultaneously and silently that they had no responsibility to deal with whatever disaster unfolded, and went back to their vigorous thrusting.

Shortly thereafter, another fire alarm sounded toward the north. That would be the rail car in the depot. Again, the pause, the silent consideration, and resumption of fervent activity.

Mary Jane had gained the ability to relax in such situations. All the same, she was becoming sore. She did not know how much time had passed before she heard shots fired in the victualing yard. Both men pulled away from her instantly.

"What—?" Nagel began.

"Firearm," Overton said, "In the yard."

The two men pulled up their trousers.

"Go," Overton said to Mary Jane. "Dress quickly and go!"

The men hurried out the back door into the yard.

Mary Jane did as the night rounder instructed. Her shawl hid the fact that her bodice and chemise were loose. She heard more gun shots as she left the gatehouse.

She met Alister the Onion and Joseph Fleming in Windmill Lane. Joseph was counting out money into Alister's hands.

"A pleasure, Fair Rose," the Onion said. He tipped his hat to Mary Jane, blew her an oniony kiss, and walked away toward the south along Hanlon Street.

"That's done, then," Joseph said, taking Mary Jane's arm and leading her toward the west. "I'm glad the job is over. I feared for your safety. The Onion told me what happened with Miss Fourth."

"And someone fired a gun," she said.

Joseph had a troubled look. "Yes, I heard, but don't know why."

Determined to be a good sport for him, Mary Jane shrugged, despite a sudden exhaustion, and a churning of her gut, a remnant of her fear that Miss Fourth would keep her from meeting the scheme's timeline.

"Now we can work up a plan to get your necklace back," Joseph said.

At any other time Mary Jane would have jumped for joy at his suggestion. With the unsettling events of the evening, all she could think of was having a deep, soothing dose of laudanum. She remained determined to resist the desire.

CHAPTER THIRTEEN

On Monday, November 22, two days after returning to their lodgings in Globe Road, Mary Jane and Joseph sat together in the Green Man pub, waking up with morning coffee, reading newspapers. She read in *The Star* that a man named Frederick Caille had been killed at the Deptford Victualing Yard on the night of November 20. Although several others were also killed, including a policeman, the emphasis was on Mr. Caille, an important man. The story said nothing about a theft.

Had Joseph been hired not to aid an effort of theft, but for one of murder? The crime occurred while Mary Jane kept in gammon the yard's night rounders. She'd heard barking irons, yet Mr. Caille had died from strangulation. The other men perished from stab wounds.

"What do you know of the murder at the victualing yard?" she asked Joseph, showing him the story.

His face as he read told her much about his innocence. Still, Mary Jane remained upset.

"I just saw that in *The Globe*," he said, tapping the newspaper he'd set aside. "I hoped you would not see it."

"You think I'm flat, do you?"

"Keep your voice down," he said, grimacing. "No, I'm not trying to hide it from you. I didn't know. I dare say Thomas didn't either. The map we made of the yard aided the killer. Could be the theft went awry or, as I now suspect, his plan had been for murder all along."

"I don't like it that you led me into something like that," Mary Jane said.

"All three of us were gulpy enough to be duped into taking part. We ought to hope the police of R Division are unable to put together our presence in Deptford with the murder, and find us."

The angry face of Sally Fourth came to Mary Jane's mind.

"*You* were gulpy," Mary Jane said. "You might be guilty. Victim of a second-hand flam, I haven't any guilt."

Fleming shook his head, stared into his cup of coffee. "Should the one who committed the crime be the man what came to the job site to talk to Thomas, I've seen the fellow. To look at him would not give one concern, yet something about him told me he was indeed dangerous. I should not ask further questions if I were you. I'm ill-at-ease with what little I do know."

Joseph was right about Thomas. He later professed his innocence to both of them, and Mary Jane believed him. Thomas was just a business man trying to get on. Fleming had been the one to disappoint her. He had street cokum, or so Mary Jane had believed. The realization that he'd been tricked into helping with a murder tarnished the halo she'd placed over his head.

CHAPTER FOURTEEN

Mary Jane saw Jennie outside the Angel and Trumpet on November 29. The older woman recounted the death of her mother, Levinia Weatherhead, a few days earlier. Then, wiping away tears, Jennie said, "The children were hungry, so I returned to the streets the next day, walking about in colorful clothing, looking for a man, whilst knowing that respect demanded I wear mourning black. Please, forgive me mum!"

Mary Jane hugged Jennie and stroked her shoulder, then offered her a shilling. The older woman refused the coin. "Thank you, but I must learn to take care of myself."

Fleming had made no further mention of recovering her necklace. She pressed him on the matter on December 1.

"I am working on it," he complained. "As I told you, the lurk shall be more complicated than what you offered. I must come up with a believable flam to give Mrs. Arseneau that will push her to hire me on the spot, without questioning the low price I offer. Something about a new plaster mix or process that need tests, that I'll do the work, repaint for free, and come back and repair it if it fails in any way. Why the Phoenix, though? I've thought to suggest that the plaster might be scented so that it spurs desire or some such thing. I haven't sorted it all out. I'd hate for her to step back and decide that indeed the work needed to be done, but she has a nephew what'll do it for free."

As the weeks passed, she kept at him about it, her harping coming between them at times. She began to develop hard feelings toward Joseph.

Although he'd paid her the ten pounds for her efforts in Deptford, she suspected he'd merely used her, that perhaps he'd known all along that she'd have to prig the night rounders and he didn't care because she was a whore.

The low cost of Fleming's room, the comfort, its location, and her damned feelings for the man had kept her there. Still finding her love for him frightening, the sentiments were also driving her away from him.

CHAPTER FIFTEEN

In mid-January 1887, coming to the realization that she might never recover the necklace, Mary Jane had begun to neglect Joseph's needs again and resumed her efforts to earn as much as possible from clients.

In early March, having increased her savings to seventy pounds, she found herself looking for reasons to leave Fleming.

The idea that he'd used her wasn't quite the reason she needed because she was also using him.

If I were on my own, I could have laudanum again, she told herself, though her desire for the drug had thankfully diminished considerably.

The thought that Joseph had unwittingly led her into danger in Deptford became the seed she needed to grow her discontent. With time, she came to the conclusion that if she stayed with him, he'd eventually get her killed or imprisoned. She'd just about persuaded herself to pack up and leave at the beginning of spring when suddenly she had all the reason in the world to get out in a hurry.

In the late afternoon of March 15, while looking through the sheer curtain over the bay window in their room, she saw Stuart Brevard moving along Globe Road, talking to some people, searching for a while, lurking in doorways, and watching the street.

Gabriella Gorse did follow me home that night. She told him where to find me!

Mary Jane felt certain Mr. Brevard watched for her. She knew he would give up if she stayed out of sight. He could not see her through the thin curtain.

If not Gorse, someone had given him enough information that he'd got close. Mary Jane didn't think she'd ever said anything about where she lived to Gabby or anyone who knew the woman.

Brevard gave up on waiting, and entered the Green Man pub

across the street. He left there after a time, crossed Green Street and entered the Fire Station. Mary Jane waited and watched to see him exit. He moved along Globe Road, talking to a few more people. He tried a few doors of tenements, and entered some buildings. She watched each time until he returned to the street.

Finally, he approached her tenement. A rattling came from the direction of the front entrance. Fearful of becoming trapped if he got in, Mary Jane left her room and stood in the darkened hallway beneath the broken gas jet, ready to flee through the back of the building into the complex of small yards in the rear. Watching the door shake, fearful that he'd somehow get in, she took care not to allow herself to think what he'd do to her.

The lock resisted Brevard's prying, and he gave up on the door. Standing at the bay window, she watched him walk away toward the south.

Mary Jane packed most of her belongings into two carpet bags and left, heading west to become lost in the stews of the Whitechapel and Spitalfields rookeries. Mrs. Carthy had once recommended a boarding house in New Street, Bishopsgate. "Mr. Buller has both a common lodging and a boarding house," the proprietress had said. "If you want a common lodging go elsewhere." She'd grimaced, which told Mary Jane that the common lodging must be truly horrid, Mrs. Carthy's standards of cleanliness being so low. "But if you give Mrs. Buller my name, she'll make room for you at the boarding house. It's quite nice there."

⚓

Mary Jane walked southwestward along Bethnal Green Road, stopped at a tavern for a meal, then made the mistake of continuing on toward her goal after nightfall. She noted that the gas lamps on the street were dark near the crossing of Bethnal Green Road and Brick Lane. On the south side of the street, she hurried forward to pass quickly through the darkened area.

Close to Brick Lane, five creatures rushed out of a building's thin through-passage. Mary Jane let out a small cry of surprise, and backed away only to discover they had surrounded her. *Goblins!* she thought, seeing merely glowing eyes in dirty faces, and the filthy tatters of their clothing.

No, she thought, getting a better look, *children.* She couldn't determine the sex of the raggedy creatures in the gloom. The two largest, perhaps ten to twelve years old, threatened her with knives that reflected the blue-gray of the night sky and what little warm light came from nearby windows. The other three grabbed her bags and pulled her toward the passage opening.

"Stop!" she cried, still holding onto the handles of the bags.

They seemed to anticipate her, and all cried, "Stop," drowning her voice with theirs. As if playing a game, they followed that with laughter, the sound echoing up the passage.

Mary Jane wouldn't let go, and they pulled her into the darkened corridor.

"Help!" she cried.

Again, they anticipated her. They all cried, "Help the little children, Lord," drowning her out, More laughter followed.

"Let go if you value your life," came a boy's voice from her left, the tallest figure, one with a knife.

"Such drama," Mary Jane said, trying to sound calm and confident. Despite knowing better, she had decided they would not harm her if she showed enough courage.

She was losing the battle of strength.

"We get ream swag from this toffer," came a girl's voice, one of those tugging on a bag. "Too bad if we have to cut her pretty face."

Another child giggled, the high-pitched sound clearly belonging to one well below the age of ten.

Mary Jane's eyes had adjusted somewhat to the darkness.

An adult appeared in the passage, an older fellow.

"Sir, help me, please," Mary Jane said, breathlessly.

"He ain't no help to you, miss," came the boys voice again on her left. "He's got to live here with us."

The man walked by without a word.

Mary Jane prepared herself to yank her bags free with great force, to push past the children, and go on her way.

As she planted her feet firmly to make her move, the boy on her left stabbed her in the arm.

Mary Jane cried out again, and went into a slight crouch. Not a deep wound, just enough to draw blood. She could feel it running under her sleeve.

She thought of the knife in her boot. *I won't have to use it on the children, just frighten them with it.*

She reached for it. The child on her right kicked the boot where the knife was hidden. Mary Jane cringed with pain as the point of the blade punctured her ankle. The sheath she'd fashioned for it was lightweight because her boots were already tight.

The boy on her left, swung his blade in threat a couple times, with a warning look in his wide eyes, the circles of whites the only part that showed in the dimness.

Mary Jane realized she was about to lose everything she had.

"Do it now, fancy woman," he said, "or we shall take it."

They closed in.

Mary Jane let go of her bags, backed away quickly.

The one with the knife on her right let her pass. The boy on her left waved his knife and lunged toward Mary Jane to dislodge her from the passage.

She continued to back away into Bethnal Green Road, turned toward Brick Lane, and ran.

Mary Jane wept, feeling cruelly molested, and ashamed for having suffered such treatment from children. She'd been slow to appreciate the severity of the threat. Gaining distance from the nippers, she discovered gratitude for finding herself alive. Her savings and other possessions could be replaced.

Her right ankle stung from the puncture the knife had inflicted. Mary Jane slowed to a walk.

Most of the Ladybirds she knew didn't carry weapons because clients were known to take them and use them against their owners on occasion. The little bit of training Fleming had provided hadn't prepared Mary Jane to face true danger. If she hadn't been able to use the knife against children, what further disaster might come from drawing it on an adult? Another item she could add to the list of failings she held against Fleming. Disgusted, she crouched, extracted the blade, and threw it in the gutter.

Mary Jane gave up the idea of going to Buller's. Some funds remained in the pocket under her top skirt. She would find a doss house and a bottle of laudanum.

Joseph found Mary Jane a week later at Cooley's Lodging House in Thrawl Street, Spitalfields. They sat in the common room between meals with no one else about.

"Why?" he wanted to know.

Mary Jane didn't want to tell him about Stuart Brevard. Not having spoken of the man's pursuit of her before then, she'd be ashamed to reveal that she'd kept that a secret. Joseph might have protected her from Mr. Brevard, if she had given him the chance. Of course, the ginger-haired man was only part of her reason for leaving.

"You hold me too close," Mary Jane said, "when you know what I am and what I must do."

"I earn enough for us both," he said. "You don't have to solicit any longer."

"I cannot depend on you forever. Life has shown that I am a fool to depend on anyone but myself."

"You don't mean that." Joseph had a terrible sadness in his eyes.

Mary Jane turned away so she didn't have to see him.

She had nothing to say because he was right. The excuse that if she'd stayed, he would have led her into danger had not held up to further consideration. Unwilling to admit to herself that she'd left because she feared the power and the worth of the love she felt for him, she had latched onto the second most plausible reason as an excuse to leave: She'd wanted her freedom purely for the laudanum.

He ought not to have told me to give it up.

As if Mary Jane needed the habit to justify her thinking, she'd returned to the drug with a vengeance, her consumption already greater than what she'd known the previous fall. Considering her plans for leaving London to settle elsewhere, she'd had to wonder what particular *elsewhere* would allow her continued easy access to laudanum. Large cities were the best candidates, yet those were also the costliest in which to live.

Given time, I will have savings again. Then I can make the big change.

"You prefer this?" Joseph asked, gesturing around at the dingy common room that served as dining hall and parlor for all the lodgers at Cooley's. The room had random stains from floor to ceiling. A smell of mildew and rancid food hung in the air.

Stuart Brevard will not easily find me in Spitalfields. She imagined he might be too proud to enter such a rookery.

"The rooms can't be much better," Joseph said. "How many strangers share your bed?" He frowned as he seemed to see the flaw in his question.

"I pay for a room of my own."

"You want me to check your hair for chats?"

Mary Jane shook her head, looked down at the table top, and stopped talking, though he continued.

Finally, his arguments ended. "I won't give up on you," he said, and walked out.

In her room afterward, she took thirty drops of laudanum, and enjoyed a deep, dreamless sleep.

CHAPTER SIXTEEN

On Good Friday, April 8, 1887, Mary Jane watched a couple of men playing Mumblety-peg at Spitalfields Market. One of the two clearly had more skill in the game. She'd never seen anyone so comfortable and capable with a knife. He noticed her watching. She smiled for him. While his opponent mumbled the peg, he introduced himself to Mary Jane as Seph Barnett. A licensed fish porter at Billingsgate Market, he'd come to Spitalfields to make a delivery to a fishmonger, the fellow still trying to pull the peg from the ground with his teeth.

Mary Jane and Seph had drinks at the Britannia pub, also known as the Ringers, and later had a dinner together at the Golden Heart, a tavern in Commercial Street with tall windows and numerous skylights. They got along well. She saw him again the next day, and he asked her to take up with him. She surprised herself when she accepted his invitation. Or had that been Miss Laudanum's choice? Mary Jane told herself that the nagging feeling that she needed protection had not driven her into his arms. Still, having a man on hand who was good with a knife couldn't hurt.

A slim, dark-haired, blue-eyed fellow, she found him appealing enough, though he frequently smelled of fish market. She called him simply Barnett. He had a funny habit of repeating the last word anyone said.

Mary Jane removed from Cooley's to Barnett's lodgings in George Street, a miserable little cell at the back of an old wooden house. Because he didn't wash his clothes right after work each day, the place smelled of the fish market.

Her dislike of the lodgings must have shown. Barnett said, "I'll begin the search for a better room tomorrow."

To reach the chamber, they passed through a hallway rented as lodgings to an old woman, Mrs. Hollis, who slept on a narrow straw mattress on the floor. Her few possessions were neatly stacked against the wall so Barnett and Mary Jane didn't tread upon them. By day, Mrs. Hollis begged beside Christ Church wearing a placard that told of the loss of her son, a midshipman aboard HMS Penelope. Something about the story seemed familiar to Mary Jane, but she didn't know why.

The room had rotten floorboards, a coal grate that didn't quite fit the large old-fashioned fireplace, and one small window that gave a view across a paved yard to the backside of Satchell's Lodging House. Barnett pointed out the soft spots in the floor so she could avoid them. He enclosed the firebox with stacked bricks until the flue drew better and the air they breathed while heating the room improved. Nothing could be done for the view.

To improve the smell in the room, Mary Jane insisted that his work apron should hang outside the window, and that his work clothes would remain in a barrel with a tightly fitting lid if he wasn't wearing them.

Barnett could be sweet when sober, angry or maudlin if drunk. He didn't mind the laudanum, probably because she hid the drug from him most of the time. He wasn't pleased with her soliciting.

"One day," he said, "you'll give it up for me."

Mary Jane had no intention of abandoning her means of independence just for him. She kept that to herself.

Quite different from the affection she'd had for Fleming when she'd taken up with him, she knew she'd never love Barnett.

Will be easy to leave him when I'm ready.

He was a man of few words unless in his cups. They quarreled then, and he struck her a few times.

Although she hadn't decided she deserved that sort of treatment or the wretched living conditions, she supposed she believed it all the same. The laudanum helped make it all tolerable.

⚜

In mid-April, Barnett and Mary Jane heard about a larger room that would become available in a house in Little Paternoster Row, Dorset Street at the end of the month.

The week before, she had written to Jennie, giving her the

George Street address. She had been about to write again to give her the future address, when, on April 29, Jennie turned up on the doorstep in George Street.

"May I come in to talk?" she asked.

"No, my room is not suitable." Mary Jane said.

She took her friend to the Ringers and they sat down together with glasses of bitter.

"He seemed a friendly gentleman," Jennie said, seeming out of sorts. "Please forgive me!" She covered her face with her hands.

"Who?"

"That man! The red-haired one."

"Stuart Brevard, the one after me?"

"Yes. He showed me a drawing of you with the name, Andriette. I took it to be one of your assumed names and thought little about it. He said he was an old friend of yours visiting London for a short time, and asked me how to find you. Though he might know you by that name, I wasn't going to inform him otherwise. I said simply that the picture looked like a friend of mine that lived at the crossing of Globe Road and Green Street, since I remembered you saying that once. Only afterward, almost a month, did I remember him from the attack on Bale Street. He must not have recognized me."

So, Gabby had not chased me, had not led Stuart Brevard to me in Globe Road.

"You did not give him the name Ginger or Mary Jane?"

"No," Jennie said. "I most humbly beg your pardon. I am not used to the ways of the streets. I am *not* clever. Forgive me, please."

"There's nothing to forgive," Mary Jane said

"What do I do should I see him again?"

"Say you have not seen me. Do you know who might have put him on to you?"

"No."

Jennie took on a worried look. "You look as if you're not feeling well."

"I have not," Mary Jane lied, "though I am getting better now."

She knew the unhealthy look came from too much laudanum.

"I am currently lodged with a man named Seph Barnett," Mary

143

Jane said. "We are about to remove to a room in Little Paternoster Row. I wanted you to have the address."

"I should think you might not want to give it to me after—"

"Nonsense."

"We must find other, less expensive lodgings," Jennie said, "Clarissa, my niece, nephew, and I. What do you pay in George Street?"

"Four bob per week, but the crib is a wretched hole."

"Less than what we ought to pay in a doss house." She paused, became thoughtful. "Yes, the cost is a good bit less than what we pay now, and, being here, I might lose Brevard. Would you ask your landlord if he'd consider us?"

Mary Jane could see the advantage, and nodded. "Yes, if it would help."

Leaving the Ringers that day, the two women chanced upon Mary Jane's neighbor, Mrs. Hollis. She stood on the footway beside Christ Church with her placard, begging.

"Mrs. Hollis," Jennie said.

The old woman seemed surprised.

"It's me, Jennie Weatherhead."

Mrs. Hollis dropped the imploring look she gave passersby.

"Oh, Miss Weatherhead," she said, "What a delight."

"You two are acquainted?" Mary Jane asked. "Mrs. Hollis is our neighbor, perhaps soon to be your neighbor."

"I've known Mrs. Hollis for some time," Jennie said. "She and her family joined ours in the civil suit against the man, Caille."

The name sounded familiar to Mary Jane.

Mrs. Hollis had a nearly toothless smile. "My son, John, were a midshipman aboard HMS Penelope with Jennie's brother, Lieutenant Weatherhead, a fine officer."

Mary Jane remembered that her friend's brother had died, poisoned somehow.

As Mrs. Hollis's smile disappeared, Jennie took the old woman's hands into her own.

"My poor John," Mrs. Hollis said, "two other midshipman, and the Lieutenant died at sea. Were bad victuals supplied by Frederick

Caille's company what killed them."

Caille, the victualing yard! Mary Jane almost said the words aloud, but thought better of it.

"Caille was murdered not long ago," Jennie said.

Mrs. Hollis's jaundiced eyes grew large. "Good!" she said with surprising force.

So, Jennie knows!

The two women hugged for a time. Mary Jane stood, uncertain what to do with herself.

Finally, Mrs. Hollis and Jennie separated, and discussed the possibility that they might become neighbors.

"That would be most welcome," the old woman said.

Jennie smiled and seemed to remember that Mrs. Hollis had been begging. With a look of embarrassment, she gave Mrs. Hollis a ha'penny, then looked to Mary Jane expectantly. She gave the old woman tuppence.

"God bless you both," the old woman said.

Jennie and Mary Jane walked south along Commercial Street, the noise of traffic and the many people using the footway oddly giving a sense of privacy.

"What do you know about the murder of that man, Caille?" she asked.

"Only what I read," Jennie said. "He got what he deserved after his fraud against the Royal Navy cost the lives of my brother and the others."

"Did you also come to Spitalfields to find a room?" Mary Jane asked.

"No. I'm glad I did, though. I came to warn you and to see how you're faring."

"How *I* am?"

"Yes," Jennie said with a look of surprise. "You're not the only one who can look out for others. With your help, I've settled into a routine that earns a small income. I can bring that to Spitalfields. I don't like what I do, but I am grateful for your help, and I've *missed* you."

To hear that warmed Mary Jane's heart.

"I haven't yet built up my weave of friends here," she said. "I'm working on that at the Ringers. I miss the dressing screens. Have you been taking clients to Dresser's so the girls can look them over?"

As Jennie nodded her head, Mary Jane caught a glimpse of another cut, a deeper one under her chin. She stopped walking. When the older woman stopped and turned toward her, Mary Jane gestured toward the cut. "Nick Shears again?" she asked with some outrage, thinking Jennie didn't take paying the protection money seriously enough.

She nodded sheepishly, then said with clear defiance, "I was late paying."

Mary Jane saw that Jennie pridefully thought she'd got away with something. Perhaps she hadn't heard what failing to pay had got other ladybirds, the gruesome mutilations they suffered. Mary Jane knew that some had been killed. She took Jennie by the shoulders and shook her. "You must not make light of the matter!" Mary Jane said angrily.

The older woman shrugged her off, retreated toward the wall of a building, a frightened look in her eyes. Jennie glanced around, probably to see if they were watched. No one passing on that street cared what the two women did.

"He is a terrible leach!" she cried. "Someone must stand up to him. At least I made him wait. And hopefully I'll leave him behind, should I remove to Spitalfields."

"No," Mary Jane said, trying to pull herself together. "He and the Gully Bleeders work the whole of the East End. There's no escaping him. He drew blood again. The cut is a further warning. He shan't always warn. Should you be unable to pay, come to me. In the future, he will—"

"*You weren't there!*" Jennie said, loudly interrupting, "and *I* didn't have the funds. I am *trying* to help support Clarissa and her two children."

With the older woman's angry tears, Mary Jane had to tell herself that she wasn't obliged to protect her friend. The thought did little to change the sense of duty she had. "Promise me that won't happen again."

"I promise."

The look of hurt in Jennie's eyes pained Mary Jane.

"Will you speak to your landlord?"

"Yes," Mary Jane said coldly. "But should you come to Spitalfields you must still pay your protection money. I will not have your blood on my hands."

She took Jennie's right hand and tried to put two shillings into it.

"I don't mean to frighten you," the older woman said with a look of hurt.

Mary Jane could not help showing her fear and anger. "You do."

Jennie turned away quickly, and walked back the way they had come.

Finding that the two shillings remained in her hand, Mary Jane nearly went after her friend, then decided not to bother—she was too proud to take the money.

～❦～

Jennie and her family removed to the George Street address in early May, once Barnett and Mary Jane had gone to the new lodgings in Little Paternoster Row.

Throughout 1887, Mary Jane concentrated on her efforts to rebuild her savings. She located cribs in the area that rented by the hour and saw as many clients as she could. To help insure her safety, she did her best to organize the ladybirds of Spitalfields, using the Ringers much like she had Dresser's in Stepney.

Infested with insects and rodents, the new room in Little Paternoster Row, though larger, was worse than the last. Mary Jane and Barnett didn't stay there long. They took lodgings in Brick Lane in July, 1887, and lost that because Barnett, while drunk, had an argument with the landlord. Mary Jane contacted Mrs. Carthy and asked if her husband, John McCarthy had anything. He offered a room in Miller's Court, number 13, another Spitalfields address. Mary Jane and Barnett settled into the room in February, 1888. All the places in which the couple had lived being within easy walking distance of the George Street address, Mary Jane had the claustrophobic feeling that her world had shrunk.

To her utter dismay, she spent little time with Jennie. Though many months had passed since their harsh words about Nick Shears and the importance of paying protection money to the Gully Bleeders, their friendship had never recovered. Even so, as Mary Jane developed her weave of friends and associates, she drew Jennie into the work and introduced her to all the women who took part.

On a gloomy day in late March, 1888, alone in the room in Miller's Court, Mary Jane closed the curtains over the windows and retrieved the Chinese tea tin that she kept in an inner pocket of a jacket she rarely wore. From the tin, she extracted her savings, and set it out on the table. She stacked the coins and folded the soft together as she counted the funds.

Seventy pounds—just what I had when I left Joseph Fleming and the children robbed me. Took about a year to recover that. By summer, I'll have a hundred pounds. Then I'll leave Barnett and London behind.

The goal of one hundred pounds seemed arbitrary.

I would be more comfortable if I made it one hundred and fifty pounds. Then I might stay a little longer.

Mary Jane had yet to decide where she would go to live. Unfortunately, she couldn't think of anywhere she'd rather be than London. She hadn't liked Paris. The idea of traveling to America frightened her. Even staying in Spitalfields was preferable to returning to Cardiff. She could find arguments against any city she considered.

Mary Jane returned her savings to their hiding place. As she'd done before many times, she put the decision off.

CHAPTER SEVENTEEN
Wednesday afternoon, April 6, 1888

On Whitechapel Road near Saint Mary's Church, Mary Jane paused to look at the selection offered by a hawker of books, Eliza Cooper.

"You've heard about the woman murdered," Eliza asked, "Emma Elizabeth Smith? Lived at Bewley's Common Lodging, I believe."

"No!" Mary Jane said, more a rejection than an answer. She nearly dropped the copy of *A Crystal Age* by W. H. Hudson she'd picked up. To hear the name gave her a heart-thumping fright, it being close to the one Jennie Weatherhead had assumed for use on the street.

Eliza looked at Mary Jane with sympathy. "You knew her?"

"No," she said again, because the name wasn't exactly the same.

"Two nights ago she were attacked," Miss Cooper said. "She died in hospital yesterday."

Jennie keeps a room at Bewley's!

"Elizabeth or *Lizabeth*?" Mary Jane asked.

"Don't know her," Eliza said. "I'd *heard* Elizabeth."

Distressed, Mary Jane set down the book, and left the hawker, crossing Whitechapel Road and moving north. She intended to go to the Weatherhead family lodgings in George Street, to see what she might find out. The building was but a few doors away from the passage that led to Bewley's.

Unless she'd done so unknowingly, perhaps on the street, Mary Jane had never met Jennie's family—her sister-in-law, Clarissa, nephew, Benjamin, and niece, Maisie—and didn't know what she might say to them if her friend were not home.

Instead of going to the Weatherhead family lodgings, Mary Jane decided to go to Bewley's Common Lodging. Jennie did her soliciting late at night and took her clients to Bewley's so her family would not know about her activities. At times, she did not return home for a day or more. She'd given Clarissa to believe that she worked nights as a housemaid for a Jewish family in Poplar. To explain away her periodic overnight absences, she said she stayed with the Jewish family to help out when they entertained their many friends from abroad.

Bewley's Common Lodging consisted of an ugly set of wooden structures that squatted in the interior of the block of buildings that faced George Street to the west, Thrawl Street to the north, Brick Lane to the east, and Wentworth Street to the south. A through-passage into the paved yard before the entrance to Bewley's ran beneath the second floor of an old, stone building facing George Street several doors north of the one in which the Weatherhead family lived. Confident that her family would not see, Jennie could enter even in daylight if she chose the moment with care.

In Osborn Street, Mary Jane saw an acquaintance, a prostitute named Francis Booth, walking the opposite direction. She didn't participate in the weave of associates at the Ringers.

"Do you know anything about the woman murdered?" Mary Jane asked.

"Emma Smith," Francis said. "I've met her, but that's all. Wouldn't know her to see her."

"Emma *Elizabeth* or Emma *Lizabeth*?"

"I don't know." Francis pointed out a trail of dried brown drops that continued along the footway running into the distance northward. "That's her blood," she said. "I heard she removed her shawl as she struggled along the lane, were holding it against the flow from between her—uh, well…you can imagine, I suppose. She wouldn't let anyone help her. The blood continues on Wentworth Street."

"Thank you." Mary Jane said, and hurried on.

How can she do the work and not be able to speak of that part of the body? She realized her feeling of disgust toward Francis was an effort to distract herself from thinking the worst had happened to Jennie.

Just before she got to Wentworth Street, a greater stain appeared, what had clearly been puddles and spatters. Mary Jane could tell that much of the violence had occurred there. She hoped the victim had gone south from that point, and that she'd already seen the extent of the blood.

But, no, the trail turned the corner toward the west and George Street. Her imagination sent tears welling up in her eyes. She wiped them away, and took a deep breath, nearly tasting the odor that came from the chocolate and mustard mill, Taylor Brothers Limited, on the corner.

Nearing the crossing of George and Wentworth Streets, she saw that the blood trail continued north toward both of the rooms Jennie rented.

Fresh tears obscuring her view, she had to pause and collect herself before entering the busy crossing to make the turn into George Street.

Once across, she felt some relief to see that the trail did not enter the building where Jennie's family lodged. Further on, she saw that the stains did enter the passage that led to the yard before Bewley's. Still, she followed the blood, holding in sobs that tried desperately to escape.

The lodging house has lots of tenants. Any one of them might have done the bleeding.

Mary Jane entered Bewley's and found the deputy in her office, a middle-aged woman with hollow cheeks, and oily hair pulled too tightly into a bun to be attractive. Sitting, having tea and biscuits, the woman glanced up quickly, then returned her eyes to her food and drink.

Mary Jane stood beside a chair facing the desk, trying to gather herself together enough to speak. She knew she presented a red face and pained eyes. "My name is Ginger," she said, voice unsteady. "I am a friend of Emma *Lizabeth* Smith. I've heard that Emma *Elizabeth* Smith were murdered. Both may be lodgers here."

"Mrs. Mary Russell," the woman said flatly, not rising from her seat. She aimlessly pushed papers around on her desk in a manner clearly meant to give an impression that her work shouldn't be interrupted.

"I mean to find out with certainty that the woman killed were

Elizabeth, not Lizabeth." Mary Jane said forcefully, her voice rough and cracking. She feared that her tone gave an impression of anger and that the woman might become unwilling to answer. She took deep breaths. "Can you give me assurance of that?"

Still looking at the papers on her desk, Mrs. Russell said, "Yes." She had a troubled look, though, one that Mary Jane might not have noticed had she not had such a clutching need for answers.

"Are you being honest with me?" Mary Jane asked, the words somewhat garbled as they caught in her throat. "Please look at me."

The deputy lifted her gaze. In her eyes, the lie could be seen clearly.

Mary Jane collapsed in the chair opposite her, weeping. "Tell me," she cried.

Mrs. Russell stared at her in horror, then with resignation, a deep sadness troubling her eyes and the left corner of her mouth.

Waiting for the woman to speak, Mary Jane began to shake. She struggled to regain control of herself. Mrs. Russell pushed her plate of biscuits across the table.

Mary Jane shook her head, more a product of her quaking than anything else. Deciding that having something to do with her hands and mouth might calm her, she took a biscuit anyway.

"Miss Emma Lizabeth Smith came in very early Tuesday morning," Mrs. Russell said carefully, "about four o'clock. She were bleeding heavily, had her woolen wrap—"

Mary Jane cried out, her pent up sobs suddenly released with great force. She knew what it was to be violently abused and considered herself hardened to such experiences. Not Jennie, though. Mary Jane's awareness of the room fell away as she pictured her friend, deeply wounded and struggling along the street, frightened and in severe pain.

Finding her fancy too agonizing, she pushed the vision aside, found herself back in the deputy's office, staring downward from her seat at the deputy's worn boots beneath the desk.

Mrs. Russell got up, and closed the door of her office. She leaned against the edge of the desk, and laid her hand warmly on Mary Jane's cheek.

They both wept.

Mrs. Russell pulled a bottle of scotch whiskey from a drawer, poured a generous amount of the drink into each of two glasses on the desk. One she handed to Mary Jane, the other she lifted to her mouth and quaffed all at once. Mary Jane did the same.

Some time elapsed before she located her voice. "Please tell me what happened," she said.

Mrs. Russell had an apologetic look as she began. "She returned here about four in the morning on Tuesday. She were bleeding heavily, said she'd been attacked on Osborn Street. I couldn't imagine her walking so far in that state."

Mary Jane hid her face in her hands until she realized that the darkness allowed her imagination to visualize Jennie's suffering all the better.

Mrs. Russell poured more whiskey in each glass.

"I found my boy, Harold, had him fetch his barrow, and with the help of Annie Lee, we prepared to haul Emma in it to the London Hospital." She shook her head. "'I don't want to go there,' Emma said. 'I don't want my family to find out. I'll just go to my room and rest.'" Mrs. Russell wiped the tears from her eyes. "We took her there all the same. On the way she told me what happened—said she were returning from the docks when a scarred man come for her with sheep shears. She seen him in the corner of her eye, and wanted him to get close because she had a knife. He were faster than she expected. Clipped her right ear nearly off."

Nick Shears, Mary Jane thought.

"She turned quickly and gave him a cut across the face. They fled in opposite directions, and she thought she'd got to safety. Then some young men appeared, and began following her near Saint Mary's."

Trying to hear the words, yet not wanting to further imagine Jennie's suffering, Mary Jane concentrated on things within her immediate experience: the faint residue of peat smoke from the scotch on her tongue, Mrs. Russell's slight lisp, the varying shapes and sizes of triangles formed by the overlapping pieces of paper on the woman's desk, the occasional rumble of footsteps coming from movement on the floor above.

"They set upon her across the street from the chocolate factory."

Mary Jane remembered the larger area of bloodstains where Osborn Street became Brick Lane at Wentworth Street. She winced and her eyes filled again with tears.

"I suffer a deep sadness for her loss," Mrs. Russell said in a manner Mary Jane took to be a conclusion of the tale.

"No," she said, "You must tell me all of it."

The woman breathed deeply for a time. She wiped her tears away again before continuing. "They beat her. They raped her, then jabbed an iron bar—" She covered her mouth, struggled to swallow. "I cannot say—"

Mary Jane could readily put the story together, yet kept her personal vision of the incident at arm's length. Though she'd been irritated with Francis Booth's inability to speak of such matters, she found herself grateful that Mrs. Russell could not say the words.

"I understand," Mary Jane said.

"No, not until I'm done, you don't." Mrs. Russell had a look of frustration. "You must help me keep her secret."

Confused, Mary Jane sat up, focused more intently on the woman.

"She asked me not to tell anyone for fear that the truth would harm her family." Mrs. Russell looked down, rubbed her brow, and shook her head. "Once, I were one who judged. Since taking this position, I have learned what many spinsters and widows must do to get on. I judge no longer."

She poured more scotch into both glasses, raised hers and drank it down. "Her face were terribly battered. I would not have recognized her. Until she spoke, I had mistaken her for Emma *Elizabeth* Smith, who lodged here until Sunday when she absconded, owing a week's rent. She were a dishonest person, always looking for advantage over others. I regret allowing her to stay without paying, but now saw I could put her absence to good purpose. On the way to the London Hospital, I told Emma Lizabeth Smith that she ought to say to those who asked that she were Emma *Elizabeth* Smith. I said that I'd do the same, and explained to her that the woman had gone away. Lizabeth said that was good, that her family would think she were staying at the place she worked, a Jewish family, and she'd clear it all up after she got better."

Mary Jane knew that the Weatherheads did not know Jennie's assumed name. "When my friend doesn't return home," Mary Jane said, "the reason for her loss being unknown will torment her family."

"Better that," Mrs. Russell said, "than knowing the truth, don't you think?"

Mary Jane thought about that for a time, found that she agreed, and nodded.

Again, they sat in silence for a while.

"I stayed with her in hospital as long as they permitted," Mrs. Russell said. "There came a time I think she knew her end was nigh. She said Ginger would look for her, and that I ought not to tell you. 'If she gets the truth out of you,' she said, 'tell her that I love her, and that I know she'd done her best for me.'"

Mary Jane had lost her mother again. Even as an adult, she'd failed to protect her.

"Thank you," she said, weeping anew. She rose unsteadily from her seat, stumbled out of Bewley's, through the yard and passage to the street. Dusk had settled with deep shadows that helped her avoid seeing the blood trail. Mary Jane turned north, intent on returning to the wretched hole she and Barnett currently called home in Miller's Court.

Alone with her thoughts, she ignored the many others using the footways at the end of their work day. Instead of the ever-deepening sadness she'd experienced with Mum's death, an anger welled up inside her. Recognizing her inability to protect Jennie, she knew a disdain for herself, but she also saw a larger picture of the conspiracy to destroy her loved one. Mary Jane had been an unwilling part of the scheme, insisting that the protection money must be paid to those who committed the crime.

Too weak to take on Nick Shears and his bullies, she wondered who else supported them. Possibly, she might find someone to harm who was key to the conspiracy, yet still vulnerable to her limited power.

As she turned into Dorset Street and made her way west,

something tugged at the edges of Mary Jane's memory, suggesting she did indeed know of such a person. With time, perhaps she would remember.

Resentfully, she thought that Emma Elizabeth Smith had got away with a crime, small though the offense seemed, because Jennie's corpse provided an alibi of sorts.

She walked through the Miller's Court passage, and entered her room.

Thankfully, Barnett had not yet returned home from Billingsgate Market.

Intent on escaping into sleep, Mary Jane took thirty-five drops of laudanum.

CHAPTER EIGHTEEN

Despite the large dose of narcotic, Mary Jane could not find insensibility. She left the room at seven o'clock in the evening, stumbled through the Miller's Court passage, then east into Dorset Street toward the Ringers through a heavy downpour of rain. Slow and awkward with so much intoxicant in her, she felt as if she moved through water up to her neck.

The gutters along the street flowed with heavy runoff. Thinking of Mum in the River Towy, she entered the Ringers, and ordered violets to toss into the water outside.

"We don't have violets," the barmaid said impatiently.

"Irish whiskey, then," Mary Jane said.

She would later recall that women she knew greeted her and asked her to sit with them, but would not recollect their names or faces. After drinking her whiskey, she had a row with someone and struck that person in the face, yet she would not remember anything about what had started the fight or who the person might have been. The publican, Matilda Ringer, had Mary Jane put out in the street.

She awoke near dawn the next morning in her bed, lying next to Barnett. He stank of the fish market so badly, her gorge began to rise. She got out of bed, lit a lamp, and went out to the privy. Head aching and gut churning, she vomited into the privy vault. Her stomach calmed somewhat and she sat. Too backed up from the laudanum, she succeeded only in passing water.

Mary Jane noted that her right hand hurt and had bruised knuckles. The few memories of the night before brought a distant feeling of embarrassment for the way she'd acted at the Ringers, one eclipsed, though, by her grief over the loss of Jennie.

Mary Jane returned to her room.

Barnett gave her a look. He rose to begin his day as she got into the bed.

Trying to return to sleep, something of memory kept suggesting that Joseph Fleming had helped her home the night before. A mere fancy perhaps, she still found the idea comforting, in spite of her desire to stay away from him.

Barnett moved about the room, washing with a flannel at the basin, preparing a cup of coffee, packing and lighting his pipe. Eventually he took a seat at the table beside the largest of the two windows.

Unable to sleep, Mary Jane made some decisions. *I shall wean myself from laudanum.* Should she somehow find a way to avenge Jennie, she'd need a clear head.

"I'm giving up soliciting," she decided aloud.

"Soliciting," Barnett repeated, blowing smoke from his mouth and nose. She knew he was trying to wake up before heading out to the market to begin the day's labor. She didn't usually rise early enough to see that. With the curtain pulled back, he sat looking out into the court. The view offered little of interest; the wooden privy stall, the rusted pump with its peeling blue paint, and the whitewashed brick of the facing building. He looked toward the left, beyond the bend in the court beside their room.

Why does he bother? Mary Jane had to wonder. *The view gives merely more brick. We live in a sad, little hole.*

She remained in Miller's Court because she felt somewhat safer hidden in its shadowy depths from the likes of Brevard. The only entrance to the court's thin, L-shaped paved yard was from Dorset Street by way of a three-foot-wide, twenty-foot-long through-passage under the second floor of the building that held their landlord's chandler's shop.

"That's good you're giving it up," Barnett said after a time.

As usual, he'd had much to drink the night before and had little desire for conversation.

"I shan't be contributing much to the household accounts until I find a position."

"Position…" he said. "That's fine for now. I can work longer hours at market."

He knocked the ash out of his pipe into a tin on the table.

Mary Jane had decided to give up soliciting because of what had happened to Jennie. She could not escape the fact that helping her friend learn to work the streets, she'd contributed to her death. Mary Jane had insisted that Jennie pay the protection money the Gully Bleeders demanded, as if that were all that was needed to keep her safe.

I might have seen that she could not afford to pay. I should have persuaded her to give up soliciting and find a position.

Somehow, she found that her mood fit with Barnett's silent contemplation of bricks—a mute acceptance of a grim world. That didn't please her.

The grief is too hard. To bear up, I ought to take action.

Someone had to pay for what had been done to Jennie. Mary Jane knew that to become the instrument of the revenge she sought, she'd have to be secretive because of her limited strength.

She would spend time gathering information from the ladybirds of Whitechapel and other districts within the East End.

My savings will allow me to move freely, at least for a while.

She would watch the Gully Bleeders and look for an opportunity to strike out at them. Though she had given up soliciting, she would pay her protection money so those she watched would be none the wiser.

Barnett finished his coffee, and put his pipe in his pocket. He donned his hat and jacket, took up his apron, and headed toward the door.

"This evening, then," he said.

"I'll be gone much of the time, looking for work." Mary Jane said. "I'll look for night shifts too, so I might not be home till late."

"Good luck," he said, and left.

Making the rounds, talking with her ladybirds and trying to make new friends and widen her territory, Mary Jane saw Gabriella Gorse at the Black Eagle Pub in Brick Lane. The prostitute spoke to a young, thin, dark-haired woman.

Again, Gabby talks to the green tail. She saw that the younger woman had the gaunt consumptive appearance. *She ought to do well.*

Plenty of fools attracted to that helpless, hopeless look.

She had presumed Gabby lodged in Stepney, but didn't remember anyone ever saying where she lived.

Seeing her over the following weeks at other pubs in different parts of the East End—the Bricklayers Arms in Poplar, the Black Dog in Shoreditch, and Bunch of Grapes in Limehouse—Mary Jane grew curious. In the ensuing summer months, she followed the woman whenever she turned up.

While following Gabby, Mary Jane had a stalker as well. She first noticed the shadowy figure following her along Market Street in Poplar, then again among the foot traffic at several other locations in the East End. The stalker stayed in the distance, keeping well enough to the shadows that she could not make out any definite features. She saw the silhouette clearly a couple of times framed against a brighter background, and became certain the figure was male. The shape did not have the thicker build of Stuart Brevard. Fancy told her he might show himself more clearly any time. She feared he might be one of the Gully Bleeders. Were they somehow on to her desire to harm them?

Ridiculous.

Numerous men had stalked Mary Jane in her short life. She didn't let fear of them stop her.

Gabby visited streets where Judies plied their trade. She went from pub to pub, and a couple of taverns that had back rooms with entertainment. Everywhere she went, Mary Jane saw her approach and try to talk to the green tail.

Since Gabby rarely took a cab anywhere she might walk, she remained easy to follow. Her eyes seemed to fail her with much distance. Not seeking clients, Mary Jane did not dress as a ladybird. She wore a bonnet and sensible clothing. The one time Gabby noticed Mary Jane, they were at the Horn of Plenty pub in Poplar.

The sound of the coarse saw dust crunching beneath her tread took away from the graceful approach Miss Gorse attempted. She asked, "What are you doing here?"

"I needn't be surprised to find I'm here for the same reason you are," Mary Jane said. She glanced around the half-empty establishment as if looking for someone. The rainclouds outside brought heavy shadows inside among the age-darkened wood furnishings. The men at nearby tables stared at the two women.

Gabby looked Mary Jane up and down. "You're not dressed the part."

"I'm dressed for the client what hired me."

With a contemptuous curl of the lip, Gabby turned away.

Mary Jane wasted no time moving beyond the woman's range of vision.

Because Gabriella Gorse, another fallen toffer, reminded Mary Jane of her own failure, she'd always considered her dislike of the woman unfair.

No, there's more to the feeling, something wicked *about her. I just don't know what that is.*

Mary Jane remembered the words of the prostitute, Sally Fourth, whom she'd met in Deptford: "I haven't seen you try to earn a single farthing." In Deptford to help Joseph Fleming with his criminal scheme, Mary Jane hadn't been soliciting, but wanted to appear to be. The prostitute had caught her out.

Mary Jane thought she was on to something like that. She'd never seen Gabriella Gorse take a man up on an offer; never seen her "disappear" with a man, as ladybirds were wont to do.

At the King of Prussia in Shadwell, while watching Gabby talk to an older woman, Mary Jane got an odd feeling that raised the small hairs on her neck and gave her a chill. She couldn't say whether that feeling had something to do with Gabby's appearance or what she did. Still, intuition seemed to be trying to tell Mary Jane something.

The ladybirds of Stepney had given Gabriella Gorse her nickname for talking so much, particularly to the new girls. They joked that she acted like a mother hen, taking poor young chicks under her wing. They thought that foolish, but kind. Somehow, Mary Jane had always known that was a sham.

She suspected the woman had got herself into something sinister, having seen her in conversations with Nick Shears.

The Gully Bleeders bled prostitutes a little at a time; not so much that women would balk after learning something of the consequences, and not enough that the gang's efforts were worth the trouble for the take from just one. Yet taking a little from all the women engaged in soliciting in the East End each week amounted to a fortune. And that fortune grew with each new woman who turned to working the streets as a means of making ends meet, something that happened more and more as the growing ranks of the unemployed competed for positions, day labor, and piece work, driving wages down. Earning a living by legal means had become more and more difficult. Still, prostitution being a secretive pursuit, a woman entering the trade would not take it upon herself to inform the Gully Bleeders of what she did for a living. No, she wouldn't want to. And one woman engaged in prostitution without paying the protection money could inspire others to do the same. A spy was needed to collect the names of those just joining the ranks of the East End ladybirds, one that looked like a ladybird herself.

Once Mary Jane had reasoned out the lay, Gabby's betrayal seemed obvious enough. She knew the business. She could recognize all the signs of fresh, budding tail. Who better than that for the Gully Bleeders to have as an informant?

Those ideas about Gabriella Gorse solidify but slowly over the summer of 1888. Even though Mary Jane had always disliked the woman, she'd believed the kind face the prostitute showed the new Judies to be pure cokum, Gabby's way of looking for opportunity and advantage, nothing more.

Perhaps she'd been scornful toward Mary Jane to keep her at arm's-length. Gabby would know that Mary Jane could do the same job for the Gully Bleeders. With that ability, she might also easily discern what Miss Gorse was up to.

Almost two years earlier, Mary Jane had seen her in the East London Cemetery with Nick Shears and some of his bludgers. She'd watched Gabby counting out something on her hand. On that day, had she counted off the women she'd told the gang about that week? Did she get paid a little of the take from each new Judy?

Not long before sighting the woman in the cemetery, Mary Jane had seen Gabby nodding her head toward Jennie's table at the Angel and Trumpet to direct Nick Shear's attention. He must have seen

Jennie. Shortly thereafter, he'd come to her for protection money.

Mary Jane felt foolish for taking so long to fit the pieces together. Gabriella Gorse was a blower for the Gully Bleeders. She put the gang onto Jennie. If Mary Jane could not take on Nick Shears, harming Gabby was a more manageable goal.

Standing there in the King of Prussia, watching Miss Gorse laugh with the older woman, the pitch of Mary Jane's anger rose. She fancied murdering Gabby and trembled at the thought.

Should I not go after the one who directed his gang to kill Jennie?

Nick Shears was always a threat, an obvious one. Gabriella Gorse knew the cruelty of his gang's methods. She pretended friendship among innocent and needy casuals, and then betrayed them to the Gully Bleeders.

She *must be the target of my wrath.*

Not seeing clients, traveling about the East End, frequently in cabs, purchasing meals while on the move, Mary Jane's funds had diminished over the summer. What in the spring had been about seventy pounds, had become forty-five.

At present, she didn't care about growing her savings. She realized that her goal of leaving London had been replaced with one of exacting her revenge. Her anger over the death of Jennie had pushed aside her fear of Stuart Brevard.

Before I leave London, I shall see Gabby pay for what she's done.

CHAPTER NINETEEN

In late July, 1888, Barnett lost his fish porter's license at Billingsgate Market. He'd been stealing fish for Mary Jane to cook at their lodgings.

"Don't worry," he said, "I'll look for work."

She gave fifteen pounds of her savings to Barnett to help with household expenses. He looked at her with surprise. "You finally found work?"

"No," she said, "'tis from my time soliciting. I haven't been able to find anything that pays nearly as well. That should see us through for a time, but I could always return to—"

"No," he said quickly, "I don't want that."

Barnett seemed to have accepted her explanation for the source of the funds. Thankfully, he didn't ask if Mary Jane had any more.

She would not return to earning until money became tight.

Continuing to follow Gabby, Mary Jane looked for opportunities for revenge. She had a notion to push her in front of a moving vehicle or throw her from a height. She tried to think of ways to destroy the woman's reputation and possibly sabotage her efforts with the Gully Bleeders so they might turn on her. Nothing she imagined seemed remotely possible for her to pull off. The more times she pictured the woman's demise, the more sympathy she seemed to gain for the horrible creature. She remembered that Gabby had once taken a beating meant for Mary Jane. Her heart wanted the woman to suffer, but her conscience told her that intentionally harming others was wrong and would scar her own spirit.

Frustrated, she watched Gabby climb into a cab, an old-fashioned cabriolet, and ride off down Whitechapel Road.

"You have lost your quarry," came a voice from beside her.

She looked at the man, took a step back away from him.

How does he know?

Though his presence seemed nonthreatening, she felt uneasy. Mary Jane wanted to think of him as a gentleman. His voice, his bearing, his fine dark gray suit, black shoes, and black felt hat, all suggested a proper gent, yet something about him forbid such a term. She found herself unwilling to look him squarely in the eyes.

Feigning confusion, she said, "Sir?"

"I have certain requirements," he said.

"Of what do we speak, sir?"

A woman walking past accidentally bumped against Mary Jane's shoulder. She moved toward the nearest building, a tobacconist's shop, to get out of the busy walkway.

Unfortunately, the man followed. "You appear to be familiar with the streets. Am I correct?"

A policeman, a private investigator? Mary Jane wondered.

Somehow, she didn't think he was the one she'd seen following her on and off throughout the summer.

Perhaps he was a potential client who saw through her disguise, recognizing her as a ladybird.

"What gives you that impression?" she asked.

"Not what you'd think."

Not a potential client—good! Something about him did not sit right.

Mary Jane said cautiously, "I know something of the goings-on hereabouts. What are you looking for?"

"Anything out of the ordinary," he said. "Things that don't sit well with you."

Like you? she wondered.

His eyes narrowed slightly, and she had the oddest notion he'd heard her thought.

"What tells you I know about such things?"

"What I see, or think, are none of your concern. I require a sense of changes, disturbances—the gutter-talk, the huddled conversations. Rumour."

With the coldness of his tone, Mary Jane felt threatened. Sensing that he was indeed a dangerous man, she had an impulse to run, yet knew better than to show her fear. She pushed the feeling down and leveled her gaze at the man's black eyes. They were not black after all, merely gave that impression. They appeared a light blue or gray.

"Are you a policeman?"

He didn't answer.

"You need a blower?"

"I need an informant, yes."

Did he have something to do with Brevard? Her heartbeat quickened, and she struggled to conceal her fear again. "Do you work for someone?"

"If you do not want coin for such services, there are others who no doubt shall, such as the woman you follow." He turned away and began walking in the direction Gabriella Gorse had taken.

No, he might tell Gabby I follow her.

"Please," Mary Jane said. "I mean only to know something of the terms of our communication."

He stopped and turned back. "Communication is my business. I will find you when I need to. On each encounter, I will provide a guinea, assuming you provide, in return, such snippets as interest me. Do you have anything for me now? You speak to me as you might to a priest. Consider me a servant of God."

He gave a faint, cold smile, the first time his features had given anything away. Mary Jane knew that he was not a servant of God and that he had contempt for such ideas.

She thought of what she knew about Jennie's death, and decided that might be worth a guinea. "The woman attacked on Osborn Street on April 3, and died two days later, she wasn't Emma Elizabeth Smith as reported. She were Miss Jennifer Weatherhead."

The man held out his hand. She extended one of her own, dismayed to see it shaking. He dropped a coin into her hand. The golden relief of the Queen's likeness flashed briefly at her. Excited to see a gold sovereign, an 1888 Victoria Jubilee minting no less, Mary Jane slipped the coin into a concealed pocket of her bodice.

The man turned and seemed to instantly disappear among the foot traffic.

She didn't know what to make of the encounter, but knew with a dread certainty that she'd see the man again. Unexpectedly.

Mary Jane sat in the Ringers pub, having a glass of bitter with ladybirds, Madeline Grissette, and Merrilee Sweeney. A tatterdemalion woman, possibly sixty years of age, approached them.

"May I sit?" she asked. "I am Mrs. Glory Sagebart." A bit mushy, her words came so quietly that Mary Jane barely heard them over the hubbub of conversations among the patrons of the busy pub. "Mrs. Maria Harvey said I'd do well to talk to you, should I want to take up soliciting."

Mary Jane didn't like the uncharitable look of scorn Merrilee gave Mrs. Sagebart.

The publican, Mrs. Matilda Ringer, appeared. "You are not in a condition to be in here," she said to Glory. "You must leave."

Mary Jane gave Matilda a look.

"She reeks," The publican said flatly.

Glory kept her head down. The weary, hungry look about her suggested she didn't eat well. With the way her lined face collapsed when she shut her mouth, her lips folding inward to create a thin seam, she probably had few teeth, limiting what she might eat. She wore several layers of clothing; a couple of chemises beneath a ragged wool jacket, three skirts, two thin cotton bonnets, one inside the other, both rotting from exposure to hair oil, and brown boots split at the toes between the uppers and the soles so that her darned black wool socks peaked out.

Mary Jane had spent her money freely on herself and others in the Ringers lately. "Do you want *me* to leave?" she asked Matilda.

The publican hesitated, then shook her head and went back to the taps.

"Of course you may sit with us," Mary Jane said. She pushed the chair beside her out and the raggedy woman sat.

The Maria Harvey of whom Glory spoke, a woman of about forty-five years of age with dark hair and brown eyes, had left her eight children with her brother in Shoreditch and come into Spitalfields to earn through soliciting.

"Foolishly, I thought the police could make my husband stop beating me," Maria told Mary Jane the day they met. "Instead they sent him to prison. His wages gone, we have nothing. Should I miss those beatings?"

Mary Jane had spent a little money helping the woman because she saw something of Jennie in her. She justified her charity in part with the notion that she currently had extra funds that came from little effort. Twice in two weeks, she'd seen the odd man who asked her to be his informant. She'd given him information about the streets on both occasions, earning a gold sovereign each time. She thought of him as the black-eyed man. Mary Jane did not tell Barnett about the income because she truly didn't know what to say about her new client, and she wanted control of the funds for her own purposes. She would contribute more to the household as the need arose.

The experience of losing Jennie also drove Mary Jane to persuade Mrs. Harvey not to take up soliciting. She had allowed Maria to sleep in the room in Miller's Court while Barnett worked at the market. Then, after he'd lost his fish porter license, Mary Jane had shared her bed with the woman on the nights when Barnett was away looking for work in other districts. She had felt good about helping Maria.

Casting the need for justification aside, Mary Jane had then helped Julia Venteney, another middle-aged woman who had recently considered soliciting. Julia was rawboned and freckled all over, had pale eyes and graying ginger hair. With Mary Jane's help, providing funds for meals and occasionally paying their doss at Cooley's Lodging House, both Maria and Julia had been able to find work at White's Laundry. The work was daily, and irregular because they weren't always needed. Nights, they repaired damaged clothing for the laundry, sewing buttons back on and stitching torn seams.

If Miss Harvey had told Glory Sagebart to talk to Mary Jane about soliciting, that no doubt meant that Maria didn't want the older woman to become a prostitute.

In such poor condition, Glory could not earn the going rate of a casual: Four pence. Her aspirations of earning as a prostitute were hopeless. Mary Jane hoped to persuade the woman of that.

"May I get you a cup of soup?" she asked. "They have a lovely fish and potato."

Glory's eyes brightened. "Yes, thank you." Saliva drooled down her chin. She wiped the spittle away with her hand.

Mary Jane signaled to a barmaid, who came and took the order. "Can you write?"

"Yes," Glory said. "I taught at Saint Mary Magdalen National School."

"Oh, my," Mary Jane said, surprised. "How did you—" She had intended to ask how the woman ended up in such a state, but stopped herself.

"My husband, Roderick, gambled," Glory said, seemingly unashamed, "had a large debt, and decided to remedy that with a robbery. Something went wrong. A policeman caught him in the act. Roderick struck him in the head and accidentally killed him. He was among the last to get *the boat.*"

"The boat?" Mary Jane asked.

"Transportation to a penal colony in Australia," Merrilee said.

"Twenty-one years ago, that was," Glory said. "I lived with family until they could no longer help."

So many ways women end up on the streets, Mary Jane thought.

She remembered what the black-eyed man had asked for: "I require a sense of changes, disturbances—the gutter-talk, the huddled conversations. Rumour." He'd also said, "Anything that doesn't sit well with you," and had been interested in her revelation that Emma Elizabeth Smith was Jennie Weatherhead. If he were somehow involved in law enforcement and could do something about the bad apples among the Ladybirds' clientele, assembling a list of such would be helpful.

"Do you think you could help me begin a record," Mary Jane asked.

"I could if I had pen and paper." Glory said. "I used Pitman shorthand as a secretary for a time. Really quite fast."

"I'll get those for you."

The next time Mary Jane saw the black-eyed man, she had just exited the Whitechapel Public Baths. He wore spectacles that looked at if the glass were coated with a thin layer of lamp black. In the warm summer air, with the disturbing man approaching along the hot granite footway at midday, she began to sweat in her fresh clothes.

My feeling of being clean were too brief.

Even so, she eagerly handed over what she'd prepared for him. Without a word of greeting, he briefly looked at the pages she'd offered, then gave her a gold sovereign. For his payment, he'd received a list of violent ladybird clients Mary Jane had put together with Glory Sagebart's help. With utmost secrecy, and assuring confidentiality, they had interviewed as many of the ladybirds of Spitalfields as they could find, and recorded what names and description the women could remember. Mary Jane had made certain that Stuart Brevard's name was at the top of the list.

In return for the woman's help, Mary Jane had paid Glory's doss at a common lodging and kept her fed for the week.

Rubbing the gold sovereign between her fingers, Mary Jane wondered if the black-eyed man might help her in some other way. "And should I need more than the coin?" she asked.

"Then you should find a more remunerative trade," he said while glancing at the pages.

Undiscouraged, Mary Jane pressed on. "I might need a bit of muscle instead."

She tried to look him in the eyes, though that made her uncomfortable. He remained busy, his eyes scanning Glory's fine script.

"*Please*," she said.

Her last word had no evident effect.

He seemed to think nothing of her concerns. If her interests did not promote his, he would probably not consider them.

"I shall gladly help without coin," she said, "should you consider payment of another sort."

"What would that be, this other currency?" he asked, still considering the pages.

"Doing something about the woman you saw me follow."

Finally he looked up. "I am not unreasonable." He held up the pages she'd given him. "More of this. I want a greater part of the East End."

"Yes," Mary Jane said, "I can do that."

He turned around and walked away.

I shall take Glory with me to Stepney.

They would go to Dresser's coffee shop and interview the women there. Mary Jane would dress conservatively, a disguise of sorts to throw off Brevard, should he still be rooting around those parts for her. If that went well, they could work on interviews in other parts of the East End.

Something about the black-eyed man's manner suggested he didn't value the lives of others. From his reaction to Mary Jane's words, he did not seem opposed to doing something about Gabriella Gorse, yet he had not truly said as much.

Nonetheless, Mary Jane's fancy had him harming and even killing Gabby.

Then it occurred to her that she might also employ him to kill Stuart Brevard...and Nick Shears, as well.

CHAPTER TWENTY

On Friday, August 17, Mary Jane took her last dose of laudanum. Over the past three months, she'd systematically weaned herself from the intoxicant with smaller and smaller doses, rigorously measured by droplet and taken at regular intervals. Feeling confident that she was free of the habit for good, she entertained thoughts of seeing Joseph Fleming, then decided that would be a terrible mistake.

Mary Jane's appetite, uncertain in recent days, had returned. About ten o'clock that morning, she sought something to eat at Spitalfields Market. Allowing her nose to lead her, avoiding the eyes of the hawkers and duffers, a chapmen, a badger and his plant, she made her way between the rows of vendors through the many browsing the market. The odor of cooking meat caught her. Within moments she found herself watching German sausages sizzling in a pan on a small stove.

As she stood considering a purchase from the old, gray woman preparing the food, the black-eyed man approached. Mary Jane quickly turned away from the food, thoughts of delivering the information, and all the emotion surrounding her dealings with the odd man, having replaced the drive of hunger.

The folded leaves of paper she had for him barely fit in a pocket beneath her top skirt. She extracted them and kept them folded small. Watching to make certain no one saw, and that the quickest of thieves, little nippers, were not nearby, she made the exchange. He received Glory's written record of information gathered in Spitalfields about the tragic Martha Tabram, a woman stabbed thirty-nine times ten days earlier, a quarter of a mile away in George Yard. Also included in the pages was the fifth list of dangerous clients the two women had assembled, and whatever additional information they had thought unusual or disturbing in their interviews. They had even included flights of fancy people had conveyed that might hold a grain of truth.

Without looking at the pages, he gave Mary Jane another gold sovereign. Perhaps he'd come to find her dependable.

Concerning Martha Tabram, no doubt most of the information he might have got for himself from the press or the police, had he tried. But the interviews the two women had conducted with the ladybirds of Spitalfields had turned up traces of the woman and her circumstances that the interviewees might not have willingly given up to those bodies.

With work at the laundry less regular, Maria and Julia had found time to help with the Spitalfields interviews, while Glory and Mary Jane had gone into several other neighborhoods. Within a short time, they had secretly covered a large part of the East End in their quest for information. Then Julia landed work as a charwoman, and took up with a lumper named Harold Owen in Miller's Court. They occupied the room nearest the one where Mary Jane and Barnett lodged. With her new charring position, Julia couldn't help with the interviews as much, yet Mary Jane and her "girls," as she liked to call them, still did well because they had got better at the work.

Though his manner was difficult to fathom and he hadn't said a word, Mary Jane had the impression the black-eyed man got from her what he wanted. After they parted ways, she turned back to the sausages. They no longer looked tasty. None of the smells of the many foods available seemed appealing.

Dodging a patterer trying to sell some trifle to make embroidering easier, and a mountebank offering a bottle of what he called "liver cleaner," she made her way through the many browsers to exit the market at Commercial Street, and from there to the Ringers.

Mary Jane felt at home sitting in the pub with her girls. Within a short time, they had coffee and warm food in their bellies.

"Were quite a row between your Barnett and that man, Fleming," Maria Harvey said. "I wanted to slip out, but they blocked the doorway."

Maria had stayed the night in their room. Barnett didn't want her there. To make matters worse, Joseph Fleming knocked on the door in the early morning, rousing everyone from sleep.

"I need to talk to Mary Jane," he said.

"Mary Jane," Barnett said, shoving her aside and standing in the doorway. He looked Joseph up and down, must have seen the plaster on his clothing. "Are you Fleming?"

"Yes."

Barnett had turned surly on the few occasions she had spoken of Joseph, so she'd ceased to say anything about him.

"She wants nothing to do with you."

"She might speak for herself," Fleming said.

"Herself," Barnett said.

Mary Jane pushed past the two men on her way out to the privy.

Fleming tried to take her hand. Barnett grabbed his right arm. Fleming swung his left fist. Barnett ducked under it, caught Fleming's other arm, twisted the limb up behind his back, and escorted him through the passage to Dorset Street.

As angry as he'd been about losing his job, Mary Jane thought Barnett showed restraint not striking Fleming while he had the advantage. Instead, he shoved him away, said, "Don't come back. I've a knife what's gutted better fish than you."

After the privy, Mary Jane returned to the room, discovered that Maria had left.

Barnett said, "I don't like sharing the bed. 'Tis small enough you don't keep putting bunters in it."

"You mustn't talk about my friend that way," she said. "She hasn't been soliciting for over a month now."

"Now," he had grumbled, but added nothing else.

"Barnett said Fleming were cruel," Maria said, "that he'd been in the habit of hitting you."

"Told me that too," Julia said.

Why Barnett had lied, Mary Jane didn't know. *Probably to turn them against Fleming, should he show up again.* She wasn't interested in defending Joseph and kept silent.

Thomas Morganstone approached their table. Mary Jane's surprise and delight left her speechless. He had dressed down for the coarser neighborhood. His checked black and red wool coat with holes at the elbows and his bent brown felt hat reminded her of the times when, as a young man in Carmarthen, he'd worn old clothing to visit the worksites where he learned about construction. With his handsome, clean-shaven face and the curling locks that fell from beneath his hat, Mary Jane again knew her girlish crush on him had not gone away.

She finally found her voice, and introduced Thomas to Maria Harvey, Julia Venteney, and Glory Sagebart. "Please sit," she said. "How did you find me?"

"That's not for me to say," he said. "Indeed, I ought to speak with you privately."

The other woman excused themselves quickly, got up, and left the table, taking their coffee cups with them.

Thomas looked surprised. "They didn't—" he began.

"They left us for me," she said, "not for you. We are in the habit of seeking privacy in certain communications. They're following a discipline we've imposed upon ourselves."

"Perhaps the need has something to do with what I've come to say. I hope I'm not too late. I let the matter go too long."

"How mysterious," Mary Jane said. "Too late for what?"

Thomas craned his neck, looking around the Ringers. A Friday afternoon, the place had few seats not taken and many people standing, drinks in hand, milling about and talking, the ten-day-old news of the Martha Tabram murder still the most discussed topic. Mary Jane had arrived early enough to take a corner table. Tobacco smoke hung in the air like fog, and the murmur of many voices created sufficient confusion of sound that conversations remained intimate with little effort.

Matilda Ringer approached the table. "Good afternoon, sir," she said, taking a good look at Thomas. She nodded her approval to Mary Jane. Apparently the publican could see through his disguise. Mrs. Ringer didn't seem to like the company Mary Jane kept lately; older women with no money. Not that the matter was any of Matilda's business. She stepped to the wall and yanked a bell-pull. A barmaid perked up and headed toward the table as Mrs. Ringer went back to the taps.

"What'll you have?" the barmaid asked.

"Your inkiest porter, Thomas said.

"More coffee," Mary Jane said.

The barmaid nodded and went away.

"I'm afraid I may have got you mixed up in something dangerous with that Deptford job," Thomas said.

"More than just the murder?" Mary Jane asked. She laughed to give him the impression that she wasn't concerned, that she didn't blame him for her exposure to risk. She had given that role to Joseph Fleming, however unfairly.

Thomas had a troubled look. "Should the situation have ended with that, and we heard no more, no. The one who hired me to map the victualing yard, and asked for the distraction that you and Joseph pulled off, he came to see me, and asked about you."

"Did you ask about the murder?"

"No!" Thomas said, his eyes briefly wide-open, "of course not."

"What did he want?"

"I'm not entirely certain. When I told him I didn't know anything about you, he went away."

"What is his name?"

The barmaid returned with a pint glass of porter and a pot of coffee. She placed the glass on the table, poured coffee into Mary Jane's cup, and left.

"I don't know that either." Thomas looked embarrassed. "I never did. Sometimes I get paid to do a task for people who never reveal anything about themselves." He shook his head. "I'm not proud of that sort of thing, and I hate to think you might be hurt because of it."

Mary Jane shook her head, denying the possibility that he might bring her harm. "What does this man look like?"

"That's difficult to say. He's a rather ordinary-looking fellow."

Mary Jane remembered Joseph Fleming telling her of a man talking to Thomas about the extra work at the victualing yard.

"He doesn't *look* dangerous," Thomas said.

"Yes, I remember Joseph saying he was an ordinary cove."

"That's right. I let that impression settle my fears when I knew I should not have done. To deal with him, though, one gets the impression that he *is* dangerous. I ought to have found you and told you about his query immediately. I've allowed a couple of months to pass. Finally, my conscience would not let me sleep until I located you."

Thomas had the most distressing look of shame.

Mary Jane reached across the table and clasped his hands. "You believe he is the one who killed the man, Caille, in Deptford," she said. "Am I right?"

"Yes."

Mary Jane shrugged. "No one has tried to harm me, but I suppose I ought to know who to look out for."

"Not much about him stands out. In truth, the feature of his that most comes to mind is one that seems to withdraw rather than stand out—his eyes seem…I'm not certain how to say it. They are rather—"

"Black?"

"*Yes,*" Thomas said with a look of surprise. "Have you seen him?"

He is the one who murdered Caille. The ordinary cove and the black-eyed man are one and the same!

Mary Jane held back her surprise. "Yes. The blackness is only an impression. He has blue eyes. When he's not looking you in the eye, he's just an ordinary cove."

Fear had returned to Thomas's expression.

"He's not a threat," Mary Jane said quickly, squeezing his hands. "I've spoken to him."

Thomas seemed to relax, and finally took some of his drink. "Hmm—that's good porter."

"She gave you the good stuff. Most of their mild drink is watered."

"You're right about his eyes," Thomas said. "Something of his character is reflected in his gaze and gives the impression. Somehow, he knew of your involvement at Deptford and wanted to know where he might find Fair Rose. I told him you had moved away and that I didn't know any more about you."

For some reason, Mary Jane didn't want to say much about her encounter with the black-eyed man, possibly because of her desire to have him harm Gabriella Gorse. "He offered me funds in exchange for information from the rumor mill. I don't think he's a danger to me."

"Well, that's a relief." Thomas, said. Then he became thoughtful for a moment. "Later that day, at a job site, I saw him talking with Joseph Fleming."

Mary Jane wanted to ask after Fleming, but didn't want him to find out about her interest. Although she'd wanted to learn something of his wellbeing when he came to her room that morning, she had done her best to ignore him for the same reason.

"In truth, I suppose that is what troubled me. The man had walked away once I'd said I knew nothing about you."

"What do you mean?"

Thomas had a sad smile. "Poor Fleming has gone to pieces since you left. I believe he truly loves you. Watching Joseph talk to the man, I saw a spark of hope in his eyes not seen for a long while. I grew fearful that he'd somehow help this fellow find you. And perhaps he did."

"I have a feeling the man in question is resourceful. Joseph would do nothing to betray me."

"I quite agree, at least not intentionally. He's been queer lately, though, disappearing for days on end. I didn't want any of this to come as a surprise to you."

"Thank you for finding me. I'm happy to learn that someone is looking out for me."

"Joseph would too, should you let him."

Mary Jane merely smiled in response. She didn't want to explain herself.

"Would you allow me to take you for a fine meal?" Thomas asked.

"No, thank you. I've cast my lot with these women for now, and feel the need to stay close to them for a time."

"Well, come and visit when you can," Thomas said. "I miss you."

Mary Jane nodded.

He left the Ringers.

Anticipating the return of her girls, she drew the remainder of his porter, most of the glass, to her side of the table.

Though Julia, Maria, and Glory, helped her put together information for the ordinary cove, they knew nothing of the source of the money that Mary Jane spent on them. If she gave the funds to the women, Maria would drink rather than eat, and Julia's part would end up in Harry Owen's pocket. Thinking of her past need for laudanum, Mary Jane chose not to judge Maria. All three seemed to trust Mary Jane. She'd bought them new clothes and fed them. She had also provided them with shelter, including Julia before the woman had taken up with Owen. They had all expressed their gratitude, and seemed quite willing to follow her advice for keeping their efforts secret.

Mary Jane's intuition had been correct. The ordinary cove with the dark gaze most certainly was *not* a policeman, nor a private investigator.

Of all the millions of people in London, I was unwittingly involved in the black-eyed man's scheme to murder the man, Caille, the one Jennie believed responsible for the death of her brother. What a rum coincidence.

Jennie and Mrs. Hollis thought the murder of Caille a good thing.

Did Mary Jane's gathering of information for him somehow serve the side of decency and good? Most likely not, but she wanted to think he could perform further good services for her.

Either the ordinary cove had something against Caille or someone had hired him to kill the man. Certainly, that had not been Jennie, although she might have done, if she'd had the price.

The black-eyed man had somehow known of my involvement in his scheme.

How?

And does he see me as a lose end, a possible threat should the police somehow place me at the scene of the crime and question me?

Again, she worried about the hatred of Sally Fourth.

Mary Jane told herself that if he considered her a threat, he might have got rid of her any time within the past couple of months.

She preferred to look to the future she hoped to see.

She had been saving back some of the funds received from the black-eyed man for the coming time when her payment from him might instead be retribution for Gabriella Gorse. Though she knew that in her conversations with the man she had never fully discussed the matter, somehow Mary Jane believed he had not forgot.

While she didn't like him, strangely, she did trust him in their business arrangement. He was dependable as clockwork, showing up lately on Mondays and Fridays. She gave him whatever information she had and he paid her.

Mary Jane intended to earn the ordinary cove's good will, if that were possible.

Once he's got enough from me, she told herself, *he will consider further what I want done to Gabriella Gorse—perhaps he'll help with Nick Shears and Stuart Brevard too.*

He *did* know what she wanted regarding Gorse. Of that, Mary Jane remained confident. She'd needed a killer, and found one, yet she couldn't seem to bring herself to speak directly to him about the matter. Perhaps that suited him.

CHAPTER TWENTY-ONE

Mary Ann Nichols was murdered in Buck's Row in the dark hours of early Friday morning, August 31, 1888. Polly, they called her. She'd been about the age of Martha Tabram and Jennie Weatherhead. Talk of the killing everywhere, Mary Jane and her girls did their best to collect it.

Some women they spoke to saw a pattern that fit with the murders of Martha Tabram and Emma Elizabeth Smith, as they knew her, one that suggested the Gully Bleeders had decided to come down harder on the women of the streets. Yet the gang did nothing to encourage the belief. Since their business turned on fear, they missed an opportunity if indeed they'd done the Nichols murder. From what Mary Jane and her girls gathered, she did not believe the Tabram or Nichols killings were warnings to prostitutes from the Gully Bleeders.

Friday September 7, while in Spitalfields Market, Mary Jane saw Stuart Brevard at a distance talking with two men, a tall one in a blue and black striped suit and bowler, and a stouter one in a brown and tan checked jacket, black trousers, and pale straw hat. As if giving commands to the men, Brevard gestured, first north, then south. One man went in the first direction the other the second. Though he had not seen her, Mr. Brevard headed eastward, in her direction, looking all about.

Did he hire punishers or private investigators to help him?

Mary Jane exited the market into Commercial Street and headed south toward the Ten Bells pub at the crossing with Fournier Street. She thought to lose herself among the patrons of the public house, then decided against entering for fear of becoming trapped.

The ordinary cove approached her at the corner, turned his black eyes on her.

"I must keep moving," she said, walking swiftly eastward into Fournier Street. "I have something for you, but there are men following me."

"They are of no consequence," he said. The black-eyed man did not move with urgency. The distance between them grew.

"They are to me. One has been after me for almost two years." With the noise around them in the street, she wasn't certain he'd hear her. Still, she had to get away.

"Yes, Stuart Brevard," he said, his voice quiet, yet somehow focused well enough to reach her.

Mary Jane turned to look back at him. He'd stopped some twenty feet away.

Glancing around, looking out for Mr. Brevard and his men, she approached the ordinary cove. Strangely, she feared her pursuers less while she stood in his shadow.

"Who hired you to kill the man, Caille, at the victualing yard?" Her boldness surprised her.

"You have something for me," he said.

Mary Jane recognized one of Brevard's men, the taller one in the black and blue striped suit and black bowler, moving toward them on the footway.

"He will not see you," the ordinary cove said, "if I become the brother you haven't seen in a month."

Mary Jane thought of Jack, gone to Australia so long ago, and imagined meeting him on the streets unexpectedly. "I thought I'd never see you again," she said, as if surprise and delight were equally caught in her throat. She thought to catch the black-eyed man's hands up in her own, to hug him toward her, but couldn't seem to bring herself to do that, nor did she believe he'd tolerate such intimacy. "Have you returned to stay? Does Mum know?"

The ordinary cove turned, and Mary Jane with him as Brevard's man walked past. She glanced at the fellow's back. He kept moving eastward.

How had he known the man approached?

In a rush, Mary Jane extracted the pages of information she and her girls had put together about Polly Nichols and her circumstances.

Again, they had included in the record whatever other strange goings-on they came across while interviewing people.

"Do not hurry," he said.

She took a calming breath, said, "Stuart Brevard will kill me if he catches me. Can you do something about him?"

He provided no answer.

Mary Jane handed over the folded pages.

He palmed to her another gold sovereign.

"Your friend, Jennifer Weatherhead's, cousin," he said.

Mary Jane was confused. Then she remembered the question she'd asked him: *Who hired you to kill the man, Caille, at the victualing yard?* He'd provided an answer to her question!

Dumbfounded, she stood for a moment, lost in thought and memory.

Jennie had talked about a cousin, Catherine Weatherhead. Mary Jane pictured a tall, dark-haired woman, and recalled that she'd met Catherine briefly a couple of years ago. They were about the same age. Jennie had said that her cousin helped her family with funds from time to time.

When her full awareness returned to the street around her, the ordinary cove was gone. In a panic to disappear before her enemies spotted her, she dashed into the road, passed between carriages and a car loaded with bushels of potatoes, and got across Fournier Street with little dung caked to her boots.

Taking to the footway and glancing back, she nearly bowled over Mrs. Hollis. She stood, as usual, beside Christ Church with her beggar's placard. Mary Jane held the startled old woman by the shoulders to steady her. She had seen Mrs. Hollis there many times, but had avoided speaking to her since Jennie's death out of shame and a desire to avoid the painful thoughts of loss.

"Forgive me," Mary Jane said. "I didn't mean to frighten."

"N-not at all, uh...Ginger. I-I—"

Face to face with Mrs. Hollis, Mary Jane suddenly knew that she had questions for her.

"Please walk with me for a time and answer my questions, and I'll give you a shilling."

The old woman nodded her approval, and the two walked to the crossing, then south on Commercial Street.

"Do you know a cousin of Jennifer Weatherhead's named Catherine?" Mary Jane asked.

"Yes," Mrs. Hollis said.

"And has she private means, a good position?" Mary Jane recalled something about the young woman being a widow's companion. That would not pay very well, she presumed.

Mrs. Hollis had an awkward look. "There are rumors that she is a spiritualist or fortune teller of some sort, though the family does not know this."

"Oh?"

"Is what I've heard," Mrs. Hollis said. "I last saw her at the funeral of Jennifer's mother, Levinia."

Mary Jane had no notion as to what earnings came from such pursuits. She didn't know what she believed about spiritualists. Many people considered them swindlers. She wondered if she ought to be suspicious of any information that came from Catherine Weatherhead.

"I want to know if she hired someone to kill Frederick Caille at the Deptford Victualing Yard, and, if so, what she knows about him."

Mrs. Hollis's eyes became large. Her near-toothless mouth gaped.

"I believe I have become acquainted with him," Mary Jane said. She described the black-eyed man to Mrs. Hollis.

"I will write to her and ask. She may not be willing to say. I don't know how long it will take to get an answer."

"Thank you." Mary Jane gave Mrs. Hollis a shilling and they parted company.

On Saturday, September 8 in the early hours of the morning, the body of Annie Chapman turned up behind a house in Hanbury Street. She'd been murdered and mutilated. Mary Jane and her girls continued their interviews in an effort to gain information about the murder.

Although she worried they might catch up to her anytime, Mary Jane did not seen Stuart Brevard or his two men Saturday or Sunday. Even so, she carried a sick feeling in her gut. Suddenly her past had caught up with her again. The need to escape London and start over elsewhere had returned, while she still had unfinished business with the ordinary cove and Gabriella Gorse.

Until the previous Friday, Mary Jane's fear of Mr. Brevard had diminished consistently throughout the year and a half she'd not seen him. With a renewed sense of the threat he posed, she thought again about how to fund a relocation. Still not seeing clients, and having spent much of the money she'd earned on her girls and their interviewing efforts, she had little savings left, at present about ten pounds. Her thoughts circled back to ideas of recovering the necklace from the Phoenix gay house, though that seemed hopeless. Surely by now, someone had discovered the hidden jewelry.

On Monday, September 10, she and her girls had just concluded an interview with a friend of Annie Chapman's, a woman named Amelia Palmer, when the black-eyed man appeared in the Ten Bells pub. He approached their table as Mrs. Palmer got up and left. Mary Jane's girls excused themselves and left without explanation. She would later learn that the man had so unnerved Maria, Glory, and Julia, that they could not stay.

He sat across from Mary Jane.

"I must finish my work here and make a fresh start somewhere I am not known," she said to him, "unless you can do something about Stuart Brevard."

He made no response.

"Shall I have any hope that you will deal with Gabriella Gorse?" she asked.

"I am paid in coin for my services," he said.

Most of her funds were hidden away in her lodgings. She had little in her pocket. "How much do you require?"

"Whatever token amount is to hand."

"You make a jest of my need?"

Again, the ordinary cove did not respond.

Holding back a desire to show her disgust, Mary Jane slipped the hidden pocket out from beneath the waist band of her top skirt. She raised the pouch to the table, and turned it out to display the two shillings and one tanner within. "A token amount," she said as flatly as possible. He deserved no better than he gave.

"That would be sufficient," he said.

Mary Jane sat back a bit hard, her seat rocking.

He didn't make any sense!

She put her hand to her mouth for fear that she might say something rude to him.

His black gaze remained unwavering. Mary Jane turned away from the terrible sight.

Had she gained his trust?

In some ways, perhaps. More likely he'd gained leverage over *her*. She still knew almost nothing about him.

She'd trusted him enough to do business with him. So what had changed?

His suggestion that a life was worth no more than two and a tanner.

Yet Gabby's life is worth less than that to me.

He does not *make a jest. The truth is* there *in his eyes.*

Again, she turned away, looked down. "Then allow me to pay you for Stuart Brevard instead."

"As I told you, he is of no consequence."

Is he afraid of Brevard?

No.

Mary Jane stared at the dented wood grain of the table top, unable to think of a winning way to press her need. The black-eyed man didn't respond to her charms as other men did.

He stood as if to leave.

"No, please," she said quickly. "The woman, then."

He sat.

Mary Jane carefully plucked the three coins from her pocket, hearing her decision to have Gabriella Gorse killed in the metal on metal sound of each coin touching its neighbor. She slid them across the table to the ordinary cove. They stayed in a small puddle of spilled coffee for a time before he picked them up and wiped them carefully with a handkerchief.

"When shall you do the job?" she asked.

"When I am ready."

She wanted to ask why he would kill for so little, but knew the answer, or lack of one, would trouble her more, and she'd have to live with the knowledge for possibly many years. Better that she didn't know.

The proper question is, does Gabriella Gorse deserve to die for what she's done?

Yes.

After the ordinary cove had gone, she realized she had not given him any of the information she and her girls had gathered about Annie Chapman and her circumstances. All they had so far were Glory's shorthand notes, not yet transcribed into a legible document.

He shall reappear on Friday.

Having paid him to commit the monstrous act, Mary Jane already knew the shame she would experience every time she had to look at the man, whether he committed the crime that day, the next, or never.

Still, she would suffer that shame for Jennie.

CHAPTER TWENTY-TWO

In the afternoon of Friday, September 14, having just emerged from a urinal on Booth Street, Mary Jane saw the black-eyed man standing in a doorway along the lane to the east. She approached, gave him the record she and her girls had assembled of the Annie Chapman murder, and received another sovereign, all without looking directly at him.

Annie Chapman had been an acquaintance of Mary Jane's, someone she had seen at the Ringers on occasion. The woman had been one of countless casuals, an unfortunate with a kind though wary smile.

Mrs. Chapman and Mrs. Nichols had had their throats cut and their guts laid open. They were left in open view, in positions that suggested that the murderer found a certain sexual delight in the cruelty. One such killing had little power to hold the public's imagination for long, but two similar murders indicated that someone hunted in the East End with a mysterious and depraved motive.

With the ensuing confusion, fear, and panic in the streets, the information Mary Jane and her girls gathered became widely varied and more difficult to parse. Some saw Mary Jane and her girls as possibly in league with the killer. Others could not talk enough about the matter, turning to fancy when the facts ran out—stories of demons, murderous immigrants, slumming nobles, and political factions trying to start riots or foment rebellion.

The whole of the East End seemed to go mad in September of 1888. People called the fiend the Whitechapel Murderer. Bloodstains on the streets, a common enough sight ignored before, turned into evidence of his further crimes. Rumors of new murders or suspects arrested drew crowds this way and that within the East End, blocking traffic and stirring the growing fear. The Whitechapel Vigilance

Committee made noise in the streets and in the press, spurring anger that the killer had not been caught swiftly. A reward offered for the capture of the murderer further fed the frenzy.

In their interviews, Mary Jane and her girls had met numerous people who described Jewish men as somehow more capable of inhuman violence. Some said they took part in hounding Jews through the streets.

A man with a knife attacked a woman in the open, and she suffered several wounds. The angry crowd that formed around the violence insisted on lynching him. The police arrived in time to save the victim and her attacker.

Someone cried out about a theft, and a young man ran from the scene. In little time, a large crowd formed, even in the midst of giving chase. But for the constable who caught the thief, the fearsome horde might have run the young man to ground and torn him apart.

A Jewish man called Leather Apron, thought to be the killer of Polly Nichols, was said to be loose in Whitechapel, terrorizing prostitutes. The descriptions of him that appeared in the East London Observer terrorized more than the man himself. Captured, questioned by the police, and found to have an alibi for the night of the murder, he'd been released. A boot closer, he used the leather apron in his work. Other arrests of suspects for each murder occurred, yet all turned out to be innocent.

The city first heard the name Jack the Ripper from a letter that appeared in the newspapers, one taunting the police and signed with that moniker.

The night of September 30 brought the worst night of murders, if only because two killings occurred within the span of an hour. Elizabeth Stride, who had come to London from Sweden when much younger, had her throat cut. Catherine Eddowes's throat had been cut, her face mutilated, and she'd been disemboweled.

Mary Jane briefly wondered if Stuart Brevard were the one doing the killing.

No, he is bold in his attacks, not secretive.

Reason kept telling her to leave London before Mr. Brevard found her. Her heart insisted on staying to see Gabby's demise.

On Monday, October 1, Mary Jane had little more to offer the ordinary cove about the new murders. Even so, she gave him what she could from the rumor mill.

October 2, the trunk of a woman with no head or limbs was discovered within a structure on a construction site in Whitehall.

More rewards were offered for the capture of the murderer. The feeling of severe unease in the streets continued into October. As if suffering symptoms of a new contagion, the people Mary Jane saw walking the footways hurried when walking alone and clustered more tightly when in groups. They more frequently whispered their words, and cast suspicious glances in all directions.

With such horror common in the streets, Mary Jane thought her crime of hiring a killer ought to trouble her less. Though her heart had won the argument, her conscience would not let the matter rest.

She told herself that the black-eyed man was not the killer terrorizing Whitechapel. He made little show of his work, while the one known as Jack the Ripper left his victims in the open, placed proudly on display.

Maria Harvey continued to spend nights with Mary Jane on the occasions Barnett went away seeking work in nearby districts. That saved funds that would have gone to paying doss. Barnett came home early from one of those searches drunk and angry that he'd had no luck. He and Mary Jane had a row about Maria being in his bed, and he threw her out. Mary Jane went with her to Julia's room across the court. The man she'd taken up with, Harold Owen, had been away for several days, and she was glad for the company.

Mary Jane had spoken with Mrs. Hollis each week since she'd said she would write to Catherine Weatherhead. On Friday, October 26, beside Christ Church, Mrs. Hollis handed Mary Jane an envelope addressed simply to "G." Inside, she found a hand-written letter. She did not pull the letter out completely. Instead, she tucked the envelope into her bodice, turned to the old woman and said, "Allow me to take you for a meal."

They moved south along Commercial Street to the Golden Heart tavern. On such a gloomy day, the tall windows and skylights of the establishment provided a welcomed brightness. From the side service, they chose cold chops, pea's soup, buttered bread, and hot tea. Since Mrs. Hollis had few teeth, Mary Jane helped cut the chops into small pieces.

"What can you tell me about Jennie's brother, Lieutenant Charles Weatherhead?" Mary Jane asked.

"I didn't know him, and can tell you only what I've heard." Mrs. Hollis told all that she knew about the life of the man, her few words on the matter easily fitting between the mostly gummed mouthfuls of her meal. Mary Jane wished she had taken more interest in Jennie's family.

"Can you tell me about what happened to your son and the Lieutenant?" Mary Jane asked, hoping the request did not stir the woman to further grief.

Mrs. Hollis took a deep breath, wiped her eyes, and said as if reciting, "On the last day of October, 1885, my son, John Hollis, were among three midshipman and an officer killed by bad victuals aboard the HMS Penelope, God bless their souls, while the ship was on coastal guard duty out of Harwich." She paused for a moment, wiped away tears.

Mary Jane imagined that Mrs. Hollis, having offered the tale many times while begging, had unknowingly acquired the sound of recitation in her delivery of the words. Also that way of speaking of the events perhaps helped the woman keep her distance from them.

"Lieutenant Charles Weatherhead were invited to dine with the midshipmen," she continued, more at ease. "Frederick Caille, committing fraud against the government, supplied those deadly victuals. When we took the case to court, he bested us, and we all lost everything we had."

They stayed quiet for a time eating, until Mrs. Hollis broke the silence, an embarrassed look on her face. "I have become uncomfortably full, and after you purchased so much."

"Not to worry," Mary Jane said with a smile.

Poor woman, her stomach has shrunk away from lack of good food.

She helped Mrs. Hollis load the remainder of the chops and buttered bread into handkerchiefs and sent her on her way.

Alone, Mary Jane moved south toward the River Thames, eager, yet strangely unwilling to read the letter. Somehow, the communication seemed a message from Jennie—her last—and Mary Jane wasn't certain she wanted to know what it said.

She got the feeling someone followed. Glancing behind her quickly a couple of times, she saw a figure at a distance among the foot traffic, one that aroused her suspicion. Each time she caught sight of him, he seemed to hide, once behind a stack of barrels at the opening to a back lane, and then into a building entrance the next. She had the impression that the ordinary cove wouldn't do anything as undignified as duck out of sight. Remembering Stuart Brevard's previous attack, and his willingness to rattle locked doors and enter buildings in Globe Road, Mary Jane didn't think he would merely stalk her. No, he wanted to get his hands on her.

Could be one of Brevard's hired toughs—not the tall one, though. Wrong shape.

A member of the Gully Bleeders might have been sent to keep an eye on me. Did they discover that she had kept Julia, Maria, and Glory off the streets? That didn't seem to represent a loss of income sufficient to anger them. Might they have somehow caught wind of her efforts at information-gathering? Would they care about that?

Mary Jane realized the stalker could be Barnett. Though she thought he'd be looking for work, he had the free time and clearly wanted to keep her from talking to Fleming.

And that left Joseph Fleming. Thinking briefly that he might be the stalker, she had a desire for him to catch up, but knew better than to wait and find out.

Glancing back, she saw the figure once more, across the street. He ducked out of sight, just as a red haired gentleman, moving swiftly, turned into the street at a crossing directly behind Mary Jane.

Stuart Brevard!

His eyes locked on hers. His straining features showed that he clearly recognized her. He rushed toward Mary Jane, closing the distance between them to a few yards.

Without looking first, she entered the road. A passing carriage clipped her and she spun around, but kept her feet. She dodged her way across, and didn't look back until she'd gained the footway on the other side. Hearing an angry cry, and the complaint of a horse, she turned.

A hansom had stopped, its driver climbing down. Stuart Brevard lay just beyond, his head stove in against the granite kerb. Blood pooled beneath his head quickly.

Mary Jane froze. The man was gone. He would never rise, would never trouble her again. She could see that he was indeed dead.

The Black-eyed man's confident words came back to her, "He is of no consequence." *Did he know Brevard would end this way? Did he have something to do with it?*

As pedestrians gathered around to gawk at the tragedy, Mary Jane stumbled away, her heady feeling of relief a confusion while her heart still pounded and her trembling continued.

At the next crossing, she looked back at the knot of stalled traffic around the calamity, and saw the stalking figure once more.

Mary Jane turned away, took deep breaths to calm her racing heart.

Pure fear and fancy. I have nothing to fear anymore!

No longer must I leave London!

I shall remain in Miller's Court long enough to see that Gabriella Gorse pays. Then, I'll leave Barnett, find lodgings of my own, and improve my situation. Once I have the chink, I might remove to the West End and reestablish myself there.

Within a half an hour, she found herself at the river. She suffered a puzzling melancholy in the midst of elation over the death of her tormentor.

Though she felt that luck had served her, and that Mr. Brevard had got what he deserved, after seeing such a chance death she felt small and fragile within an uncaring world.

The feeling will pass, and my life will get better.

Standing on the east Customs House stairs that led down to the muddy bank, she heard the drone and grumble of the city behind her, across the river, and in the water below. Above, the gray, overcast sky threatened rain. She watched the living water roll unconcerned beneath the bustling activity on the Thames. Ships moved slowly, ponderously through the current, some maneuvering into position for mooring, while smaller boats moved more swiftly around them. Many inactive vessels lined the banks, moored to docks or dolphins.

A wonder they don't jam up the waterway.

A bell drew her gaze to a crane in motion at a dockyard to the east. She watched the machine pluck cargo out of the belly of a steamship. *Like a red kite enjoying a meal,* she thought. A steam-powered signal horn sounded at the construction site of Tower Bridge less than a half mile further downriver. Though they were indeed building and not dismantling, the men and equipment on and around the bridge's black skeleton put Mary Jane in mind of carrion-eaters going after a carcass.

The breeze brought her the unpleasant stench of rotting fish and other river life atop an ever-present, but light odor of night soil. She caught a smell of something burnt, probably a remnant of the docks fire that had occurred the night of Polly Nichols's murder.

Thoughts of death and destruction—I must banish them.

Mary Jane finally pulled the envelope from her bodice, unfolded the letter from within, and read:

> *I know not how to address you because I do not know your true name. Perhaps that is for the best. Although our poor J defended you as a true friend and I only know what she told me, I had misgivings about her involvement with you.*
>
> *I have trouble deciding whether to love you for befriending and helping her or hate you for teaching her the business that killed her. I would like to include you among those I blame for her death, but know that her situation was complicated by her own grief, anger, and pride. I might just as well include myself for being single-minded in pursuing elusive notoriety in a dodgy business of my own, while I should have helped her more than I did.*
>
> *I know from speaking with the woman who delivered this message to you that you seek answers only*

I can provide. Should you have questions about our shared tragedy, she can answer them.

Yes, I hired a man to dispatch the one responsible for our family loss. From the descriptions conveyed to me, it seems that you know him. I was drawn into using him after hearing J's mother, my aunt, request such a resolution on her deathbed. I know almost nothing about him, and suspect that I will never know more.

I do not anticipate consequences from the hire, beyond the torments of my own conscience. Of that, I warn you, should you find yourself considering business with him.

Perhaps we shall meet one day. I remain uncertain how I might feel about that.

All the same, I wish you good fortune,

So much did Mary Jane share the misgivings conveyed in the letter, she could have written the message to herself.

Self pity!

She wiped away her tears.

The message didn't seem like words that might come from a swindler.

Mary Jane realized that she was relieved to find little new information about the ordinary cove. Now that she'd paid him to kill, she had some fear to learn more about him.

Though hard to resist, better not to pick at that scab.

"You have something for me," came his voice from directly behind Mary Jane.

Startled, she let go of the letter. A breeze sent the paper sailing up and northward, past the ordinary cove, who stood three steps above her. To her relief, he made no move to catch it.

She watched the letter go, not wanting to turn and face his black gaze for fear that he might read from her eyes or expression Catherine Weatherhead's message.

An unreasonable fear, yet he might well see that I hide some new knowledge of him.

"Yes," she said following an uncomfortably long silence. Out of the larger pocket Maria Harvey had sewn for her, Mary Jane pulled the pages that she and her girls had assembled concerning the lives and murders of Elizabeth Stride and Catherine Eddowes. The number of pages had grown because of all the increased fear and fancy they had recorded, not just involving the two murders, but all sorts of tales of crimes and oddities from the Whitechapel rumor mill. Increasingly, Mary Jane and her girls could not decide what held a kernel of truth and what was mere chaff.

The black-eyed man had killed at least one murderer: Caille. Perhaps Mary Jane's efforts with her girls would help him kill more of them. She handed the pages over with a glance in his direction, then quickly returned her gaze to the activity on the water.

With that short glimpse of his eyes came the notion that he *had* somehow read Catherine Weatherhead's message before Mary Jane did and that he didn't care what it said. She didn't know why she thought that, and she wasn't going to bring the matter up with him.

"Someone follows you," he said.

"Brevard?" she said without thinking.

The ordinary cove didn't respond.

Not just fear and fancy, then—I did see another man.

Again, she wondered who else might be after her. She didn't think Barnett dangerous. If Fleming stalked, he did so with amorous intentions. That left innumerable members of the Gully Bleeders, including Nick Shears, and possibly unknown persons. Fear began to well up inside her again.

"What can be done to stop him?" Mary Jane asked, hoping he might offer to remedy the problem.

He merely extended his right hand toward her.

She looked at him, concerned that if she took his money, he might not deal with Gabriella Gorse.

"I will deal with the woman," he said.

Oddly, his evident lack of concern calmed her fears somewhat.

He wouldn't bother paying me if he thought my life was in danger, she thought.

Mary Jane held her hand under his and received another gold

sovereign. The Saint George and the Dragon image on the coin's tail flashed dully at her, bringing with it a sense of danger.

"The Whitechapel Murderer...," the black-eyed man said.

Is that the man following? Mary Jane's heart took a rapid turn in her chest. She held her hands out for balance. The air cooled on her exposed flesh.

"...as part of my plan for the woman, Gorse," he said, "he will be on to you."

"No!" Mary Jane cried. Her vision shifted dizzyingly—trying to take in everything at once—and a wave of nausea took her to her knees.

The ordinary cove remained impassive.

"Is he now?" she asked, words barely a whisper.

He didn't answer. Perhaps he did not hear.

"Is he!"

Again, nothing from the man standing above her.

In her horror, Mary Jane dropped the sovereign and folded in the middle. She hugged the stair, the chill granite all the world offered in that moment that felt certain and solid. Her life had come undone and seemed to fly apart with the sound of the golden coin rolling and bouncing against the stone stairs in its increasingly mad dash to the muddy bank below.

I cannot continue!

"Should you want to live...," he began.

She barely heard him for the thoughts churning in her head of the recent murders; what she'd learned of the cruelty of the killer, and the mutilations of the victims.

"...if you don't want to end up like those women..."

Those words came to her clearly, and she listened.

"... you will do as I say and ask no questions. Stay close to home and people you know until I instruct you otherwise. You must go on as if nothing is amiss. I will be watching."

He still needed her for something, but what? She knew he wouldn't answer if she asked.

What had Thomas said on the day Mary Jane discovered him in London? "Misery loves company. Criminals need coconspirators, and they'll get them by hook or by crook. Once you've worked for them, they'll hold it over you or find some other way to make you do it again."

Mary Jane had had a strange confidence in the ordinary cove before. Without something of that again in that moment, she might have thrown herself in the Thames. Finally, she gained the courage to ask him to remove the threat stalking her. She glanced up, only to discover that he had gone.

Mary Jane remained, clutching at the stone stair.

Did he trick me? Did he want me dead all along? Does he have any reason for that?

He'd said he'd deal with Gabriella Gorse, and somehow Mary Jane still believed him. Why fulfill his contract with her if she would soon be dead? He said he'd be watching. Would that be to protect her, or for pleasure in seeing the cruelty that might unfold?

She found no answers to the questions.

The coming of the dark got her moving.

Mary Jane abandoned the gold sovereign. Some lucky mudlark would find the coin.

She had to get home to Miller's Court before nightfall.

CHAPTER TWENTY-THREE

Mary Jane's last conversation with the ordinary cove left her wanting to return to laudanum. Instead, she drank heavily in the following days.

He had said, "As part of my plan for the woman, Gorse, the Whitechapel Murderer will be on to you."

Because the black-eyed man had not responded when she asked if Jack the Ripper were the one following her, Mary Jane tried unsuccessfully to persuade herself that the Whitechapel Murderer was not indeed after her.

I could pack up and run out, catch a train, and start over somewhere else with nothing.

If he wasn't then after me, he may be now. She realized that fleeing the city might give him a chance at her in a place with fewer potential witnesses. *Better remain where I might have the help of those I know.*

She would have spoken of her fears, yet to do so she would have had to speak of the ordinary cove. Considering that, she wondered what might be said that anyone would believe. He seemed a figment, indescribable. She didn't even know his name. Even though her girls had helped her, she'd never told them who had charged her with the task of gathering rumor. They knew nothing about him.

Above all, Mary Jane knew that he would not want her to speak of him. She would do as he'd instructed because, oddly, she feared the black-eyed man more than she did the Whitechapel Murderer.

With her distress and disquiet over the looming threat, Mary Jane took out her frustration on the one who might have protected her. She started drunken rows with Barnett over nothing. She chided him for knocking over and breaking her only wine glass. She could not let go of her outrage over the burn spots in the bedclothes, a consequence of his drinking too much and falling asleep in bed while smoking his pipe. An affront to a woman who "ought to be seen with a handsome man," Mary Jane could not abide the length of his mustache ends not matching. She laughed at him for what she saw as his need to always repeat the last word anyone said.

Repeating *his* last words, she mocked him on and off, until the early evening of October 30, when he'd had enough and gave her a shove. Mary Jane fell back, putting an elbow through a glass pane and cracking another in the smallest of the room's two windows. Her sleeves protected her. She stormed out angrily to have more drink at the Ringers. Worried about the Whitechapel Murderer stalking her, she fairly ran all the way to the pub, a distance of about twenty-five yards.

The next day, Barnett's side of their bed felt cold. He had gone, taking some of his things with him.

Mary Jane never dreamed he'd leave her.

I used and abused him, but he is not the fool I am!

Trying to remember how she'd got home the night before, she found either fancy or hazy recollection of Joseph Fleming coming to her aid. Had he seen her home, tried to pay her for services, and kissed her while standing at her door?

Fancy, she decided. *Wishful thinking! A desire for a protector, though I had one and drove him away!*

The next day, November 1, Barnett came to Miller's court. Upon answering the door to his knock, Mary Jane thought hopefully that he was returning.

"I've come for the rest of my belongings," he said. "I've taken a room at Buller's boarding house." He moved about the tiny room, stuffing clothing and a few items in a sack.

Disappointed, she stood in the doorway, hoping to keep him there. She could not feel good about her motives—she did not want the man himself, just the protection he might provide.

"Please forgive my horrid treatment of you and come back," she said.

"Back" Barnett said. He offered her two shillings. "Please take this. Won big on the dogs for once."

"No," she said, "you'll need the funds."

He approached the door to leave.

"Won't you reconsider and stay?" she asked, still blocking the threshold.

"Reconsider," he said. "I've paid for a week at Buller's. Perhaps when that's done."

That may well be too late.

The look in his eyes suggested he could not be persuaded. Mary Jane stepped aside, and he left.

⚓

For the next few days, Mary Jane remained near home. If out, she stayed close to friends and acquaintances. She kept a wary eye out for her stalker, and wondered when the ordinary cove might come to her with further instructions.

He did not appear on Friday, November 2 to gather the information Mary Jane and her girls had collected. He had what he needed, she supposed.

Barnett visited the room that day, and repeated his offer of shillings. She didn't take them, and he seemed troubled. Again, she asked him to come back to her, and he declined. On the third day of the month, he found her at the Ringers. When she refused his funds again, he turned frightfully insistent, drawing concerned looks from those with her, Madeline Grissette and Sarah Lewis. He appeared so distraught, Mary Jane felt relief once he'd gone.

The next time she saw him, November 4, he acted worse still. She had accompanied Maria Harvey, who was on her way to look at possible new lodgings in New Court, another thin avenue off the north side of Dorset Street accessed by a tight through-passage. Barnett saw them as they emerged from Miller's Court. Maria, perhaps not wanting to further upset him, had continued on toward their goal.

"I don't want you going back on the street," he said, grabbing Mary Jane by the shoulders.

Passing nearby, a man paused to watch with a scowl. Barnett showed him a fist, and the fellow moved on.

"I'm afraid of what might happen to you with that fiend loose," he said, a queer, feverish look in his eyes. "I don't know what I'd be

202

willing to do to stop you. You *take* these shillings!"

"Should you be willing to come back," Mary Jane said, "I would have no need of them."

He did not respond to her statement. The look on his face frightened her. To calm Barnett and quiet his fears, Mary Jane took his money.

Having presumed that the information gathering for the ordinary cove had concluded, she could use the funds to keep from dipping further into her savings.

She watched Barnett walk away.

He wants me safe, and knows he's better off without me. He knows I were merely using him. Still he cares. I don't deserve it.

I did the same to Joseph Fleming, even though I love him. Admitting her feelings for the man to herself in no uncertain terms brought a pang of loss. *He, too, is better off without me.*

Mary Jane caught up with Maria. Her friend decided to take the room they visited when it became ready.

On November 5, Maria, Julia, Glory, and Mary Jane sat together again at the Ringers.

"We are done with our efforts to gather from the rumor mill," she told them.

"Why?" Julia asked.

"The need for the information has passed, and we shan't be paid for more."

From the start, they had all seemed to think it best not to question the source of the income Mary Jane shared. The present, apparently, was no different.

Clever Glory wondered aloud, "Possibly the newspapers would be interested in our work."

Maria and Julia showed interest, and seemed confused by Mary Jane's silence. Still, they let the matter go.

"Will you stay with me until your new lodgings are ready?" Mary Jane asked Maria.

"Yes. The room shan't be ready until Wednesday."

In the overcast afternoon of November 7, Maria Harvey removed to her new lodgings.

Alone in her room following Maria's departure, Mary Jane saw the ordinary cove enter Miller's Court. The mustache he wore had to be theatrical, because he hadn't had time to grow one since last she'd seen him. The spectacles he wore did not have darkened lenses. She decided they were probably theatrical as well, since she'd seen him more without glasses than with them. He carried a paper-wrapped parcel tied with string.

Watching the man through the small window, she began to shake with a fear of having to face him again. Mary Jane had decided that Jack the Ripper fit into the black-eyed man's plans, yet she could not fathom how. While she wanted further instructions to aid her survival, she didn't want to know more about the murder of Gabriella Gorse.

He walked the "L" of the court, looking all about the damp, moldy brick, then came to her door. Mary Jane reigned in her fear, steadied herself, and answered his knock. Without a word, he entered and looked at the room.

She had left the door open so she might have an escape.

Indian Harry, the man who worked for John McCarthy, the landlord, walked by and looked in briefly. Once he'd gone past, the ordinary cove shut the door.

"Regarding the plan for the woman, Gorse," he said, "you shall give me the key to this room."

No! was her answer, but she held her tongue. What a frightening thought, that the black-eyed man would be able to enter her lodgings. Even so, Mary Jane decided to say nothing, and handed over the only key she had. Following that, to use the lock on the door, she'd have to slip an arm through the broken window to reach the mechanism.

"She will have to be christened," he said. "You know the term from thieves' cant."

Mary Jane believed that the expression meant to remove identifying marks from something stolen—an inscription perhaps from a ring or watch, an owner's mark from a firearm, a name stitched into a garment—to reduce the possibility that the item might become a damning piece of evidence.

How does one do that to a human being?

"If you have had a change of heart..." he said.

With a murderer pursuing her that she did not know, Mary Jane found herself afraid to cease her dealings with the one who'd shown a willingness to kill for her.

"No," she answered quickly.

"You will learn little of my plan," he said. "Tomorrow night, you must resume soliciting, be seen to see clients until after midnight. Since your man has left you, no one will be surprised. If you are in the room late at night and do not have a client, keep a candle lit, and make what sound you can to remind others who live in the court that you are here. You shall keep this up until half past one o'clock in the morning. At that time, you must be prepared to vacate your lodgings immediately and quietly, never to return. You will leave London and take a new name. Before leaving, you must put on these clothes. Fold the clothing you've removed and place them on a chair. Take nothing else with you." He handed Mary Jane the paper-wrapped parcel.

If not for the continuing mystery of his plan, she'd have been relieved to hear him speak with such confidence about her escape from London. She remembered him saying while they had stood on the stairs at the river, "Should you want to live, you will do as I say and ask no questions."

Mary Jane closed her mouth, and nodded her head to show she understood.

Exiting her room without another word, he made one more circuit of the court, walking slowly, flipping a coin and catching it several times. The man's black eyes that were truly blue, seemed to look past the tumbling gold disk, another sovereign, as if absorbing all the details of the yard.

She took a deep breath of relief when he left the court.

CHAPTER TWENTY-FOUR

Unable to sleep, Mary Jane spent most of Wednesday night in nearby pubs. Wanting to confuse her trail some, she decided to go to the Blue Coat Boy instead of the Ringers. The entrance to the pub was on Dorset Street, six doors west of the passage to Miller's Court on the same side of the street. She had little fear since she wasn't out in the night for long.

In the pub, she sat with Pearly Poll Conolly and Frederick Simons, and drank watered bitter. That cost little, and provided something to do. Once Pearly Poll, who had been with Martha Tabram the night of her murder, began talking about the killing, Mary Jane excused herself and went to the Ringers. Even with the drink in her, she felt a rising panic on the way to the pub, though the establishment sat even closer to the entrance to Miller's Court than the Blue Coat Boy. Mary Jane decided she ought not to stay out late or there would be few people in the street when she wanted to go home.

Once at the ringers, she sat with Eliza Cooper, Alice Lacroix, and Madeline Grissette. They sang songs, and she had more bitter and a couple quarterns of gin. Mary Jane knew she would not sleep even if she returned to her bed, and stayed much later than intended.

She set out for her room about four o'clock in the morning. The streets were nearly empty. Mary Jane had less than twenty-five yards to walk. Even so, time passed too slowly, giving the Whitechapel Murderer too much opportunity to strike.

Despite the gaslight in the court, she had shadows at her back. Mary Jane could barely quiet her trembling enough to slip her hand through the broken window and unlock the door. In the room, she got in bed with her clothing on in case she had to get up and flee into the night to get away from an intruder.

As she'd feared, Mary Jane failed to find sleep. She became lost in dreadful thoughts, running over possibly unanswerable questions. She wondered what would happen to Gabriella Gorse at the hands of the black-eyed man. He'd asked for the key to the room while talking about Gorse, so Mary Jane supposed he would somehow bring her there.

Did his plans for Gabby have anything to do with the Whitechapel Murderer?

Why would the ordinary cove take it upon himself to find out who were Jack the Ripper?

Having made that determination did not mean the killer would be easy to find or catch.

Cokum—he's too wary and clever to be caught easily.

Yet the black-eyed man has his own cokum.

Is he *the Whitechapel Murderer?* Considering what she knew of the killings on the street, she discounted the notion. *He does not show his work proudly, and he might have killed me anytime.*

Mary Jane's thoughts shifted to examining what she knew about the ordinary cove, a frustrating exercise at first.

I know next to nothing about him. I suspect he's in the business of killing, an assassin of sorts. I know he has killed at least once.

Thinking back over her experiences with the man, a few of his traits occurred to her. He was exacting in a strangely compelling way, and seemed always in control. His ability to find her, as he'd done, and his awareness and knowledge of Stuart Brevard and his toughs—how did he acquire such information? Did he have other teams of information gatherers, like Mary Jane and her girls, or did he have access to police files?

That would explain a lot, but certainly his manner held something of the uncanny. Thinking of Catherine Weatherhead's business as a spiritualist, Mary Jane couldn't help wondering if the woman had allies that were more than human. From which side of the veil did the black-eyed man hail? Was he indeed an agent of the supernatural?

The intelligent command of situation and circumstance that he demonstrated appeared to be otherworldly, yet that didn't make it so.

No, he's too much of the grit and grime of the cruel world I know. He belongs *here.*

Cokum, he has. The ordinary cove has uncanny cokum, that's all.

He wanted her to make a show of herself Thursday night. He wanted her soliciting to be obvious to those living in the court as well as her presence in her room in the late hours.

To what purpose? Is he trying to lure Jack the Ripper here? Am I his bait?

Does he have a deal with someone to kill the Whitechapel Murderer? If so, what does Gabby have to do with that?

What if Barnett had not left her? When did the black-eyed man come up with the plan?

Mary Jane got the strange notion that he had given her a role in a drama, one that he deftly directed without having given the full script to any of the actors. Had he told her that Jack the Ripper would be after her so that, in her distress, she'd drive Barnett away? Was he that good at reading character?

Again, no answers presented themselves.

Her thoughts fixed on Gabriella Gorse.

My killing. Though he will commit the act, I shall own it.

With no ability to control her fancy, she had little success turning away from countless visions of the woman being strangled, knifed, bludgeoned to death.

My killing, she thought again, but instead of her thoughts of owning the act, Mary Jane found herself wondering if the Whitechapel Murderer would catch up to her before half past one o'clock Friday morning, or even as she tried to make her escape at the appointed time.

So listless that she had insufficient will to rise, and still vulnerable to unwanted fancy, thoughts about the promised killing intertwined with the one she imagined happening to her. She *was* Gorse. The terrible visions commenced again, a jumble in which she and Gabby, combined, endured innumerable, horrifying deaths.

When she began to feel a kinship with the woman in their shared suffering, she could stand the visions no longer. She rolled to the edge of the bed and allowed herself to fall to the floor. A jolt of pain from her left knee striking the hard wood brought her to full wakeful awareness of herself within her room.

Mary Jane stood awkwardly and backed away toward the larger window. Daylight had come at last.

The half-light coming through the closed gray curtains illuminated her bed in a manner she found disturbing, though she could not have said why. She didn't want to look at the dilapidated piece of furniture, yet couldn't quite turn away. Something about the sweat-stained, rumpled linens on the lumpy mattress, the scarred wood of the frame, and the crooked headboard, gave her an unaccountable dread that if she ever used the bed again, her greatest agony would find her.

The ordinary cove had given her too little to do and she was going mad!

A knocking came from her door.

Mary Jane cautiously approached. "Who's there?" she asked.

"'Tis Maria, what's brought you breakfast."

Mary Jane opened the door immediately, relieved to have a smiling ally on her doorstep. She hid away her fears. "Come in."

"I brought stirabout for us to share." Holding a pot wrapped in a towel, along with a couple of mugs, Maria entered and set it all on the table by the large window. She opened the curtains.

Mary Jane shut the door.

Maria glanced around the room, her nose wrinkling. "Odd smell. Shall we air out your room a bit?" She stepped over and opened the door.

Mary Jane moved to close it.

Before she succeeded, Julia Veneteney walked past, glancing in. "Good morning," she said.

"Join us for breakfast," Mary Jane called out.

"Thank you, but I'm expected—" Entering the passage, apparently in a hurry, her words grew unintelligible.

Maria had cleared a spot on the table by the window, and spooned some of the milky corn from the pot into the mugs. She pulled another spoon from her pocket, handed that and one of the cups to Mary Jane, and sat.

"Thank you."

They ate in silence for a time.

"Are you out most of the day?" Maria asked.

"No, I'll be staying in."

"Shall I bring my mending to work on in your room this afternoon?"

"Yes, yes," Mary Jane said. "I'll help. I'd like that very much, indeed!"

Maria chuckled. "Look at your grin. I have never seen such eagerness for dull toil."

Mary Jane's smile wilted as her friend took up the remains of their meal and left.

∼❦∼

Mary Jane hoped that the mending work would distract her from her worst thoughts. Maria arrived with a bundle of clothing from White's laundry in need of repair: shirts, a black overcoat, a black bonnet, and a girl's white petticoat.

They talked for a time, her friend rattling on, but Mary Jane found herself slipping into silence. The work took too little concentration, and her dark mood returned. She could not escape the feeling that leaving her room, her life, in the middle of the coming night, taking nothing with her, represented death of a sort. With the sense that despite whatever the ordinary cove had planned, doom awaited her at the hands of a murderer, she had difficulty looking forward to anything. Mary Jane had an urgent desire to put her affairs in order before the end.

Time gets away from me, while much is left undone.

Even with the desire, she had to wonder what there was to do? The ship of her life had no crew and no anchor as the vessel entered dangerous waters. She had no heirs and nothing of worth to pass on. No one who loved her would remain, save perhaps the Morganstones, and they didn't truly know her and what she'd become. Fleming might suffer for a short time, then move on with his life. Surely, she would be forgotten.

"No!" she said aloud in an effort to banish self pity, and accidentally poked herself with the needle she used.

"Don't stain your work," Maria said.

Mary Jane set the petticoat aside. She watched a small red droplet form before wiping the blood away.

Again, she thought of catching a train, and starting over somewhere else with nothing.

No, my heart would not let me live with that. For Jennie and the countless other women Gabby betrays, I must stay and play my part to make certain she pays.

"Thank you for your help," Maria said when they'd finished their work.

Mary Jane lit a candle and drew the curtains closed over the large window after her friend left.

The dark came too early.

Barnett arrived with fried fish and potatoes. He placed the food on the table and sat. Wanting to take the other seat, Mary Jane noticed that Maria had left the clothes they had mended on the chair, all except for the coat which she'd also forgot after hanging the garment on the frame of the small window.

Mary Jane set the clothing on the chair aside and she and Barnett ate in silence, sitting at the table before the large window.

Lizzie Albrook knocked upon the door, and came in.

"Good evening, Lizzie," Barnett said. "You been a good girl?"

"Why, yes."

Mary Jane gave him a look. She'd confided in him that the young woman had asked her advice about solicitation.

Lizzie also lived in Miller's Court. She was a slavey at Crossingham's Common Lodging, four doors west of the passage to the court. A flaxen-haired saucebox, all of twenty years old, she'd treated Mary Jane with undue deference since they'd met over a year earlier, and had asked numerous questions about soliciting. Lizzie would have been a delight if not for her adoring fascination for Mary Jane. She found herself unsettled to see in the girl so much of what she'd been at eighteen in Cardiff: naive, yet hard-bitten and willing to risk for a little adventure.

Working as a maid of all work at a common lodging house,

Lizzie would be accustomed to long hours of exhausting, at times disgusting, even degrading toil. The work would wear her down over time, expose her to vermin and disease.

At first, she'd no doubt felt lucky to find the position at Crossingham's. No secret that stable employment in London had become a rare beast, especially in the East End. While true enough for men, that was ever more so for women. Most jobs offered back-breaking day labor of little variety that could not be done for long without harm to one part of the body or another, depending on the task. If Lizzie didn't know that from watching members of her own family go through the experience, then she'd seen the effect in the lives of others.

With the notion of soliciting, just like Mary Jane had done when young, Lizzie probably saw past the unpleasant task of sex with a stranger to the coin at the end. Knowing she'd start out at the rate of a casual or little better, she possibly saw beyond the low pay to a time in which she might gain a reputation that brought her more.

Seeing her take a seat on the edge of the bed gave Mary Jane more of the foreboding she'd felt earlier, but she said nothing.

"I seen a possible earlier today," Lizzie said brightly. She had an excited look about her that Mary Jane didn't like to see.

In the past, when they had talked about soliciting, Mary Jane had done her best to discourage her. She had told Lizzie that if she must engage in the practice, to always walk her possible clients through the Ringers so the other ladybirds might provide warnings about the bad ones. Mary Jane had introduced her around.

"He made eyes at me at the crossing with Commercial Street. I says, 'Take a drink with me at the Ringers.' He must have had a change of heart, 'cause he walked on. But he almost decided in my favor."

In that time and place, the young woman's hope broke Mary Jane's heart.

"Favor," Barnett said, turning to her and frowning. "You're teaching the young ones how it's done, are you? While I'm trying to keep *you* off the streets, and there's a madman loose?"

"No, I would not have her start," Mary Jane said, "yet

circumstance may put her there whatever I say. She has a desire, and should she follow it, I want her prepared."

"Prepared," he said. "She's just a girl, what ought to find a beau to buy her a tussie mussie. You needn't talk to her about the streets at all, unless to frighten her notions away telling the dangers." He threw his hands in the air in disgust. "*Jack the Ripper!*"

"I know," Lizzie said, "I'm not a *child*."

Barnett looked down, shook his head, mumbled "Child."

"Yes," Mary Jane said, "the murderer is out there…hunting up casuals…cutting their throats, and, well…*worse*." She said the words slowly, hoping they might lodge uncomfortably in Lizzie's mind.

"Odds of meeting him are slim," the young woman said. She acted brave because she needed to persuade herself as much as anyone else. That backbone would serve her well, if it didn't get her killed. She had little else in life.

Mary Jane shuddered, thinking of Lizzie alone on the street at night.

"Barmy girl is what you are," Barnett said. "You don't know what you're about."

Lizzie hung her head.

"Don't pretend you know what it's like," Mary Jane told Barnett, turning a fierce gaze on him. "You don't know much about the choices women have to make."

He did not look her in the eye. He grumbled, huffed, and said no more.

She knew plenty of women willing to take the risk, and so did Lizzie. If the madness of the East End, the ceaseless talk of the Whitechapel Murderer hadn't changed her mind, Mary Jane would not succeed in dissuading her with fears.

She gripped the edge of the table to steady her shaking hands. A tear of frustration rose to her eye. She wiped it away before they saw, turned to Lizzie. "You don't want to turn out as I did. I am a poor, wretched creature by my own estimation. *I have nothing.*"

"Nothing," Barnett said. He gave Mary Jane a look that said he'd found insult in her words. He gathered the remains of their meal, made his goodbyes, and left. When he had gone, Mary Jane discovered two shillings he'd left on the table. Despite her poor treatment of him, he would still provide what he could for her.

He deserves much better than he got from me.

Lizzie smiled sadly. "I *shall* take care."

"*Please* do," Mary Jane said, holding down a rising anger. Her ire was not for Lizzie. Mary Jane was disgusted with herself, and angry about the state of affairs in London's East End, an order of things that left many women, young and old, with so few expectations that prostitution became appealing.

Again, she thought of Barnett's generosity. *What did he expect, taking up with a whore?*

Perhaps sensing the older woman's mood, Lizzie grew uncomfortable, and soon made her goodbyes. Once she'd gone, Mary Jane's anger faded and the dread returned.

Weary from too little sleep and considering a nap, she looked at the bed.

Don't you ever get in that bed again! she told herself. Once more, she could not have said why.

Instead, Mary Jane did as she hoped the younger woman would not do, and went out to find a client, all the while knowing full well that Jack the Ripper was indeed after her.

CHAPTER TWENTY-FIVE

Remembering that the only candle in her room was reduced to a short nub, Mary Jane stopped at McCarthy's Chandler shop and bought a new one from Indian Harry. Leaving the shop, she walked East on Dorset Street to Commercial Street, then north to the crossing with Fournier Street, to spend time out front of the Ten Bells pub. The lighted clock on Christ Church said five minutes past nine o'clock. Rain had come and gone, leaving a dampness in the cold night air. Feeling fairly safe, standing near the entrance to the busy pub with people coming and going, she bundled into her plum-colored woolen shawl to keep warm, and looked for a client.

Mary Jane tried something ladybirds had taken up in recent days; asking for the loan of a tanner as a way to indicate the price they were willing to take. The scheme had its problems. Should a man misunderstand the true message, and offered a tanner, one had to decide whether to keep the money, or give it back right away. If kept...well, the dangers in that were easily imagined.

Deciding that she could always drop her price, Mary Jane asked for a shilling.

The rain came on again. She gave up and went into the Ten Bells for a glass of bitter. She sat with Elizabeth Foster, a friendly face from the neighborhood.

"Any luck?" The woman asked.

"Can't say I deserve any," Mary Jane said, shivering.

"Let me get you a whiskey," Elizabeth said. "Irish?"

"Yes, thank you."

Miss Foster had the same. When they'd finished, Mary Jane bought another round. Others joined them; Louisa McGregor, Maggy Evans, and Faye Holmsford. Along with more drinks, they had songs together. Then Mary Jane found herself singing for her companions. The song "Myfanwy," by Joseph Parry, with lyrics by the

Welsh poet, Richard Davies, told of the sadness of a man confused that his beloved, Myfanwy, had lost her feelings for him. The lyrics asked, "Where has your love for me gone? Why do you give me dark looks? What have I done?" The song concluded with the message, "I only wish you well."

Though they no doubt did not understand the Welsh lyrics, they praised Mary Jane's singing.

She became subdued, thinking of how she'd treated Joseph Fleming. He might just as well have written the beautiful, sad song about her.

Remembering that she ought to be soliciting, she excused herself, and decided to leave the pub altogether during a lull in the rain. She walked south, used the urinal beside the churchyard, then looked up at the clock on Christ Church again. Ten till eleven o'clock, it said.

Mary Jane felt safer than she had the previous night. A moment passed before she understood the reason: She was doing what the ordinary cove had told her to do, and, though she did not see him, she believed he watched her.

Mary Jane crossed Commercial Street, and entered the Ringers. After fetching a glass of bitter, she looked for a place to sit. She shied away from the few people she recognized, and felt lucky to find a small table against the eastern wall vacated by a couple headed for the exit.

The damp air, much warmer inside the establishment, brought out the worst smells of the place, even with the heavy tobacco smoke. Sodden with wet foot traffic, the saw dust on the floor gave off odors of mold and mildew. As always, the furnishings reeked of whatever food and drink wasn't entirely cleaned off of them, and from contact with countless human beings, their often unwashed clothing, and bodily fluids. A long brown spatter on the floor nearby suggested that an American was present in the pub or had been recently. Matilda Ringer kept spittoons beneath the bar for the Americans and the few locals with the disgusting habit, but they frequently went unused.

The odors got in Mary Jane's head and moved her gut uncomfortably.

I shall not miss Dorset Street, she thought, drawing a hand over her surprisingly moist face, and hoping she would not lose her fish and potatoes. *Indeed, I shan't miss the whole of London's filthy East End.* The thought, while not entirely true, told her that she had reconciled herself with the black-eyed man's plan for her departure in the early morning hours. *What choice do I have?*

Removing her hand from her face, she found Joseph Fleming standing across the table from her. He'd grown a mustache, and dressed in a manner perhaps meant to impress her.

Mary Jane stood to leave. She could not abide her feelings for the man.

"Please, talk to me, Mary Jane," he said, his earnest expression clearly meant to appeal to her.

She got up, made her way between the tables and patrons, and left the Ringers.

Fleming followed her outside, caught up and said quietly, "I'll be at the Horn of Plenty." He walked away toward the west along Dorset Street. The pub he mentioned stood at the other end of the short lane.

At least she'd know how to avoid him.

Mary Jane returned to the Ringers and resumed her search for a client.

The glowing clock on Christ Church read half past eleven as Mary Jane stepped out of the Ringers having landed a client, something of a whale. She'd become drunk in an effort to suppress thoughts of what would happen to Gabriella Gorse that evening. Despite her intoxication, pride would not allow her to take less than a shilling, and that left her with few choices. Finally she'd settled for the heavy man of thirty years and more. He wore a long, ratty top coat and a billycock. His round red face held ginger side whiskers, a mustache, and numerous blebs. He'd been too drunk to care about her price. She'd made him show that he had the coin before they left the pub.

Neither of them walked with any confidence. Hanging onto her as they both staggered along, he spilled splashes of bitter from the pail he'd taken away from the pub. They made their way west on Dorset and into Miller's Court. He wanted to stop in the darkness of the passage and kiss her, but she would have none of that until he paid.

At the door of Mary Jane's lodgings, Mary Ann Cox surprised her, coming through the corridor and pushing past. "Goodnight," she said.

"Goodnight to you, Mary Ann," Mary Jane said, banging awkwardly into her door. Her hand searched the pocket under her top skirt. She couldn't find her key.

Ah...gave it to the ordinary cove.

She remembered that he wanted her to make noise—at least, that was how her drunken mind remembered his instructions.

"I'm going to sing," she called out to Mary Ann, who had reached her door, the last on the left, in the darkest corner of the court.

Ah, the window.

Mary Jane began to sing "A Violet from Mothers Grave."

Her client turned away to urinate on the wall of the passage.

Mary Jane moved around the corner to the small window, reached carefully through the hole in the glass. She pushed aside a sleeve of the coat Maria had left hanging like a curtain, and unlocked the door. She was glad her client had been occupied with his toilet so he didn't see her method of opening the door.

She got him inside, and left the door open. "Sit on the bed, sir," Mary Jane said.

He sat, then lay back.

By the light of the gas lamp on the wall of the court outside, she pulled out the candle she'd bought, and lit it. Mary Jane shut the door, and set the candle in the wine glass Barnett had broken. Turning to the man in her bed, she found him asleep and snoring.

Good.

Mary Jane took the near-empty pail from his right hand and set the container on the floor. She sat in a chair and resumed her singing:

> Scenes of my childhood arise before my gaze,
> Bringing recollections of bygone happy days,
> When down in the meadow in childhood I would
> roam;

No one's left to cheer me now within that good
old home.
Father and mother they have passed away.
Sister and brother now lay beneath the clay;
But while life does remain, to cheer me I'll retain
This small violet I plucked from mother's grave

Only a violet I plucked when but a boy,
And oft' times when I'm sad at heart, this flow'r
has given me joy,
But while life does remain, in memoriam I'll retain
This small violet I plucked from mother's grave.

Well I remember my dear old mother's smile,
As she used to greet me when I returned from toil;
Always knitting in the old arm chair,
Father used to sit and read for all us children there.
But now all is silent around the good old home,
They all have left me in sorrow here to roam;
But while life does remain, in memoriam I'll retain
This small violet I plucked from mother's grave.

Mary Jane heard the church bells ring midnight. An hour and
a half would have to pass before the time of her departure. Having
had little sleep, she struggled to stay awake.

Mary Jane hoped the man in her bed didn't wake up until close
to half past one o'clock, and that when he did she'd be able to get
him out in time and quietly.

She sang the song twice, sang other songs, then "A Violet from
Mothers Grave" once again. With the song, she wept for Mum, for
Jennie, for Lizzie Albrook, for herself, and Gabby too. After all, the
woman had once taken a beating meant for Mary Jane.

With time, she rose and undressed, folding her clothing
neatly and setting them on a chair. She placed her boots before
the fireplace. She gathered the clothes Maria had left behind and
set them beside her boots. Reaching under the bed to retrieve the

package of clothes the ordinary cove had given her, she disturbed her client's sleep. He awoke with a start. Mary Jane backed away, still naked.

"I'd just got you dressed, sir," she said, thinking on the fly. "I didn't mean to wake you. You were so weary after your proud performance."

He blinked, mumbled a few words, and finally said, "I did?"

How well he possessed his own mind and memory in that moment, she did not know. Mary Jane could only hope he wouldn't see through her flam.

"I have rarely got a wapping like that." She took a few light, dancing steps. "Such a pleasant, *long* swyve. And at the end…oh, what a great flood of bliss." She giggled, as with delight. "Took some time to clean up your warm gush, it did." Mary Jane gestured to her naked madge.

He smiled with a look of pride, despite his drunken state.

She unwrapped the package and dressed.

He remained seated, gathering himself together.

The clothing would not stand out; gray skirt, petticoat, pale-blue chemise, black stockings, black boots, a gray woolen shawl, and a black felt hat.

The bed groaned as he rocked unsteadily, and she feared the crooked head board would release the side rails and the whole kife would come crashing down on the wash tub stored beneath.

"Now, I must go out to attend a sick niece," Mary Jane said. She picked up the pail, handed it to him, and gestured toward the door. "If you'd be so kind…"

She held the way open for him. He got up and stumbled out of the room, then paused and turned to her.

"Your pay," he said with concern.

"You paid when we arrived," she said.

Hoping he would not make much noise, Mary Jane watched him move away through the passage, searching his pockets. She worried that he counted his money, would remember at last, and come back for what they'd bargained.

A great relief came once he'd turned east into Dorset Street, and she no longer saw him. She shut the door.

In an overwrought state, Mary Jane sat in the empty chair, her breath coming in short, shallow gasps.

She heard the chime for the one o'clock hour. Knowing she must wait longer still, she sang again.

CHAPTER TWENTY-SIX

"Quietly," he'd said. Mary Jane thought of that as she stumbled in the passage and nearly fell on the way out to Dorset Street. The black-eyed man told her to leave with nothing but the clothing she wore. She didn't believe he'd meant that she should take no push. Mary Jane had several pounds worth in her pocket. She'd padded the coins so they would not jingle.

Her drunkenness had gone. She decided to make her way to Aldgate High Street and find a cab. Cabmen waited there near Goulston Street during the early morning hours for two reasons: People getting off the rail lines in the area looked for cabs, and there were public urinals on an island in the road. She would go to Stepney and knock on Thomas Morganstone's door. Thomas would allow her to stay while she made plans to leave London.

Mary Jane stepped into Dorset Street suspecting that Jack the Ripper had somehow been lured to the area by her efforts that night.

Can he see me now? Is the ordinary cove still watching?

No, I cannot think of those things. She had to put trust in a plan she knew little about.

He had left the route of her escape to Mary Jane. She put one foot in front of the other, moving east. Although west on Dorset Street would have been the fastest route, Joseph Fleming said he'd be at the Horn of Plenty, and she wanted to avoid him.

Moving south on Commercial Street, Mary Jane kept a wary eye out, assessing the potential danger of each person she encountered. She turned west into White's Row.

Many of the people up and walking the footways at that hour had far to go to get to a work shift that began near dawn. Mary Jane noted fewer sleepy-eyed ones than usual, especially among the women, no doubt a response to the news of the murderer loose in the streets.

At the western end of White's Row, she turned southward into Bell Lane, which would become Goulston after it crossed Wentworth Street. Once that happened, she told herself, she might run the rest of the way to escape an assailant. A murderer would not want to draw attention to himself in Aldgate High Street.

She increased her pace, knowing that she truly could not outrun most people.

A glance behind revealed the silhouette of a man following. His pace showed no urgency. Still, unlike most others using the footway, he carried nothing. Those on their way to work often carried a meal, or items necessary for their labor.

Mary Jane increased her pace again, glancing back to gauge the response, if any, from the silhouette.

The figure had picked up speed!

Mary Jane wanted to call out, drawing attention to herself, and her possible assailant, yet didn't want to feel foolish if the fellow was merely in a hurry to make a rail connection.

She considered moving west into the passage to Cox's Square. Then she might continue south on Short Street. The darkness of the passage discouraged her.

A glance behind showed the figure having closed some of the distance between them.

Her breath caught in her throat. The light drizzle of rain blurred her vision for a moment, and Mary Jane felt a rising panic. She quickly turned west into Montague Street, and immediately regretted the decision because the much thinner lane had fewer gaslights and much less foot traffic.

She heard rapid foot steps behind her.

Mary Jane ducked into the recessed entrance of a tenement.

Ready to scream, she held her breath as the footstep drew nearer.

"Mary Jane," came a familiar voice.

She exhaled and gasped for a breath, feeling lightheaded, her heart pounding in her chest.

Joseph Fleming came into view. Mary Jane leaned back against the brick wall behind her, held her head in her hands. "You frightened me nearly to death!" she croaked.

"My apologies," he said, approaching slowly. "You needn't be out in the night alone."

"That is my business," she said, realizing that she meant that in two ways.

His resigned look and the nod of his head said he understood both meanings.

"A mutual acquaintance told me to keep an eye on you."

"Who would that be?"

"I can't say."

The black-eyed man! Joseph worked for him in Deptford. Just because he said he didn't know about the killing of Caille, doesn't mean that's true. The assassin is using me as bait for Jack the Ripper, and Fleming is involved!

If he has Joseph watching me, are the ordinary cove's black eyes focused elsewhere?

Mary Jane pushed past Joseph and moved toward Goulston. He followed her into the street.

"Please, Mary Jane," he said. "What have I done to get such black-eyed looks?"

"I'm not your Myfanwy!"

"I don't understand."

She hurried on toward Aldgate High Street.

Fleming followed without further conversation.

Mary Jane felt safer with him at her back, despite not wanting him around. He'd be useful right up until the moment she climbed into a cab.

She could see the gaslights of Aldgate High Street ahead, and with the sight came renewed hope of escape. Mary Jane sprinted forward through the increasing rain, noting oddly that the boots the ordinary cove had given her fit perfectly. The pair she'd left in the room had a cracked sole that became a nuisance in rainy weather. So far, the ones on her feet had let in no water.

Approaching her goal, she looked back and saw that Fleming still followed.

Reaching Aldgate Station East, where Goulston Street ended, she was tempted to enter one of a couple of pubs attached to the station and have a drink. Seeing a hansom standing idle at the corner, the driver huddled into a pile of blankets with his hat pulled down low, she forgot about the drink. She ran toward the carriage, fearing someone else might call out first. She had no need to signal the driver. The cabby's head lifted and he moved the hansom forward to anticipate her arrival.

"The Stepney Gasworks," she said, stepping up into the carriage. Avoiding the reins, she turned and sat.

Joseph Fleming, closer than she'd expected, lifted himself on the driver's step-up to talk to the man. She could not hear what he said.

"Drive," Mary Jane said. She knocked on the trap door to offer her money. Ignored, she had decided to get out and find another cab when Fleming pushed in with her. The driver shut the doors and she felt trapped.

As the cab pulled into the road, Mary Jane opened her mouth to cry out in complaint. Joseph clapped his right hand over her mouth, while his left hand gripped the back of her neck. She struggled and he wrestled with her, shoving her down in the seat and wrapping his left arm all the way around her neck, the elbow beneath her chin. She wanted to tell him she'd give in, but she couldn't get her words past his hand. She felt his hot breath on her right ear. Though she could still breathe through her nose, Mary Jane grew lightheaded.

He *is the Ripper!*

Darkness crept into her vision, and took away thought.

Mary Jane awoke lying in a bed. She saw Joseph sitting in a chair to her left in the darkness.

Alarmed to find him so close, confused to see him inactive with eyes drooping, she noted that he didn't seem to be looking at her. Perhaps he was half-asleep.

She looked for the way out of the tiny room. The chamber appeared no more than eight feet square. A door stood closed to her left. A small coal grate occupied the same wall. Little light from the night without came through the sooty pane of the room's single window. Through the glass, she saw the back sides of a couple of brick buildings, and smoke rising lazily from chimney pots.

Joseph must have seen her glancing about. "My room in Brick Lane."

Mary Jane realized that he must have been in Spitalfields for some time if he had lodgings.

He rubbed his forehead, peered down at her in a curious way. "I beg your forgiveness. I didn't want to frighten you. You were drawing attention to yourself while I was trying to get you out of London."

And the horror of her flight to Aldgate High Street, the assault in the cab, fearing that death had found her, all came back in a rush. She struggled to maintain an appearance of calm.

The fact that her stalker had been someone she knew and he'd not actually murdered her had meant nothing. She had feared for her life in a manner she would wish on no one, yet Gabby would suffer something quite like it, and much worse. Mary Jane gasped with the realization.

I called for that.

Swinging her legs off the bed, she sat up slowly, not wanting to alarm Joseph again. Her boots, hat, and shawl had been removed. Otherwise, she remained clothed.

Mary Jane saw a poker jutting out of a bucket of coal by the grate.

A weapon.

"Should people see you after they learn of the one in your room," he said, "you might be charged with a crime." Joseph got up and stood by the window, looking out at the brickwork and the dirty sky above.

He means Gabby. Has she been killed or is that yet to come?

"You're *helping* him," she said in accusation.

She made little sound getting to her feet.

"Thomas too," he said.

No, not Thomas.

"We didn't have any choice. I don't know his name, but I know he's a dangerous man."

Yes, Mary Jane thought, *the black-eyed man is a criminal who shall kill us all in the end.*

"He knows something of our past crimes," Joseph said, "and

though a freelance assassin, he's working under a police commission. I know little of the particulars."

She made for the poker, slowly, hoping he would not hear. The floor boards squeaked, and she froze, holding her breath.

He turned toward her briefly.

As if struggling to awaken, she kept her head down, pretended to busy herself arranging her hair.

"The cove told me what to do," he said, his voice sad and weary. He turned back to the view outside. "For now, he's guv'nor,"

Perhaps Joseph believed that the feelings she had for him left her harmless.

"You'll stay here today, and we'll leave after dark."

Imagining Joseph hearing the rasping sound of iron against coal, and turning quickly, Mary Jane knew she'd have to anticipate his movement and be swift. She pulled the poker from the bucket and immediately made a back-handed swing for his head, struck him above his right ear as he turned.

Joseph toppled to the floor.

She examined him, felt his head. Finding wetness, but no deep hole, she was thankful the hook at the end of the tool had faced away from him. He appeared to be out cold.

Mary Jane discovered her boots under the bed, her hat and shawl on a chair, and donned them. She felt for her pocket and the money within, reassuring herself that her funds hadn't been taken.

The door opened easily. She slipped out and exited the building. The cold bit into Mary Jane's face and hands, while the clothing the ordinary cove had provided kept her body warm.

To determine her location, she fled along Brick Lane toward the closest crossing.

Where shall I go?

I can't go to Thomas—he's working for the black-eyed man.

To Liverpool Street Station, and away by rail—anywhere!

Mary Jane's black thoughts, like the murmuring motion of a flock of starlings in flight, flew this way and that, broke off at odd tangents, trying to avoid a firm, frightening center wherein the happenings at 13 Miller's Court might be imagined. She did not want to think about Gabriella Gorse, yet thoughts of her continued—what *had* happened, or what might *be* happening, even then, to the woman.

Her feet carried her forward while she remained lost in thought. In her mind's eye, she and Gabby had merged as one. Mary Jane had the unwanted feeling that she would suffer whatever her nemesis suffered. Their experience in life having been so similar, one might stand in for the other easily. Hadn't Gabby once suffered a beating meant for Mary Jane?

She may not know that the Gully Bleeders murdered Jennie.

Gabby's crime against Jennie truly amounted to the extortion of one tanner per week.

I have discovered as much and more lying on the pavement several times, dropped by careless pedestrians.

No one could have known that Jennie would so enrage Nick Shear that he'd have her killed. She'd cut his face!

I should have given his name to the black-eyed man instead.

Gabby is no more wicked than many I've known, and some that I've loved.

No telling what sort of criminal I'd had in Joseph Fleming. No matter what he'd told me, he were involved with a murderer.

He strangled *me!*

Had he indeed wanted to kill her? Had he resisted the urge all those nights when she lived and slept with him?

Damn my feelings for him!

People walking by on the footway stared after her.

I must have a hysterical look.

Carter Street—have to keep going.

No, that's the Black Eagle Brewery on the left. I have to turn back, move south.

Mary Jane turned around and hurried forward in the good boots, past Pelham and Hanbury Streets.

I must avoid Dorset, take Fournier and Brushfield.

Jennie were courageous, much braver than I.

If she had not taken the risk of swinging a laundry sack at Stuart Brevard, what might have become of me?

I'd be maimed or dead.

Impatient to move westward, she took a turn into Princelet Street.

I don't know the time!

Has Gabby met her death yet, or is there still a chance to save her?

Left into Wilkes Street.

No! I mustn't think of it.

Oh, give me a church bell to tell me the time!

To what end? Just *get to the railway station.*

Intent on merely passing through her old neighborhood, Mary Jane remained fearful of being seen by the black-eyed man or Jack the Ripper. She looked for a weapon as she moved.

A right into Fournier Street.

The lighted clock on Christ Church ahead and to her left said ten till four o'clock in the morning.

Hours had passed since Mary Jane left her room in Miller's Court.

Gabby must be dead by now.

Or she lingers as Jennie did, suffering, hoping help will come.

She thought of Daphne Michaels. The woman had found and taken Mary Jane to the infirmary after the man attacked her in Cardiff.

Without that aid, I might have died.

Though she hated Gabby, Mary Jane had nothing but regret for employing the ordinary cove.

Reaching the crossing at Commercial Street, she saw a broken wheel spoke in the gutter by the kerb. Mary Jane paused briefly to pick up the hard oak shaft. One end had splintered off sharp. She tucked that end under the waistband of her top skirt.

Hopping over the spreads of rutted "mud," she hurried across the street through slow, light traffic, and found herself turning toward Dorset Street.

She stopped, holding her head in her hands.

Something in me wants to go back to Miller's Court!

She didn't know when after half-past one o'clock in the morning the black-eyed man had intended to implement his plan.

Should I try to help Gabby, I could be killed.

I did not try to help Bell when Stuart Brevard attacked her. She were lucky a bystander did help or she might be dead now. The shame of that had kept her from visiting Bell in the infirmary, and had troubled her since.

Mary Jane found herself walking again, past the Ringers and turning right into Dorset. Few people on the street.

Despite knowing the time, she still did not know if she would be too late to help or too early and hurrying into danger.

Gabby caused so much suffering.

Yet I am not blameless.

Imagining Jennie's pain and fear, tears rose up, and Mary Jane stumbled half-blinded until she wiped them away.

I put her on the streets.

Still, should I suffer for that?

I hurry to my doom!

Why can't I stop myself?

Her steps faltered.

Because I cannot live with myself if I do not try.

What would have become of me if Jennie hadn't had the courage to swing that laundry sack?

Luck had been with me then, as it had been when I fended off Harris Brevard's attack.

Luck will be with me again.

Should I be careful in Miller's Court, no one shall know I'm there.

Reaching through the window, I could let myself in silently. If there is danger, I might still take the advantage, like I did with Joseph.

Mary Jane picked up speed.

Fear of darkness stopped her again—she stood before the passage to Miller's Court and her room.

Mary Jane heard a scuffling of feet coming through the passage. Unwilling to be seen by those who might be within, her view of the part of court illuminated by the gas lamp remained obscured. Fancy told her that someone had stumbled on the way to the privy, or that a murderer had positioned himself out of sight, preparing to surprise her.

While the sound further stoked her fear, she looked for reasons to prop up her courage, thought of the day her mother had drowned and died. Mary Jane had allowed the treed thicket to stop her on that day, to keep her from hurrying downstream to help Mum. She'd retreated, looking for help, and yet later passed through the thicket successfully. Too late!

If I'd had the courage to push through the difficult patch quickly, I might have saved Mum.

Fear shall not stand in my way now.

Mary Jane took quiet steps, pushing forward through the corridor, listening.

No one in the court. Quiet now, but for the murmur of the sleepless city all around.

She paused just past her room to listen more carefully.

The door to the privy stood open. Dim light reflected into its interior showed no one within.

A person on Dorset Street walked past the opening to the passage into the court.

No light came from either window of her room. The curtains were drawn over them.

Mary Jane crouched down beside the small window and tried to peer in around the edge of the curtain, her heart pounding in her throat, her vision speckled with stars that appeared briefly with each pulse. She realized she was holding her breath and let it out slowly.

The coat Maria had left behind further blocked Mary Jane's view. She had to put her hand in and push the garment aside.

Hearing the cloth of her cuff brush along the glass, she flinched, yet avoided cutting herself.

She became still, heard nothing from within.

Any moment, one inside the room would cut her arm, her hand, or grab Mary Jane and pull her through the window into the room.

Her flesh prickled, the hairs standing up, as she slid her arm between the sharp edges of the broken pane, and reached to unlock the door.

Some relief when she withdrew her arm. A smell of night soil emerged from the hole in the glass.

Curious—I left nothing in the chamber pot.

Mary Jane stood, drew her sharp wheel spoke, moved to the door, and turned the knob slowly. Even taking care, the mechanism made a small clicking sound, and she knew she would have alerted someone inside. Did he wait patiently in the darkness within?

Even so, she pressed forward, opening the door. Mary Jane gripped her spoke more tightly. The light from the gas lamp outside sent a broadening rectangle of illumination into the room.

The odor of slops grew stronger, along with a smell of metal, iron possibly.

Ready to change course in an instant, dash through the passage and out into Dorset Street, Mary Jane instead held her weapon out before her, and slid a foot forward.

Blood on the floor beside the bed! The clothing Maria had left behind and Mary Jane had placed on the floor had been scattered. The petticoat, now bloodstained, lay beside a leg of the bed.

Still, nothing stirred within. She took another step, turning, trying to see into the shadowed corners.

Someone—Gabby—lay upon the bed. Mary Jane wanted to speak, but couldn't find her voice.

She turned toward the table, fumbled for the matches and lit the candle in the broken wine glass.

Mary Jane lifted the glass and turned toward the bed, hoping to give aid, fearing the worst.

No hope!

"Oh, Murder!" she cried.

She wanted to fold in the middle and loose her roiling gut. She retched uselessly, holding herself, trying not to drop her source of light.

Finally she knew what he'd meant—the black-eyed man had indeed christened Gabriella Gorse!

Her face gone, the skin and muscle cut away. Her blue eyes, so much like Mary Jane's, shown dully from the shambles of her mutilated features. Smears of red glued once beautiful, flaxen hair to the bedclothes.

Her gut had been laid open, her cunny, posteriors, and dairy gone. One leg, like a a joint of lamb brought to the table too many times, was carved to the bone. Butchered flesh had been piled upon the table, blood everywhere.

The ordinary cove is a madman!

Mary Jane hastened to blow out the candle, stumbled back, and set the wine glass down.

The starlings of her thoughts spooked. They flew in all directions at once, the flutter of notions and concerns too swift to have meaning, a great, gray rushing sound in her mind, followed by a wide-eyed calm. She lost track of time, standing motionless as she considered what had led to that moment.

A useless effort—I have been a pawn in a ghastly scheme of murder!

Then, a moment of clear thinking.

Get out!

Hurrying from the room toward Dorset Street, Mary Jane ran into someone in the passage. He clapped a hand over her mouth. She struggled, swung her weapon uselessly. Her heart beat too fast. She grew dizzy. The more she wriggled, the tighter he held.

I shall die, Mary Jane thought, suddenly wishing it.

The thought brought relief, a hope for release. She let go of life in that moment, became limp in his arms.

Yet life did not let go of her.

"'Tis Joseph," came the familiar voice, whispered close to her ear. "We must lock the door. Your key."

"Gone," Mary Jane said, gasping.

"Go," he said. "I have a betty." Joseph shoved her in the direction of the street.

Glancing back, she saw him in the gas lamp light, crouched down beside the door, working with the tool. He didn't know about the broken window.

Unsuspecting, a couple walked past the opening to the passage without looking in. The woman laughed at something the man said.

Mary Jane hurried out into Dorset Street, and stumbled away along the lane, becoming increasingly lost within herself, her ongoing fright and thoughts all-consuming. She had little awareness of the world around her.

Later she would be told that she'd somehow got away from

Joseph and wandered until the pubs opened. Then, she visited several of them, drinking and talking with others. She wouldn't remember any of that.

With her next awareness, she found Joseph escorting her out of the Horn of Plenty. He hurried Mary Jane across Crispin Street to Raven Row and into Artillery passage. Entering the thin corridor, she grew afraid. She suddenly saw the world around her more fully. Daylight had come.

She struggled to get away from him. He pulled her right arm up behind her back. "Walk calmly and quietly through the passage," he said. "You will hurt if you don't." He demonstrated with a tug on her arm. The agony too much, she pinched her mouth shut. They passed others using the thin lane, no one appearing to suspect that Mary Jane was being forced to do Joseph's bidding.

At Sandy's Row, just across from the Hoop and Grapes pub, a carriage pulled up. The door opened and Thomas Morganstone leaned out to help her in.

Mary Jane resisted. "You worked for the black-eyed man too."

His confused look said he didn't know who she meant.

"The cove," Joseph said. "Our *Guv'nor*."

"Yes, all three of us have worked for him," Thomas said. "He is nothing like the evil he just vanquished."

Jack the Ripper? Isn't the ordinary cove just as wicked?

Again, Mary Jane struggled against Joseph's grip. Surprising herself, and him, she got away, and started running back through Artillery Passage.

Oddly, with her ability to run so well, she wondered at the need to do so. A thought out of place had occurred to her: *My boots! Why give me tidy boots if he meant me harm?*

A small thing. A foolish notion in the swarm of maddening thoughts on that day, but it stopped her in her tracks.

Yes, they had all three worked for the ordinary cove. He'd never lied to Mary Jane, and had been true to his word in all their business. He had no cause to harm her if she could not be located.

Though afraid of him, she'd trusted the strange black-eyed man until animal fear took away rational thought.

Mary Jane turned around. Thomas and Joseph had come for her, yet made no threatening move. Joseph reached slowly to take her arm. Thomas laid a hand on his shoulder. "Stay," he said simply.

They remained still for a moment.

Mary Jane no longer saw menace in their motives.

Then, she found herself in Thomas's arms. She'd not felt the few steps that took her there. She hugged him and wept quietly.

Her arms and legs had become useless. She sagged into his embrace, felt him lift and carry her. He placed her on the seat in the carriage, and Mary Jane knew no more for some time.

Epilogue
Carmarthen, Wales, 1890

A great length of rail passed beneath me, and the life of my flesh began anew in Wales.

I put it that way because I do not truly live while Gabby's remains occupy my mind's eye. I have few moments in which I am not reminded of her in my bed in Miller's Court. I eat little, and certainly no meat, as the sight of anything rent with teeth or knife takes away hunger and brings a lasting revulsion. I carry a sachet of lavender—a safe smell—held close to my nose most of the time, because I never know what other odor might carry me in recollection back to my old lodgings in Spitalfields. Any period of silence, should it be a lasting one, drives me mad. The worst silences are at night, when only severe fatigue allows me to sleep.

In October of 1888, in a scheme much more complicated than I had imagined, Thomas and Joseph had retrieved the emerald and platinum necklace from the top of the armoire in my old room at the Phoenix gay house. Fleming sold the jewelry to a fence. He gave me the funds. Once we'd arrived in Carmarthen, he and I were married and took a room together. Molly Fleming, I am now. We had every intention of exploring the love we clearly had for one another.

"You will recover your good spirits with time," he assured me.

I wanted to believe that, yet I suffer a severe melancholia that frustrates every effort toward happiness. Whilst being told and reassured many times that Jack the Ripper's career has ended, I fear that he might find and kill me. I have also feared that, after my performance on the streets and in the pubs of Spitalfields the morning of November 9, 1888, the ordinary cove will be forced to cover his tracks and kill me.

Indian Harry, John McCarthy's man, found Gabby at 13 Miller's Court that same morning when he came for the rent about eleven o'clock. The police were alerted.

Despite several witnesses speaking up to say they'd seen me that morning, common belief held that I died at 13 Miller's Court. Though the witnesses' reports appeared in print, eventually the newspapers seemed to come around to the belief that I had indeed perished.

"They say that because the police and the coroner say it," Joseph told me. "Seems some efforts were made to hasten the process of examining the murder. Whether our strange assassin had anything to do with that or not, I don't know, but I have my suspicions. He had a police commission. I believe he returned to your room after we left to tidy it up. Whatever the case, we're safe here."

He said those things well over a year ago. In the fall of 1889, Fleming left me when he could no longer take my sensitivities; my sudden bouts of anger, my cringing in fear over things as simple as the sight or smell of blood. I do love Joseph, and hold no hard feelings.

Dear Elen Morganstone took me in.

"Two broken women together make a whole," she says.

Confined to her chair, she is much more capable than I. Her mother, Peggy, having passed away in the winter of 1888, Elen finds me useful. Thomas says she considers me a godsend. Help whenever needed, I do. I cannot believe I'm good company, and I am lucky to have her.

Crying out while having nightmares, I regularly disturb her sleep.

Thankfully, I do not remember the dreams once awakened.

Perhaps Gabby sends them for revenge. I hate her still for what she did for the Gully Bleeders that led to Jennie's death.

I also love her like a sister. How could I not—we died together in the same room.

Possibly the black-eyed man also visits my dreams.

Despite his unwillingness to say as much, it seems he had indeed been working for the police in some capacity. What of his dealings with me were considered with his police commission in mind? Although Joseph never said it outright, his words had implied that the assassin had been given the task of dispatching the Whitechapel Murderer. Had the ordinary cove sought a way to satisfy that commission and his contract with me simultaneously? I suspect I will never find an answer to that.

Did he indeed get Jack the Ripper? The killings did stop.

I hated the black-eyed man for what he'd done to Gabby. He had surely been the one to christen her corpse, yet I don't know if he'd been her killer. "You will learn little of my plan," he'd said.

Without seriousness, I've wondered if he owes me two and a tanner. I would laugh at that if I could.

I hate myself more. Set the events in motion, I did, what led to Gabriella Gorse's death.

I am her murderer.

I occupy a room at the back of Elen's tidy house on the edge of Carmarthen. Well fed, kept in comfort, and even loved, I feel little of it.

When things get difficult for me I retreat to another room at the back of the house, where Elen installed Thomas's miniature town, the one we'd all worked on together as children. The small village is a pleasant one where nothing bad ever happens. The single ladybird, a ghost really, what walks the streets, is respected, and always treated well by her clients.

Some of the walls inside the houses still need paintings, and some of the figures could use better clothes, should I need distractions.

At the beginning of this record, I wrote: "Should I have another life, give me one of hardship and hatred or one of comfort and love, but not both. The knowing between the two is where true cruelty lies."

I know as I watch Thomas today, I would not truly want that. He is building a little fountain in the garden just outside my window to provide a continuous, soft noise in the night. If life had been purely pleasant, his gesture would mean little.

With the gentle sound, perhaps I shall sleep better.

To understand more fully events hidden from the point-of-view character, Mary Jane Kelly, in this story, please read the companion novel, *The Assassin's Coin*, by John Linwood Grant, also available from IFD Publishing.

About the Author

Alan M. Clark grew up in Tennessee in a house full of bones and old medical books. He has created illustrations for hundreds of books, including works of fiction of various genres, nonfiction, textbooks, young adult fiction, and children's books. Awards for his illustration work include the World Fantasy Award and four Chesley Awards. As of summer of 2018, he is the author of 18 books, including twelve novels, a lavishly illustrated novella, four collections of fiction, and a nonfiction full-color book of his artwork. Mr. Clark's company, IFD Publishing, has released 45 titles of various editions, including traditional books, both paperback and hardcover, audio books, and ebooks by such authors as F. Paul Wilson, Elizabeth Engstrom, and Jeremy Robert Johnson. Alan M. Clark and his wife, Melody, live in Oregon. www.alanmclark.com

IFD Publishing Paperbacks

Novels:

Of Thimble and Threat, by Alan M. Clark
Baggage Check, by Elizabeth Engstrom
Bull's Labyrinth, by Eric Witchey
The Surgeon's Mate: A Dismemoir, by Alan M. Clark
Siren Promised, by Jeremy Robert Johnson and Alan M. Clark
Say Anything but Your Prayers, by Alan M. Clark
Candyland, by Elizabeth Engstrom
Apologies to the Cat's Meat Man, by Alan M. Clark
Lizzie Borden, by Elizabeth Engstrom
A Parliament of Crows, by Alan M. Clark
Lizard Wine, by Elizabeth Engstrom
The Door that Faced West, by Alan M. Clark
The Northwoods Chronicles, by Elizabeth Engstrom
The Prostitute's Price, by Alan M. Clark
The Assassin's Coin, by John Linwood Grant
13 Miller's Court, by Alan M. Clark and John Linwood Grant
Guys Named Bob, by Elizabeth Engstrom

Collections:

Professor Witchey's Miracle Mood Cure, by Eric Witchey

Nonfiction:

How to Write a Sizzling Sex Scene, by Elizabeth Engstrom
Divorce by Grand Canyon, by Elizabeth Engstrom

IFD Publishing EBooks

(You can find the following titles at most distribution points for all ereading platforms.)

Novels:

The Prostitute's Price, by Alan M. Clark
The Assassin's Coin, by John Linwood Grant
13 Miller's Court, by Alan M. Clark and John Linwood Grant
Guys Named Bob, by Elizabeth Engstrom
Apologies to the Cat's Meat Man, by Alan M. Clark
Bull's Labyrinth, by Eric Witchey

The Surgeon's Mate: A Dismemoir, by Alan M. Clark
York's Moon, by Elizabeth Engstrom
Beyond the Serpent's Heart, by Eric Witchey
Lizzie Borden, by Elizabeth Engstrom
A Parliament of Crows, by Alan M. Clark
Lizard Wine, by Elizabeth Engstrom
Northwoods Chronicles, by Elizabeth Engstrom
Siren Promised, by Alan M. Clark and Jeremy Robert Johnson
To Kill a Common Loon, by Mitch Luckett
The Man in the Loon, by Mitch Luckett
Jack the Ripper Victim Series: Of Thimble and Threat by Alan M. Clark
Jack the Ripper Victim Series: The Double Event (includes two novels from the series: *Of Thimble and Threat* and *Say Anything But Your Prayers*) by Alan M. Clark
Candyland, by Elizabeth Engstrom
The Blood of Father Time: Book 1, The New Cut, by Alan M. Clark, Stephen C. Merritt & Lorelei Shannon
The Blood of Father Time: Book 2, The Mystic Clan's Grand Plot, by Alan M. Clark, Stephen C. Merritt & Lorelei Shannon
How I Met My Alien Bitch Lover: Book 1 from the Sunny World Inquisition Daily Letter Archives, by Eric Witchey
Baggage Check, by Elizabeth Engstrom
D. D. Murphry, Secret Policeman, by Alan M. Clark and Elizabeth Massie
Black Leather, by Elizabeth Engstrom

Novelettes:
The Tao of Flynn, by Eric Witchey
To Build a Boat, Listen to Trees, by Eric Witchey

Children's Illustrated:
The Christmas Thingy, by F. Paul Wilson. Illustrated by Alan M. Clark

Collections:
Suspicions, by Elizabeth Engstrom
Professor Witchey's Miracle Mood Cure, by Eric Witchey

Short Fiction:
"Brittle Bones and Old Rope," by Alan M. Clark
"Crosley," by Elizabeth Engstrom

"The Apple Sniper," by Eric Witchey

Nonfiction:
How to Write a Sizzling Sex Scene, by Elizabeth Engstrom

IFD Publishing Audio Books

Novels:
The Door That Faced West by Alan M. Clark, read by Charles Hinckley

Jack the Ripper Victim Series: Of Thimble and Threat, by Alan M. Clark, read by Alicia Rose

Jack the Ripper Victim Series: Say Anything But Your Prayers, by Alan M. Clark, read by Alicia Rose

Jack the Ripper Victim Series: The Double Event by Alan M. Clark, read by Alicia Rose (includes two novels from the series: *Of Thimble and Threat* and *Say Anything But Your Prayers*)

A Parliament of Crows by Alan M. Clark, read by Laura Jennings

A Brutal Chill in August by Alan M. Clark, read by Alicia Rose

The Surgeon's Mate: A Dismemoir, by Alan M. Clark, read by Alan M. Clark

Apologies to the Cat's Meat Man, by Alan M. Clark, read by Alicia Rose

The Prostitute's Price, by Alan M. Clark, read by Alicia Rose

The Assassin's Coin, by John Linwood Grant, read by Alicia Rose

13 Miller's Court, by Alan M. Clark and John Linwood Grant, read by Alicia Rose